HER
SECRET
SOLDIER

JULIE HARTLEY

HER SECRET SOLDIER

bookouture

Published by Bookouture in 2024

An imprint of Storyfire Ltd.
Carmelite House
50 Victoria Embankment
London EC4Y 0DZ

www.bookouture.com

ISBN: 978-1-83525-701-2
eBook ISBN: 978-1-83525-700-5

This book is a work of fiction. Whilst some characters and circumstances portrayed by the author are based on real people and historical fact, references to real people, events, establishments, organizations or locales are intended only to provide a sense of authenticity and are used fictitiously. All other characters and all incidents and dialogue are drawn from the author's imagination and are not to be construed as real.

For Craig and Aislyn

Many and sharp the numerous ills
Inwoven with our frame!
More pointed still, we make ourselves,
Regret, remorse and shame!
And man, whose heav'n-erected face,
The smiles of love adorn,
Man's inhumanity to man,
Makes countless thousands mourn!

Robbie Burns

PROLOGUE

Night would fall in less than an hour and with it, the bombs.

Rose hurried out of Victoria station and into the chaos of wartime London. Horns blared, double-decker buses revved their engines and pedestrians yelled to one another as they dodged the traffic. On the corner, a newspaper boy waved a rolled-up paper and screamed the day's headlines, over and over.

'Blitz bombing goes on all night! Blitz bombing goes on all night! Blitz bombing...'

Standing alone on the pavement, Rose felt overwhelmed. This was not a world where she belonged. Not a place she would choose to be. She ached for the soft shiver of wind through the treetops of Silverwood Vale. The call of ravens in the gathering dusk.

But she had to find the courage to do what needed to be done.

It wasn't difficult to keep track of the man for he stood head and shoulders above the crowds. She waited until he turned the corner and then she hurried after. When he slipped into a park,

Rose trailed him, keeping her distance, peering out at him from behind the trees. He strode with confidence and she wondered how he could do so, in a country where he did not belong.

Even in parkland, nature had surrendered to the demands of war. ARP wardens trained new recruits under the plane trees, victory gardens had usurped native shrubbery and lines of ack-ack guns stood to attention, their silent barrels pointed to the skies.

But the guns would not be silent for long.

Rose crossed the park, struggling to keep the fast-moving figure in sight. Then she followed him back into traffic and through a maze of streets. When they emerged onto a busy road she fought back panic, thinking for a moment that she had lost him. She coiled her waist-length black hair around her neck, running her fingers through the long strands, desperately scanning the pavement. And then she spotted him, turning right down a side street.

I didn't betray you! she longed to shout. *I could never send you to your death!*

But now was neither the time nor the place.

Rose trailed the man round the corner and then she stopped abruptly, gazing wide-eyed.

Bombs had flattened the entire street. Instead of cheery Victorian homes with their pretty wrought-iron railings and window boxes, she saw only piles of rubble. Thin spirals of smoke wound upwards from brick and mangled iron, proof that this was a very recent bombing. On the top of one teetering mound of wood and plaster, a checked tablecloth fluttered, like a flag. Next to it sat a young girl. She clutched a doll to her chest and sobbed, fat tears ploughing furrows of clean pink skin through the grime and dirt of her face.

All along the street, people gazed at the devastation, speechless and disbelieving. Then a small man burst through the crowds, scrabbling at the rubble with his bare hands, calling a woman's name, over and over. Rose willed her to appear, to announce that she had been safe underground in a public shelter when the bombs fell on their home. But that didn't happen.

An ARP warden stood beside Rose, watching the desperate man but making no move to pull him back. The warden's hands trembled as he removed his tin hat almost reverently. He was saying something about the bombs that had fallen and the spirit of Londoners, how their courage was like laughing in the face of the enemy, but Rose could barely focus on his words.

The warden reached for her arm and she felt his fingers trembling through her sleeve.

'Londoners are strong,' he said, his voice quivering, 'but there's a limit, you know? We ain't superhuman.' He turned from the wreckage to look at Rose. 'There's only so far you can push people before they give up. We have our breaking point.'

Rose knew all about breaking points. But the warden wasn't talking about a person, he was talking about a city. If Londoners gave up, what would happen? She pictured Nazi jackboots, thundering across Westminster Bridge.

Glancing over her shoulder, Rose saw that the man she was following was on the move again.

She couldn't afford to lose him. Not now.

But as Rose hurried to the end of the gutted street and emerged as if by magic into a road untouched by the air raids, the sights and sounds of the bombed homes stayed with her. She heard again the girl's sobs and the small man's stricken cries as he tried to find his family. Suppressing an involuntary shiver, she considered the air-raid warden's prophetic words.

There's only so far you can push people before they give up.

Rose knew what she needed to do, but, until this moment, she had not understood how critical her involvement might be.

She kept to the deepening shadows, her eyes trained on the man who stood head and shoulders above everyone else. She didn't know where he was going, but she desperately hoped she would find out soon.

After all, night was coming and with it, the bombs.

ONE

EMMA

June 1990

Emma stood on her balcony, clutching the letter that would change her life, and waited for her husband to come home.

From her vantage point on the eighteenth floor, she peered down on cars as tiny as remote-controlled toys, streaming by on the Queen Elizabeth Way. The retractable roof was open on the new SkyDome and she could see fans watching a Blue Jays game, the baseball players miniatures of their real selves. Only the CN Tower looked impressive from this height, for it was the tallest structure in Toronto by far.

Horns blared, fans cheered, sirens wailed and Emma felt herself to be right in the thick of things, exactly where she loved to be. But the thought gave her little pleasure, today. Mike would be home soon. She would tell him that she had made up her mind and then there would be no going back.

Emma clutched the letter to her chest. With a heavy heart, she stepped inside and closed the balcony door.

From every wall of the condo, Mike's photographs stared back at her. Behind the sofa, an almost life-sized canoe drifted through mist. On each side of the door, red maples dipped to kiss a turquoise lake and beside her desk a moose waded through a pond in the early dawn.

Mike adored the northern Canadian wilderness, but to Emma the photos were a constant reminder of misery. She accompanied him on his camping trips only out of a sense of duty and their most recent trip had been the worst of all. Frigid nights, the darkness filled with terrifying sounds. Dense forest closing in on them and clouds of black flies so thick, it was difficult to breathe. On the way back to the city, Mike had exclaimed about the wonders of nature, while Emma scratched her bug bites resentfully and struggled to untangle her thick chestnut curls.

Stepping into their tiny kitchenette, Emma poured herself a glass of Chardonnay, enjoying the way it sparkled pale gold under the fluorescent lights. It was a little early in the day for wine, but the indulgence was forgivable, given what she had decided to do. She looked down at the envelope in her hand with its English postmark and felt the same astonishment she had experienced when she first opened it, three days ago. She knew her grandparents had come over to Canada from England at the end of the war, but nothing had prepared her for the contents of the letter.

She had options, now.

With a faint click, Mike entered the condo, closing the door softly behind him. Emma set down her wine glass and stepped into the hall. He was bending over, removing his shoes the way he did most things – in silence. It was something she found unsettling: his ability to move through the world without making a sound. Emma was the opposite. She slammed doors, spoke loudly and dropped things. It had always been a source of tension between them.

Mike straightened up and they stared at each other, awkwardly. 'Have you made up your mind?' he asked.

Emma thought, *After this moment, there will be no going back.*

She nodded.

'Oh, Emma, love...' His voice cracked.

'I'm a city girl,' she said. 'My home is here, in Toronto. And my career, too.'

Mike took a step towards her. 'You could freelance,' he said. 'I'll open a studio by a lake and it'll have a room in it just for you, with your desk and your library...'

Emma shook her head, becoming bolder now the decision had been made. 'I'm a journalist, Mike,' she said. 'The best jobs are here, in the city. My life is here. I can't just move three hours north, to the middle of nowhere. And I don't crave wilderness the way you do. I don't even like it, to be honest...'

Mike stepped into the living room and perched on their sofa. Emma had chosen it in the weeks before their wedding. Creamy white faux-leather, designed for a chic city condo. She had wanted real leather, but Mike wouldn't hear of it.

The sofa would have been out of place in a country cottage up north.

Just like her.

'I don't know where that leaves us,' Mike said. 'You can't come with me and I can't stay in the city. We both know that.'

He was such a calm presence, even now. Like the herons they watched together on their canoe trips. Long-necked, long-limbed, graceful. Emma recalled the gentle way Mike's fingers had moved down her spine the night before as they made love. How they had clung to one another, knowing it could be their last time, though the words had yet to be spoken.

But now, Emma had made her decision, erecting a barrier between them. She felt herself pulling away, loosening the ties that held them together.

'I love you,' Mike said, miserably. *And I love you, too*, Emma thought, but what was the point in saying it? You had to want the same things for a relationship to work.

The silence stretched between them.

'What will you do?' Mike asked. His first concern was for her welfare and this touched Emma so much that she almost faltered in her resolve. 'We can barely afford the mortgage on this place as it is. When I'm gone, how will you...'

Emma held out the envelope in response. She'd read the letter a dozen times over the past few days, but she had shown it to Mike only that morning. He'd scanned the contents, his eyes widening in surprise, before handing it back and leaving the condo without a word.

'It took them months to track me down,' Emma said, 'so I thought I would fly to England and take care of things in person. It'll speed things up and give you the time you need to...' *Move out.* She couldn't speak the words.

'Right.'

Emma thought of how they had cherished and supported one another for almost a decade. She had lost both her parents within the space of twelve months and it was Mike who had kept her together as she clawed through her grief. When Mike had been diagnosed with anxiety it was Emma who had helped him cope. Later, she had been by his side when he accepted his first award as a nature photographer.

But separation was a challenge each of them would navigate alone.

Mike said, 'If only there was a way—' and then he stopped. When he spoke again, his tone was not the gentle, loving one he reserved for her, it was the guarded tone he used with the rest of the world. 'I can see you have made up your mind,' he said.

Emma clutched the envelope tighter in her fist and waited to see what would happen next.

Mike said, 'I only wish I could...'

There was so much pain in his voice. It occurred to Emma

that, despite their many tense discussions over the past weeks, he had never stopped hoping. That until this moment he had still believed she might join him when he moved up north. Now, he had no choice but to accept the truth.

Mike rose from the sofa and padded across the rug towards her. Emma thought he was going to put his arms round her and she almost hoped he would, but he moved past her and into the hallway. He put his shoes back on as silently as he had taken them off, hooked his jacket over his arm and left. The door closed behind him with a faint click.

Emma felt tears stinging her eyes as she returned to the kitchenette. She downed her Chardonnay and recalled the night, six weeks earlier, when everything had started to go wrong.

It was their first wedding anniversary and they'd reserved a table in the revolving restaurant at the top of the CN Tower. She had worn her off-the-shoulder Terani with its pastel jacquard print and there had been candles, roses, romance.

'I could never love anyone as I love you,' Mike had said, reaching for her hands across the table.

'I would follow you to the ends of the earth,' Emma replied and in that moment she had meant it more than anything she had ever said before.

But then, leaving the CN Tower, their dreamy date had plunged into nightmare. The SkyDome was emptying, thousands of fans spilling out of the stadium, yelling, jostling, pushing. As the crowds surged around them Mike began to shake, his breath bursting from him in gasps.

'It's okay,' Emma said. But the words were stolen from her by the singing and shouting of the fans.

Then Mike spiralled into a panic attack.

Wailing like a wounded creature, he pulled away from her, shoving through the crowds in a desperate attempt to break free. At first Emma could see him clearly, his willowy frame and blond hair, but then he was gone and she couldn't even hear his screams.

It took an eternity for the crowds to disperse. Emma searched for Mike but she couldn't find him, couldn't see anyone else left on the wide sweep of concrete that separated the CN Tower from the stadium. Then she saw a body curled in a ball by the maintenance doors, looking more like a pile of crumpled clothing than a person. She hurried over.

'Breathe,' she said, placing a hand on his heaving chest. 'I'm here, Mike. I'm here.'

There had been panic attacks before, many of them, but she had never seen him like this.

Emma listened for sounds of the natural world, knowing this was often the way to bring him back to himself, but there was nothing, not here, in the heart of the city. Then she looked up and found in the light-polluted sky a single star. She described it to Mike: a faint light, shining down on them, and he looked up, allowing the star to break through his panic and guide him back to her.

Afterwards they walked home together, holding hands, but nothing felt the same. In the madness of the crowds Emma had torn the fabric of her Terani, a jagged rip down the skirt. She wouldn't be able to wear it again but after tonight, she wouldn't want to.

Mike whispered, 'I can't do this any more.'

'What do you mean?' Emma asked, but she knew.

'All these people, hemming me in. Nothing but concrete for miles and miles. This is what animals must feel like when we put them in cages. The city is killing me.'

His words landed like a bombshell, a truth Emma had known for a long time but managed to avoid.

I would follow you to the ends of the earth, she had told Mike during their dinner, but, as he confessed how miserable he was in the city, realisation dawned on her.

The ends of the earth did not include a northern wilderness.

Now, as Mike left her alone in their condo, Emma felt the weight of her sadness and loss. She gazed around the walls at his photographs, realising the images expressed, more than words ever could, the soul of the man she loved.

How bare these walls would seem when the photos were gone.

She looked down at the envelope in her hand, lifted the flap and pulled out the single sheet of paper. It was watermarked, with an embossed letterhead: *Richard Barrow, B & N Law LLP, Wills, Trusts & Probate Solicitors, London.*

The letter concerned her Great-Aunt Rose, whose existence Emma had only learned of two years ago.

'Do we have any family left in England?' she had asked her mother, just days before she died. Emma had never asked before. She had her parents and she had Mike. What need could she have for relatives on the other side of the world?

Her mother propped herself up on her pillows, shaking her head. 'We've no family left over there,' she said. 'At least, it's unlikely.'

It was a strange answer. 'What do you mean?' Emma asked.

'Well, there was my mother's sister, your Great-Aunt Rose, but she disappeared long ago.'

'Disappeared?' Emma asked, intrigued.

Her mother nodded. She fumbled for her beaker of water, which stood on the bedside table among a dozen pill bottles. Emma grabbed it, guiding the rim to her lips.

'Rose Tilburn,' her mother continued. 'She went missing during the Second World War. She was only eighteen at the time. One day, she left home and never returned.'

'Didn't the police try to find her?' Emma asked.

'They did,' her mother replied. 'But this was during the war, remember? I suppose the authorities had bigger things to worry about than a teenage runaway. Even so, your grandmother always maintained there was more to it. That Rose hadn't simply run away from home.'

'She thought Rose had been kidnapped?' Emma asked.

'Oh, I wouldn't go that far.' Her mother drew her crocheted bedjacket tight around her shoulders. It was late afternoon on a grim November day. Night was falling, winter was coming and there was no avoiding the fact that her mother would not see spring.

'Your gran blamed herself for her sister's disappearance,' Emma's mother said, 'though I can't say why.' She extended a pale arm, pointing to her dresser. 'Pass me my parents' wedding photograph.'

The dresser held several family photos, arranged prettily on a lace cloth. In the centre stood a silver frame that held a black and white photograph of Emma's grandparents, taken on their wedding day.

Emma picked it up and handed it to her.

'For years, this sat next to your gran's bed,' her mother said. She placed her fingertips lovingly against the image of her parents. 'Evelyn and Charles Lyell,' she whispered. 'I doubt you remember much about them.' Then she turned the frame over, unclipped it and tipped the wedding photo onto her duvet.

Another photograph, barely the length of Emma's thumb, slipped out from behind it.

'Your Great-Aunt Rose,' her mother said.

Emma picked up the tiny photo. It was a portrait of a young girl, taken long ago. She was leaning against an ancient oak tree, one hand trailing across the bark. Her eyes met the camera, but timidly. They were gorgeous eyes. Huge, with long lashes.

Jet black hair tumbled over her shoulders, reaching to her waist.

'Your gran received this photo in an envelope, a few days before her sister disappeared,' Emma's mother said. 'Rose sent it. Just the photograph. No letter, no explanation. I'd catch her looking at the photo sometimes. As if it was a clue she'd never managed to figure out.'

'Great-Aunt Rose was beautiful,' Emma said.

Her mother nodded. 'She certainly was. Your gran used to tell me stories of how the two of them played in the woods when they were girls. She said you were the spitting image of her.'

Emma studied the photo again, looking for the resemblance. 'Did no one ever learn what happened to her?' she asked.

Her mother shook her head. 'The story intrigued me when I was a girl,' she said. 'The idea that I had a relative who disappeared mysteriously, so many years ago. But whenever I asked questions, your gran got upset. I know she tried hard to find her sister, in the beginning. Then the war ended, the mystery was still unsolved and it was time to move on. She married your granddad, they emigrated to Canada and that was that.'

'No one ever saw Rose again,' Emma murmured.

'No one ever saw Rose again.'

Her mother's words replayed themselves in Emma's head as she unfolded the single sheet of paper and scanned the letter.

Rose may have disappeared during the Second World War, but she had not died. She had lived on for fifty years, though Emma's grandmother had never known it. According to the solicitor, Rose had become the owner of *a vast and significant tract of land*, complete with *a small dwelling*. Then, just months ago, she had died, leaving Emma as her only surviving heir. The news wasn't just astonishing – it was intriguing. Emma thought about the *small dwelling* – Silverwood Vale, the solicitor called it. The name was lovely, even magical. She pictured a quaint English cottage with a thatched roof and a rose garden.

If it was true that she now owned a cottage in England, at least one of Emma's problems was solved. She could sell the property and the land and use the money to buy out Mike's share of their condo. And by travelling to England to oversee the sale, she could ease them both through the most painful part of the separation.

Mike could move out while she was gone.

Emma grabbed her cordless phone and stepped out onto the balcony. At once, the buzz of the city rose to meet her, frenetic and exhilarating. She sat down on one of the two patio chairs, scrolled through numbers stored in the phone's memory and dialled.

She would book her flight to London right now, before she had time to change her mind.

TWO

EMMA

June 1990

'Are you sure you haven't made a mistake?' Emma asked the taxi driver. 'Are you certain this is Silverwood Vale?'

The name had conjured an image of Great-Aunt Rose's dwelling: a cute country cottage surrounded by a manicured garden. But Silverwood Vale wasn't the name of a cottage at all.

'This is the place.' The taxi driver twisted in his seat, pointing back along the road they had travelled. 'That there's Lowbury,' he said unnecessarily, for he had picked Emma up outside the train station in the town. 'Just south of us, there's the coastal path and the English Channel. And this,' he spun back round to face forward, 'this here is Silverwood Vale.'

A vast and significant tract of land, the solicitor had said in his letter and he was not wrong. To the right of the taxi, where the driver was pointing, trees bordered the country road for as far as the eye could see. They grew together in a dense tangle, thick and impenetrable, and they towered so far above them that, when Emma tilted her head to look up, she could barely see the canopy.

'It's an ancient woodland,' the driver said. 'Oldest on the south coast, I reckon.'

Emma wasn't sure what an ancient woodland was and she didn't much care. She felt tired, jet-lagged and unbelievably sad.

All night long, as she flew over the Atlantic, Emma had replayed her final conversations with Mike. She worried for him, wondered if he was coping and whether he had already started to move out. By the time her flight landed in Gatwick, she was utterly miserable and regretting her decision to come. She had pre-booked herself a room in a bed and breakfast in Lowbury, the closest town to her Great-Aunt Rose's property and the place where her grandmother and great-aunt had spent their childhoods. However, when her train pulled into the small town and she hailed a taxi – not even certain it was legal to do that in England – she had asked the driver, on impulse, to take her straight to Silverwood Vale. Perhaps it would cheer her up to see the cottage she had inherited, she thought.

And now, here she was. Silverwood Vale, which wasn't a cottage at all, but a forest that stretched for miles, with no way in but for a narrow trail, winding into the trees and out of sight.

'Miss?' said the taxi driver, jolting her back to herself.

'Is there a road going into it?' Emma asked. 'Maybe a private road, leading to a house?'

The driver chuckled. 'You'll not find no house in there,' he said, 'and you won't find much else, neither. Folks hereabouts stay well away.'

Emma wondered why, but she didn't ask.

She opened the door and stepped out. It was a lovely early summer morning and the sun shone warm on her face. The sky above her was a dazzling blue, flecked with travelling clouds.

'Miss?'

Emma turned to look at the driver.

'If it's a walk you're after, I'd stick to the edge of the road,' he said.

Emma glanced again at the narrow pathway, winding into the trees.

'Do you want me to wait? It's just that there's no—'

'Yes please,' Emma said. 'I won't be long.'

In for a penny, in for a pound. Wasn't that what the English said?

She crossed the road. A narrow ditch ran between the road and the forest, but she jumped across it easily. By the edge of the trail, someone had tied a hand-painted sign to one of the trees, the letters crudely formed and slanting one into the other: PRIVATE. KEEP OUT. A thick rope hung across the trail.

She hesitated only briefly. Without looking back, she knew the driver was watching her.

This was her land now, wasn't it?

Emma ducked under the rope and stepped into the forest.

Instantly huge trees closed in on all sides and cool, damp air wrapped itself around her, banishing jet lag and pulling her mind into focus. The forest stank of rotting things. Layers of vegetation, half decayed. Fungus, mould and stagnant water. It must have rained in the night; when a light wind teased the branches overhead, fat drops splashed onto her hair, running down her neck. The path was squelchy, rainwater pooling in the dips, and in no time at all her lilac Converse High Tops were drenched and slick with mud.

Somewhere above her, two crows cawed, bursting from the canopy.

Emma considered returning to the taxi. Clearly, she wasn't going to find her great-aunt's *small dwelling* in the middle of a forest so dense and overgrown but she didn't want to look foolish in front of the driver, so she pushed on.

Picking her way over a fallen tree furred with moss, Emma considered the hazards that lurked in the wilderness, back in Ontario. The mosquitoes and deer flies. Hidden clumps of poison ivy. Massasauga rattlesnakes like the one she had almost stepped on last year. She had no idea what dangers she might encounter in an English forest. *Folks hereabouts stay well away*, the driver had said.

Emma wished she had asked him why.

Just a few more minutes and she could retrace her steps. She'd tell the taxi driver that a refreshing walk in the woods was exactly what she had needed after her flight and then she'd give him the address of her bed and breakfast.

As the path narrowed still further, Emma imagined how a developer might transform the tangled mess of trees. She pictured brick houses in neat rows, with manicured lawns and pretty flowerbeds. Straight roads, lined with streetlights. A golf course with sweeping views down to the sea. One thing was becoming abundantly clear: Great-Aunt Rose had owned a lot of land. Emma was going to make more than enough money to buy out Mike's share of the condo.

She would have enough to pay off the entire mortgage.

Emma walked on for several minutes, comforted by these thoughts. She was about to turn and head back to the road when, without warning, the trees thinned and the trail opened up into a clearing. It was a natural glade, not unlike the ones she had camped in with Mike. A few ancient trees had toppled and sunlight streamed down through the hole in the canopy. In a wide space between rotting trunks she saw a vegetable garden and beyond that, so ramshackle that it felt like a part of the forest itself, stood *a small dwelling*.

It was like something out of a fairytale: a crooked, one-storey building made of wood, overgrown with moss and encircled by a perfect ring of neat white stones. There were three parts to the house, if it could be called that: a very old centre portion sunk into the ground like a hobbit-hole, its wooden sidings faded with age and two newer sections flanking it, made of tightly fitting logs. A pathway of woodchips led to a front door, set in the oldest portion of the dwelling. There were two windows, one on each side of the door, with window boxes that held a tangle of wildflowers.

Emma looked around the glade and saw a second path, just as narrow as the first, winding through the trees in the opposite direction. There was no road to the dwelling and no room to park a car. No electricity cables and no telephone cables. Between the vegetable garden and the house stood a well – so, in all likelihood, there was no running water in the cottage, either.

What sort of person would choose to live in a place like this? Emma wondered. Mike yearned for a country cottage, but his dream home would have electricity, running water, a telephone. And he would never give up his car.

Emma reached into the back pocket of her jeans and withdrew the tiny photograph of her great-aunt. She thought of pretty young Rose going about her life in the crooked little cottage, a fairytale princess transforming over decades into a fairytale witch. Scanning the lovely face again, she decided that she looked a little sad, despite her timid smile. As if she had carried the weight of the world on her shoulders, even as a young girl.

Why did you choose to live secretly in a forest, just minutes from your home? she wondered. *Why did you leave your family and let them go on thinking, for years and years, that you were dead?* To Emma, who would have given anything to see her parents again, such an act was beyond comprehension.

What would turn a pretty teenager into a lifelong recluse?

Flipping the photograph over, she noticed for the first time that there was something written on the back in faded ink. She peered closer.

To the one who got away, love Rose.

Got away from what? Emma wondered. Forgetting all about

the taxi, she walked down the path to the front door, lifted up the latch and pushed.

The wooden door rattled in its frame but did not budge.

She tried again. Still nothing. There was no keyhole, no way the door could be locked except from the inside, which made no sense. Not unless there was another door in the back.

Of course. There had to be another way in.

Curious to see inside her great-aunt's home, Emma stepped off the path and walked along the front wall of the house. She paused to peer in at one of the windows, but it was too dark inside to make out much.

Emma turned right along the side wall, past a lean-to stacked with firewood. And then she stopped.

She sensed rather than heard it. A presence, just beyond the treeline.

Someone was crouched in the undergrowth, watching her.

Emma held her breath and listened. For a moment, silence. Then, footsteps. The crack of twigs underfoot and the sound of branches being shoved out of the way. The taxi driver? No. The noises came from the second trail, which ran in the opposite direction. South, towards the sea.

Emma had been followed once, in her university days, as she left a nightclub alone. Foolishly, she had taken a short cut home, along a dark alley. Five men had materialised behind her, jeering. They quickened their pace, gaining on her, their taunts growing bolder and more suggestive. Emma was about to kick off her heels and make a run for it when a second group rounded the corner in front. Fear rose like bile in her throat. *She was surrounded.* But the people who approached her were not gang members but tourists, trying to find a sports bar. By the time Emma had offered them directions, the men following her had melted into the darkness and the danger had passed.

The terror of that night had never left her and she had

promised herself she would not end up in such a compromising position again.

Except now, here she was.

All noise ceased as the stranger paused just out of sight. Was he watching her? Was he about to lunge out of the trees and attack?

Emma panicked.

She ran along the side of the cabin, her right hand trailing the coarse wood, trying to be silent but failing, as always. *We would see more wildlife if you didn't make so much noise*, Mike always said. Now, Emma wished she had learned to move as he did, without making a sound.

She rounded the corner to the rear of the house and paused, with only seconds to register that there was no back door to the cabin, before she heard the crackle of boots against mulch and knew someone was walking down the garden path. There was only one rear window and she drew herself up against it, peering in through the dark interior to the front window where she had stood moments before. She saw the face of a man who was so tall that his forehead reached the top of the frame. One cheek was pressed against the glass and he was looking directly at her.

No one knows I am here, Emma thought, *except the taxi driver*. If he gave up waiting and went back to town, how long would it be before anyone came looking for her?

The man's face disappeared from the window.

He was coming. Following her round the side of the cabin.

Emma felt the same terror she had felt behind the nightclub all those years ago, except now there would be no one turning up to help her. Her only chance was to run.

She pushed herself away from the cabin and tumbled through the overgrown strip of land that stretched between the rear wall and the treeline. A thick tangle of weeds rose waist-high, tugging at her clothes like tiny, skeletal fingers, and Emma fought against them, picturing the stranger jogging round the side wall, a knife in his hand, coming for her.

Then something changed about the ground beneath her feet. Emma wasn't hearing the squelch of mud any more, she was running over something hollow. Uneven planks of wood, soft and rotting, hidden by the tangle of vegetation.

Planks that gave way under her weight, plunging her downwards.

Emma cried out as she fell, dirt and weeds and damp wood collapsing around her. A clod of wet earth hit her hard in the face and something sharp dragged across her arm, tearing through the fabric of her jacket, bringing with it a sudden flash of pain.

She came to rest with a thud on something soft and pillowy, ten feet down.   ·

Emma coughed, swiping her hand across her nose to clear away the mud. She tried to calm herself, tried to think logically. The space she had landed in was lined with wooden planks now soft and rotten with age.

This wasn't a trap she had fallen into. It was an old root cellar, abandoned for a very long time.

Did England have poisonous snakes? Scorpions? Tarantulas? Emma didn't think so, but she was sure there must be rats. She shifted her body, listening for the scurry of clawed feet, looking for rodent eyes flashing in the gloom.

Then she sat up, stretching her legs out in front of her.

She was sore and bruised from the fall, but otherwise unhurt. Above her she saw the remnants of the root cellar's roof, cracked and splintered, and beyond that a thin strip of blue sky. She could smell rotten wood and damp earth but the tangle of vegetation growing on top of the root cellar had sealed it off effectively and the ground below her was mostly dry.

Reaching out her hands, Emma patted the floor. She felt the broken rungs of a ladder that must once have reached down into the cellar and something softer, too. Fabric of some kind, lumpy mounds of it, that must have broken her fall.

She was about to investigate when the strip of blue sky above her disappeared and she saw a face, peering down at her.

If this man meant her harm, she was well and truly doomed.

Emma blinked mud out of her eyes and craned her neck upwards. The face was bearded, framed by black hair that tumbled down through the mess of splintered planks. She pictured the stranger lying flat on his belly in the squelchy mud so he could reach across the broken roof to the hole.

'Are you hurt?' he called down.

Well, that was a good sign. If he meant her harm, why would he care?

'I don't think so,' she called back. She struggled to her feet, placing one outstretched hand against the wall of the root cellar to steady herself.

Even on tiptoe, she couldn't stretch all the way up to ground level. The man extended a hand towards her. Their fingertips touched, but that was all.

'I need to find something to pull you out,' he said.

Emma was about to suggest he head to the road and ask her taxi driver for a tow rope when she thought of something else.

'Wait,' she said.

She crouched down and gathered handfuls of the lumpy fabric that had broken her fall. It was soft to the touch, mouldy and stinking. She folded it in on itself, coiling it round and round, winding it like a rope.

'Grab this,' she called when she had rolled the fabric tightly. She tossed it upwards and two strong, brown arms reached down to grab it. The stranger wriggled backwards onto solid ground and the end of the material disappeared out of the hole.

'Cover your head,' he shouted. Emma obeyed and pieces of rotten wood showered down upon her as he cleared a gap in the roof big enough for her to clamber out. Then she gathered an armful of the lumpy fabric, winding it round her wrists. She kicked at the wall of the root cellar, splintering the wood, making a foothold.

'Ready?' called the voice from above.

'Ready.'

Emma leapt upwards, her right foot planted in the wall, as the material pulled taut. She heard the stranger grunt under the strain. Strands of the rotting material began to rip, the fibres tearing apart, and Emma knew she had only seconds before it would give way altogether. She drove her left foot into the soft wood further up the wall, creating another foothold. The strip of blue sky widened above her, the wall of the cabin came into view and she was able to scrabble up and out of the root cellar, onto solid ground.

She lay for a long time in the damp undergrowth, panting. Then a voice said, 'You're bleeding.'

Emma looked up. A man in his late twenties sat beside her in a muddy puddle, the fabric still coiled round his forearm. His hair was long and tangled and he wore a collarless shirt. Both sleeves were rolled up above the elbow, revealing tattoos on his arms. He wore a tie-dyed bandana round his neck, which he pulled off as she watched and offered to her.

'Your arm,' he said. 'You cut yourself.' The man had a thick, regional accent that reminded Emma of the actors on *Coronation Street*.

'My arm? Oh. Wow.' She looked down and saw a thick gash on her forearm, trailing blood.

She struggled to sit up.

'Here. Let me.'

Gently, the man wound his bandana round her arm to stanch the blood and tied both ends neatly above the cut. Emma met his gaze for an instant. He had unusual eyes, dark brown and flecked with gold. She looked away.

'That's the best we can do for now,' he said. 'Why were you running away?'

Emma felt embarrassed. How could she tell him she had been running to get away from him? Her rescuer had strong, sun-bronzed arms and an easy manner about him that suggested he had never been afraid of anyone in his life.

Luckily, he didn't wait for her reply.

'You look a mess,' he said. He smiled kindly as he spoke and Emma decided she had nothing to fear from him.

'You don't look too hot yourself.' She smiled back, wiping mud from her face.

'You're American,' he said.

'Canadian.'

'Oh. Sorry. I'm Tristan.'

'Emma.' She paused. 'Thanks, anyway. For helping me out.' She struggled to her feet.

'This is a strange place to come wandering,' Tristan said, also standing. 'I thought I was the only person who hung out in Silverwood.'

Emma was about to tell him that she owned the forest now and that the strange little hobbit-hole behind them had belonged to her Great-Aunt Rose when a shadow fell across them. She looked up to see a black cloud scudding across the sun.

'It's going to rain any minute now,' Tristan said. But there was plenty of blue sky left. Emma wondered how he could be so sure.

'My taxi's waiting by the road,' she said. 'I should go.'

They brushed mud off their clothes as best as they could. Emma felt guilty to see that Tristan was as thickly covered in it as she was.

'I hope you live close by,' she said, but he wasn't listening, he was looking down at the hole in the roof of the cellar and the fabric gathered in folds around their feet.

'What do you make of this?' he murmured, crouching down. 'Can you see what it is?'

And as he unfolded it, Emma could. It wasn't a dust sheet, as she had imagined, maybe used to cover vegetables in the cellar long ago. It was a parachute. A large, very old, partially rotten parachute, with a section of the harness still dangling from the end.

Emma knelt down beside Tristan and together they unfolded a portion of the mouldy silk until the parachute's original shape revealed itself.

'Why would Great-Aunt Rose have a parachute in her root cellar?' Emma murmured. She looked at Tristan, realising she would have some explaining to do, but he hadn't heard her.

'The parachute was used to wrap something up,' he said.

Emma laid her hand on it, feeling the lumps inside.

A cold wind blew in from the trees. *The weather is changing*, Emma thought, *just as he said it would.*

They untangled the folds of the parachute as huge drops of rain splattered around them.

'Oh my,' Emma said as she pulled back the last twist.

Tristan rested back on his heels and stroked his beard. 'Oh my indeed,' he said.

The parachute held bones, brown and damp and speckled with age.

Emma rubbed her eyes as if she might be seeing things. But she wasn't. There was no doubting what lay in the folds of the parachute. Something that had remained hidden in her great-aunt's root cellar for heavens knew how many years.

It was a human skeleton.

THREE

ROSE

September 1940

'The Treachery Act!' Rose's stepfather roared. 'Churchill's got the right idea. We should hang the lot of 'em.' His thick brows furrowed as he looked past Rose and her mother, through the kitchen window, as if he expected to find a German spy lurking in the hydrangeas.

You're wrong, Rose thought. *Killing is wrong and hanging German spies would make us no better than the enemy*. But she kept silent, as she always did when her stepfather launched into one of his tirades.

Norman stabbed a finger at his tankard and Rose poured him another beer. He sucked the last of the meat from a chicken thigh and dropped the bone to his plate. His lips glistened with fat.

'Hanging's too good for Nazi spies, that's what I say!' Norman banged his fist down on the dining room table and Rose's mother, wrapped in her crocheted blanket, jumped in her chair.

Rose twisted in her seat to look out of the window. She saw

the sweep of lawn that had been her mother's pride and joy, back when she was still well enough to tend the garden. Beyond it, the lane curved towards Lowbury and she could just make out the stile that led through the harvested wheat field, with its thick golden stubble, down to the coastal path.

From there, it was only a short run to Silverwood Vale. She longed to be under the lush, green canopy, listening to the whisper of the wind and the chiffchaffs singing in the trees. She longed to be anywhere but here.

'And you.'

Rose saw her mother stiffen as Norman leaned across the table towards his sick wife. 'Useless lump, you are,' he growled, his voice dropping to a whisper the way it always did when he meant business. 'Useless, like that ungrateful daughter of yours. Evelyn was a traitor to this family. Don't think she'll ever be welcome under my roof again.'

It was six weeks since Evelyn had left and still her departure was an open wound for Rose. She recalled how her elder sister had skipped down the garden path in her new sundress, her travelling case swinging back and forth, her heeled shoes clicking. The stone in her engagement ring had been the largest Rose had ever seen and her eyes had sparkled just as brightly. *I don't think she'll ever come back*, she thought, with a mixture of sadness and envy.

Rose grabbed her stepfather's plate and walked with it to the scullery, where she slid the bones and gristle into the bin. When she turned back round, Norman was standing behind her.

He was a large man whose body seemed to pulse with power. Older than his muscular strength might suggest, Norman was safe from conscription, a fact that rankled Rose.

'You'll not do what your sister did,' he said, menacingly. 'Not if I can help it.' He was standing so close to her that Rose could smell the rankness of his breath. 'Your place is here, minding my house and taking care of your mother. D'you hear?'

Rose nodded, her heart sinking as it always did when she thought of her future. Evelyn was now a warden with an Air Raid Precautions unit in London, so she was doing her bit for the war effort. But Rose would never get away. Never fall in love and never have a life of her own. Her stepfather would see to that.

Norman gave a small grunt of satisfaction and strode into the hall, where he donned his helmet and tucked his truncheon into his belt. 'Some of us have to work for a living,' he said. 'Keep this country running!' He polished the silver buttons of his tunic with the cuff of one sleeve.

Anybody would think this was London, Rose thought, not sleepy Lowbury, where the most a small-town sergeant had to deal with was petty theft.

'Get that lot cleaned up,' Norman barked at Rose, indicating the pots and pans in the sink, and then he strode out of the door and was gone.

Rose listened until she heard the engine of his Vauxhall 12 burst into life. She held her breath as he reversed the car and roared off down the lane. Only when the engine had faded to silence did she breathe easily again.

'He's insufferable,' she muttered as she wandered back through to the dining room.

In the early months of her marriage to Norman, Rose's mother would have chastised either of her daughters for criticising their stepfather, but as Norman's bullying tendencies had made themselves known all three of them had learned to fear him. Rose watched her mother gather the blanket more tightly around her shoulders as if it was midwinter, not a warm September evening, and wondered whether she was in pain, as she so often was.

'Hanging people is wrong, whatever he says,' Rose said. 'One of these days, I'm going to tell him what I think.'

'You mustn't do that,' her mother whispered, before lapsing into a despondent silence.

Thinking of her stepfather's recent promotion, Rose said, 'This war's given him too much power. It's gone to his head.' That was the problem with wars, she mused as she carried the last of the dishes through to the scullery. They turned the world into a place where hard-nosed brutality was rewarded more than compassion. People like Norman did well in wartime, while people like Rose did not.

Suddenly, she felt the urge to run. She needed to listen to the breakers on the beach, the whisper of the grasses in the dunes. To seek solace under the canopy of Silverwood Vale.

Rose hurried back to the dining room.

'I have to get out of here,' she said, with the usual pang of guilt. Whenever she made a burst for freedom, her mother was left behind. An invalid, confined to the house. Rose should stay and keep her company, she knew that. Clean up as her stepfather ordered, while outside, just out of sight, the sun set without her, pouring its fire onto the sea.

But she couldn't do it.

'I'll wash the dishes later, Mam, I promise.' Rose picked up the chicken carcass from the table. The dining room was clear now, but the scullery would have to wait. 'Just an hour. He'll never know.'

Her mother gave a small nod, accompanied by a sigh that Rose decided to ignore. She reached over to peck her mother on the cheek, grabbed her canvas bag from the pantry where she kept it hidden, out of sight of prying eyes, and hurried into the warm September night.

At last, Rose was free.

All the heaviness fell away as she crossed the tangled garden that had once been glorious, breaking into a run. She clutched her canvas bag under one arm and the early autumn wind whipped through her long hair. With a wild burst of energy, she leapt the low garden wall, bounded across the country road and clambered over the stile that led through a wheat field to the coastal path. Onwards she ran, shrugging off her fear of Norman and the guilt she felt at leaving her mother behind. Wheat stalks pricked her bare legs and she tipped her head towards the evening sun as it poured its golden waves across the sky.

Life wasn't fair. There was no escaping that. Evelyn had always been the volatile one, defying Norman, talking back to him. *You're asking for trouble*, their mother had told her. But it wasn't trouble Evelyn had found, it was freedom. A handsome fiancé and a future to call her own. She would even be contributing to the war effort as an ARP warden, helping Londoners through the air raids that devastated the city each night. While Rose, the compliant one, what did she have? A life of servitude, trapped in Lowbury. No prospect of love, nor happiness. And the most she could do to help the war effort was to keep house for a small-town sergeant.

Evelyn. Vivacious and bright-eyed, with her fashionable hairdo, her silk stockings from Woolworths and her crimson lipsticks. Evelyn, sneaking out of the window on a Saturday night, high heels clutched in one hand as she dropped down from the porch roof, into the hydrangeas.

Evelyn, who Rose had loved most in all the world.

But when she turned onto the coastal path, breathing in the fresh, salted wind, Rose's spirits lifted. She could hear the oystercatchers down on the beach and see skylarks swooping over the dunes. Ahead of her lay the cool greenness of Silverwood Vale, the treeline already shadowed as the sun slipped down towards the sea.

One look at the sky with its fast-moving clouds told Rose the sunset would be magnificent.

Coils of barbed wire separated the coastal path from the dunes, an obstacle that was supposed to hinder any German spies who landed by rowing boat under cover of darkness. But Rose had discovered a loose fence post. She grabbed at it now and pushed it over, stepping into the dunes.

Rose sank low in the grasses, looking across the white beach rimmed with seashells and the darkening blue of the sea, towards France.

Occupied France, now.

She pictured Hitler's troops amassing across the English Channel, preparing for the invasion everyone said was bound to come. It was a terrifying thought: German warships advancing like an impenetrable wall towards England.

Rose wanted her life to change, but not like that.

Placing her canvas bag beside her, she gathered her wind-whipped hair in her hands and wound it round her neck. She breathed deeply, steadying nerves badly frayed by an afternoon in Norman's presence, and waited for the wildness of sea and sky to work their magic upon her.

The colours, when they came, were magnificent. Waves of lilac and orange spread across the horizon, each shade mirrored in the spangled light that ran along the surface of the water. Rose pulled from her bag a pad of paper and her precious watercolour paints. She worked swiftly, filling the paper with thick slashes of colour and adding shades she could not see in the sky before her, so the painting became a work of the imagination as much as a reflection of the real world. It astonished her that as an artist she could be so bold when she was nothing but timid the rest of the time.

Rose sank down further into the dune grasses, clumps of flowering sea aster all around her. When the sunset colours faded to darkness she began a second painting, outlining in blue-black the ridges of cloud hovering above the horizon, until all light was gone and she could barely make out the point where sky ended and the waves began.

Then she heard something.

It was the distant putter of a plane, flying low over the water.

Rose glanced back towards the coastal path and saw that it was deserted, just a blurred line in the darkness, reaching towards the black expanse of Silverwood in one direction and Lowbury in the other. But Lowbury had disappeared, obliterated by blackout curtains as the lights in all the houses were turned on.

She was alone.

The puttering grew louder and she saw it. A black smudge in the sky, far off but moving closer.

A single plane.

A Messerschmitt.

Rose felt her heart hammer in her chest to think that the war could make it all the way here, to her sleepy corner of the world.

Should she run for the trees and hide herself there? Charge back across the fields towards home? Or stay here, crouched low among the dune grasses?

She stayed where she was, craning her neck upwards to track the plane's progress across the sky. Closer and closer it came, until it neared the beach and seemed to hover overhead. *This is how a rabbit must feel*, she thought, *when it spies a hawk in the air above it.*

Something fell from the plane and tumbled towards the ground.

A bomb? Rose felt a stab of terror. Then she saw that the falling thing was a man, spinning through the air. She held her breath and watched him tumble, thinking him doomed, until at the point where death seemed inevitable a parachute snapped open. He sailed before her, the sea wind sweeping him inland towards Silverwood Vale.

Having discharged its load, the Messerschmitt spun round and disappeared over the sea.

Rose gathered up her art supplies and stuffed them in her bag with barely a thought for the half-dried paintings. She stepped over the barbed wire and onto the coastal path, pausing to plunge the fence post back into the soft earth.

She should head for Lowbury and alert the Home Guard. That would be the right thing to do. It was what Evelyn would have done, enjoying the short-lived fame such an act of patriotism would bring. But Rose wasn't like Evelyn. She didn't think of enemies and of glory. She thought of a body, plunging to the ground, perhaps broken and in pain. In need of help.

Before she could give herself time to think, Rose started to run, following the path of the parachute along the coastal path and towards the drainage ditch that marked the boundary of Silverwood Vale.

She leapt over the ditch and green darkness wrapped itself around her, a familiar and comforting mantle. The forest floor was speckled with red campion, their tiny flowers bowing their heads in homage to the night.

In Silverwood you could sense the long arm of time. Place a palm against any of the gnarled trunks and you were touching some of the oldest living beings in England, trees that had witnessed medieval poachers hunting for venison, and spied on so-called witches as they lived out their days away from the prying eyes of the world.

Stepping into Silverwood was like stepping through a portal into another world and in that world Rose was – well, if not a different person, at least a version of herself she liked.

But tonight the forest felt different. Rose doubted it had ever, in all its centuries of life, seen a man drop out of the sky.

She stopped to listen.

Silence.

Holding her hands out in front of her, Rose pushed deeper into the trees.

It was years since she had first escaped to this forest with Evelyn. They had retreated here after their father died, to nurse their grief. Later, when Norman commandeered their mother and their home, it was to Silverwood they had taken their misery and their rage. For the past few weeks Rose had returned alone, seeking solace and freedom. She had learned that in a forest there was rarely such a thing as silence. A forest was alive with noise if you listened hard enough and that was what she did now. She heard a light breeze stir the branches. A rodent, scurrying through the bushes. A nightjar, whistling in darkness. And underneath these familiar noises, another that was entirely out of place.

The sound of fabric, flapping in the wind.

Rose looked up.

The oak tree beside her was one of the oldest in Silverwood. Centuries ago, lightning had cleaved it in two and both halves of the enormous trunk had continued growing separately. She and Evelyn had named it the Thunder Oak, feeling dwarfed by the size, the wizened age of it.

Now, Rose looked up through its canopy and saw the parachute lifting and falling in the breeze like an enormous bird. And hanging from a harness at the end of the parachute, cradled in the fork of the great Thunder Oak, was the body of a man.

He hung just above head height, but in the darkness, Rose had not seen him. He had fallen with force through the canopy, breaking off a bough as he tumbled. One of the man's arms dangled over a branch and his left foot was bent behind him. His head was a mass of black curls that had fallen like a curtain over his face and he wore a jumpsuit made of coarse fabric.

Rose's gaze settled on his chest. She waited for the rise and fall of his breath, but saw nothing.

My first dead body, she thought, feeling a mixture of relief and sadness that the man was not alive. Feeling also an unexpected sense of loss. It had been foolish to run after the parachute and she had astonished herself by doing it. If the German was dead, she was not in danger and that was surely a good thing. But because he was dead, her life would go on as it had before. She would alert the Home Guard and that would be that. Evelyn would still be gone, her mother still sick, Norman as nasty as ever, and Rose would be trapped in a predictable future without the courage to change it.

On impulse, she reached out to brush curls from the dead man's face. It was a gentle face with an unexpected kindness to it and his expression was almost peaceful, as if he had died in his sleep and not by falling from the sky. The man was not much older than she was and he had a well-trimmed beard as black as his curls. Tentatively, Rose touched it, feeling how soft it was. His lips were soft, too, and still warm.

She drew her hand away, almost reluctantly.

Based on his serene expression, Rose decided the man had been a gentle soul, amenable and generous. But that was fanciful thinking, of course.

'Rest in peace,' she whispered to him.

And the man's eyes snapped open.

the one who always seemed to have all the answers, while Rose drifted into a future others shaped for her.

But really, her decision came down to just one thing: what sort of person *was* she?

As Rose searched for an answer, she recalled an incident from her childhood. She had been about ten years old, living in fear of a mean girl newly arrived at her school. The girl's name was Mildred and her father was a police officer, working alongside Norman.

Mildred had a perpetual frown, a nose that turned upwards as if she found fault with everything and a posse of girls who followed her everywhere. Timid Rose became Mildred's target at once. She liked to wind Rose's long hair round her wrist, cry, 'Giddy-up!' and run her along the road like a pony, while the others fell about laughing.

One day, on the way home from school, Rose came across Mildred and her posse standing in a circle, looking at the ground. They were prodding at something with sticks.

'What are you doing?' she asked.

Mildred looked up, eyes full of hatred. Rose had never questioned her before and she knew at once that it was a mistake.

'My little horsy spoke,' Mildred sneered.

The other girls straightened to look at her, giving Rose a clear view into their circle.

A tiny rabbit sat cowering in the middle of the group.

'Let it go!' Rose cried, realising too late that if she wanted to save the rabbit this was the worst thing she could have done.

Mildred scooped up the creature, a malevolent expression on her face.

'Let it go!' Rose repeated, unable to stop herself. This time her voice held an unaccustomed note of authority.

Mildred's eyes iced over. 'Rabbits are vermin,' she said. 'They munch away at crops – isn't that true, girls? Munch, munch, munch.'

Her posse joined in dutifully with a chorus of '*Munch, munch, munch!*' but Rose could see they were hesitant. They knew what Mildred intended to do and they didn't like it any more than she did.

'Plus,' Mildred went on, 'this baby bunny is injured. It's a kindness to put it out of its misery – isn't it, girls?'

This time, none of the others echoed her sentiments. 'Killing the rabbit wouldn't be nice, Mildred,' whispered one of the girls and, before Mildred could turn on her, the others were muttering similar objections.

Realising she had misjudged the situation, Mildred snapped, 'Can't any of you take a joke?' She dropped the rabbit and it hopped off into the bushes.

Rose had learned important truths about herself on that long-ago afternoon. She had learned that she could not bear to see a fellow creature injured and helpless. She had also learned that despite her timidity, when it was truly needed she could find it in herself to be strong.

Now, Rose looked up at the much bigger but equally helpless creature dangling from the Thunder Oak. If Mildred had found this injured man, she would have reported him to the police without considering his pain or his fate. But Rose wasn't Mildred.

And as she thought this, the man's eyes flickered open. His expression pleaded with her, begging for her help.

Rose stepped back, out of arm's reach. 'I think your ankle might be broken,' she told him.

Foreign words burst from his lips in a torrent.

'I can't understand you,' Rose said.

The man raised a hand slowly to his forehead and let two of his fingers rest there, against his temples. Then he spoke again, in clear but heavily accented English.

'You must go to your police,' he said. 'You must report where you have seen me and tell them I surrender.'

What?

'It was always my plan. To go to your British police and give myself up.'

For a second, Rose saw this as the answer to her dilemma. If this was what he wanted, she could involve the authorities with a clear conscience. But then she recalled Norman's smug words that evening as he slammed his fist down on the table.

'If you turn yourself in, they will kill you,' Rose said. 'Churchill brought in a new law a few months ago called the Treachery Act. It allows them to execute spies.'

She watched the man's face drop as he took in this news and it occurred to her that he might be telling the truth. That, as he dropped from the Messerschmitt with orders to spy for Germany, his secret intention may always have been to surrender.

'Then you must help me,' he said. 'Please.'

And when Rose thought about the death awaiting him if she informed the authorities, she knew what she had to do.

She took out the confiscated penknife and opened it.

'No...' whispered the man.

'Oh, I don't mean to...' Rose said, flustered by his reaction. 'I won't harm you, I promise. I want to cut you free.'

He regarded her warily, then nodded.

Rose reached forward to saw through the straps of the harness. When she struggled, he placed a hand over hers.

'I can do it,' he said. Rose hesitated before relinquishing the knife. He cut through the straps with ease, closed the penknife and – to her surprise – handed it back to her.

'Put your arm round my shoulder,' she said. 'I can help you down.'

She planted her feet firmly, reaching out to the trunk to steady herself, and the man twisted sideways, grunting with pain. Then he hooked an arm round Rose's shoulders and allowed himself to fall. For a second she bore his weight before her knees buckled and they tumbled to the ground.

Rose struggled to free herself, then squatted down beside him. For an eternity the man lay still, one palm held flat against his ribs and his face contorted with pain. He waited until the breath no longer burst from him in gasps. Then he opened his eyes and looked at her.

'I have been rescued by an angel,' he said, the words clipped, the accent strong. 'Perhaps I died and went to heaven, after all.'

Rose felt her cheeks burning. It was the nicest thing anyone had ever said to her. She was glad of the deep shadows, the darkness illuminated only by thin streaks of moonlight, because at least he could not see her blush.

'I am Walter,' he said.

She wondered if that was his real name and somehow felt certain it was.

'Rose,' she replied and smiled.

Walter raised a shaking hand to his temples again and winced. He was in a great deal of pain, Rose thought, and her heart went out to him.

'My head feels... and also there is, what is the word...' He glanced down, towards his chest.

'Ribs?' Rose offered.

'Yes, perhaps some ribs are cracked. And the foot...'

Rose looked down and saw that his left ankle was swelling. 'May I?' she asked and when he nodded, she unlaced his boot and eased it off.

'I don't know what I can do,' she said, examining the purple bruising.

'There is nothing either of us can do,' Walter replied, morosely. 'I have no wish to die, so I cannot seek help from your police or a doctor. It is an unfortunate situation.'

Rose said, 'Let's take things one step at a time.'

She thought again about the rabbit, cowering on Mildred's hand. She could no more leave Walter to his fate than she could turn her back on that helpless creature all those years ago.

'If you hide here in the bushes for tonight,' she said, 'I can return early in the morning with food and medical supplies.'

Walter propped himself up on his elbows and waited for her to go on.

'There's a place I know of,' Rose said, tentatively. 'A cabin, deep in the forest. Perhaps tomorrow I can take you there.'

A sudden gust whipped through the branches of the Thunder Oak, tugging at the parachute, which shuddered like the wings of a giant bird.

Walter looked up. 'Someone may see this,' he said, but Rose shook her head.

'No one comes into Silverwood except me and my sister, but she's gone away now.'

'This tree.' Walter pointed at the gnarled oak, cleaved in two by a storm so long ago. 'I believe it saved me.'

Rose nodded. The parachute had become entangled in the branches, slowing his descent.

'Will you be all right?' she asked as she clambered to her feet.

Walter offered her a strained smile. 'This will not be the first time I have slept out of doors,' he said.

'I'll be back in the morning.'

Moonshine spilled down through the fork in the old oak and onto his face. It was a kind face, Rose decided. Soft and gentle. A face that invited trust.

'I won't let you down,' she said, scooping up her bag of art supplies. Then she turned and left, running out of the forest and along the coastal path towards home, with only the glimmer of moonlight on the dark sea to guide her.

FIVE

ROSE

September 1940

It did not take long for the doubts to set in.

This man was sent to England to spy, Rose thought, tossing and turning in bed that night. It was his job to deceive people and he needed her help, so of course he would try to convince her he meant no harm – and she had fallen for it. Left to roam at will, there was no telling how much damage one German spy could do, nor how many lives might be placed in peril. *If I help him, I will be a traitor to my country.*

And, as Norman had told her just hours earlier, the punishment for treachery was execution.

The night was still and warm. With her window open, Rose could hear, faintly and far off, the rush of waves on the beach. Several times, she thought she heard the distant putter of Messerschmitts crossing the Channel and she held her breath to listen, but if England was about to be invaded, it wasn't tonight. The sound of enemy planes was only in her imagination and what she could hear was the breakers on the shore, a peaceful sound that was normally enough to lull her to sleep.

But not this time.

Pulling the blankets over her head to block out the noise, Rose thought again of Walter. This time, she recalled the warmth and kindness she had read in his eyes. The softness of his beard and lips. In the darkness she pictured his hands stroking her face as she had stroked his.

Rose sat bolt upright in bed. What had come over her? How could she allow herself to imagine such a thing? This man was at best a stranger and at worst, an enemy spy.

She turned on the bedside lamp and looked at her clock.

Dawn was still hours away.

Across the room stood Evelyn's bed, now stripped of its counterpane, and as Rose gazed at it, she felt a sudden longing for her sister.

'Look at you, my darling,' Evelyn had said one evening, a few days before she left for good. 'If I ever saw anyone in need of a little fun, it's you.' Rose recalled how she had crossed her legs prettily at the ankles, leaned against their dresser and looked her up and down with a critical eye.

There had been a huge row that afternoon, when Norman accused Evelyn of stepping out with an airman. She had laughed in his face, as if the idea was too preposterous for words, though it wasn't, of course. It was all true, and more.

Evelyn spun round to open their bedroom window. She lit a cigarette and leaned out so the smoke drifted off into the warm evening air. 'You must come with me next Saturday night,' she said, 'to the town hall dance. It will be a lark and you need it, darling, you really do.'

Evelyn was right. Rose was eighteen years old and what had she done with her life? After leaving school, she had worked in the local haberdashery but, when her mother's health worsened, Norman had ordered her to stay home and mind the house. Now she rarely even went to town, except to stand in endless queues with their ration books.

'I'm not like you,' Rose said miserably. She caught sight of herself in the mirror on the dresser. Sensible, brown tweed skirt and a cream-coloured blouse that hadn't been in fashion since long before the war. Nothing about her appearance was memorable, except perhaps her hair: jet black tresses that fell to her waist. Refusing to have it cut had been a minor act of rebellion, but a pointless one that paled in comparison to everything her sister did.

'You could be beautiful,' Evelyn said. 'Stunning, even. All you need is the right clothes. You can borrow my blue chiffon. Come on, Rose – come to the dance with me. There are plenty of dashing airmen to go round!'

Rose was shaking her head even before her sister had finished speaking. 'I don't even know how to dance,' she said and she sat down heavily on her bed, smoothing her skirt over her knees.

Evelyn stubbed out her cigarette and tossed it into the garden. Before Rose had time to resist, she leapt across the bedroom to grab both her hands, pulling her off the bed.

'Dancing's easy-peasy,' she said, 'and with your long legs and tiny waist you'll have every man in uniform swooning over you! Here, let's try the foxtrot. I'll be the man.' She clamped a hand down on Rose's shoulder. 'Look lively, here we go!'

Rose found herself propelled around the bedroom, her reluctance giving way to giggles as Evelyn shouted, 'Slow, slow, quick, quick! Slow...'

Only her sister could do this to her. Only Evelyn could make her forget her self-doubt and believe anything was possible.

They were laughing now, whirling so fast that Rose felt giddy with excitement. Maybe she *would* do as Evelyn suggested! Maybe she would defy their stepfather and sneak out on Saturday night. Maybe she—

'What the hell's going on up there!' roared Norman from

the bottom of the stairs. 'Shut it, the pair of you, or I'll give you both something to squeal about!'

Evelyn and Rose stopped dancing and fell still. Rose looked at the floor, fearful that Norman might charge up the stairs and make good on his word.

'At the dance,' Evelyn whispered, 'you're going to meet—'

'No,' Rose said.

'You can't let Norman—'

'No.' She sat down heavily on her bed. 'I'm not coming with you on Saturday,' she said. 'I'm not like you, Evelyn. I can't do the things you do.'

Evelyn was silent for so long that Rose felt compelled to look up, to meet her gaze. Something in her sister's expression had changed.

'Norman's a tyrant,' Evelyn said. 'I'm not taking it any longer.'

Rose felt herself go cold.

'Charles is going to propose soon, I know he is, and once we're engaged, I'll be gone.' Her voice was steely with determination. 'I'm off to London, to stay with his sister, Penny. And once we're married and this awful war is over, he's taking me to Canada.'

But only if he survives, Rose thought.

'None of us know how long we'll be alive,' Evelyn said, as if she could read Rose's mind. 'We have to seize every opportunity.'

Rose recalled her sister's words now as she looked around the small bedroom that seemed so empty without Evelyn. A deep sadness swept over her. Evelyn had loved her – but not enough to stay. She had taken her chance and gone, walking jauntily down the garden path with her travelling case swinging by her side. She had left Rose to care for their mother alone and she had left her at the mercy of their stepfather, too.

It was hard not to feel bitter.

. . .

Rose was still awake in the early hours when Norman returned from work. He stomped up the stairs, slammed the bedroom door behind him and moments later, his snores melded with the distant sound of the sea.

At some point, Rose must have fallen asleep too, for she found herself walking through Silverwood Vale in the moonlight, not at peace as she usually was in the forest, but filled with a sense of impending doom. She saw the Thunder Oak ahead of her, but something was in the way, something that did not belong in the forest. She knew, even before she reached it, what it was. It was a hangman's scaffold and dangling from it was Walter, his neck in the noose.

Rose shuddered awake. The night was almost over, giving way to a grey and drizzly dawn.

Shrugging off the horrors of her dream, she slid out of bed and padded down to the kitchen, taking care to do so in silence. She had made up her mind: she would take food and medical supplies to Walter, but that was all. She would not notify the Home Guard because she could not bear to have his death on her conscience, but that didn't mean she had to get involved. She would wash her hands of the whole business and walk away.

Rose put together a small bundle of food. She grabbed an old sheet that she could tear into strips for a bandage, and a bottle of her mother's painkillers. Then she let herself out of the front door and walked round the house to the garden. She was almost at the gate leading through to the country lane when something made her turn.

Her mother stood at the bedroom window, gazing down at her.

Rose hesitated only briefly, then she turned and ran for the coast.

SIX

ROSE

September 1940

Rose half expected to find Walter gone, thinking his injuries may have been no more than a ruse, a way to buy himself the time to get away. But he was there, under the Thunder Oak, exactly where she had left him.

'How are you feeling?' Rose asked. Rain had come with first light and he was drenched to the skin and shivering. His breath burst from him in gasps.

He scrunched his eyes shut and held a hand to his ribs.

Just give him the supplies and go, she told herself. She knelt down beside him, holding out the bread she had taken from her mother's pantry, but Walter shook his head. Then she showed him the painkillers and he emptied several into the palm of his hand, swallowing greedily. Finally, Rose turned her attention to his ankle, tearing the old bedsheet into strips and binding it, gently.

When she had finished, she looked up at Walter again and their eyes met.

'I have had all night to think about my situation,' he said, hoarsely, 'and I have decided that I must surrender to your police, as I always intended to do.'

Rose said, 'You can't! They will—'

'I know.'

He leaned back against the tree, one hand pressed against his ribs, in a futile effort to ease the pain.

'But if you—'

'I will not be a puppet for the German Reich,' Walter said, sharply. 'Whatever they intend me to do in your country, it will involve destruction and death. It is better for me to surrender and face execution than to be the cause of such things.'

Rose felt a sudden rush of emotion. Dread, compassion and something more. If Walter would choose execution over aiding the coming Nazi invasion, he had to be a good man. A man worth saving. She recalled the image from her nightmare – Walter's dead body dangling from the hangman's noose.

'I can hide you,' she blurted.

'But not forever.'

'Do you *want* to die?'

Walter took a moment to think about this and in the silence that fell between them, Rose became aware of the forest again. The noises were the same as they had always been and yet they were somehow changed. Trees creaked in the wind, something scurried in the undergrowth and above them, in the branches of the Thunder Oak, a chaffinch burst into song.

'There is so much beauty in the world,' Walter said at last. His eyes flickered around the clearing, where raindrops trembled like tiny gems from every leaf, and then settled again on her. 'No,' he said softly. 'I do not wish to die.'

'Then let me hide you,' Rose said, without allowing herself time to think things through. 'There's a place I know of where you'll be safe. Can you walk?'

Walter hesitated before nodding. 'I must,' he replied.

Helping him to his feet was the hardest part. He was a big man, broad-shouldered and tall, while Rose had always been petite. She couldn't bear his weight, so she picked up the bough from the Thunder Oak that had snapped clean away with the impact of Walter's body. She stripped it of its leaves and branches and Walter used it to lever himself off the ground. It also made an excellent crutch.

Normally, it only took Rose fifteen minutes to cover the distance from the Thunder Oak to the heart of Silverwood, but for Walter, each step was agony. For over an hour they struggled through the forest, Walter taking a few steps and then pausing to rest, his eyes closed tight, one hand hovering over his ribs.

Rose wondered how long she had before Norman woke and what he would do to her if he found she had left the house.

'Where are you taking me?' Walter asked on one of their many breaks.

'There's a cabin,' Rose said. 'I used to play in it, with my sister. No one will find you there. It's well hidden and anyway, most people steer clear of Silverwood.'

'Why?' Walter asked, adjusting the makeshift crutch under his arm and swiping raindrops from his eyes. His jumpsuit was plastered to his skin and his beard dripped water. Rose was drenched, too, as she was wearing only a light coat over her summer dress. She wished she had thought to sneak one of Norman's old coats for Walter to wear.

'A boy was murdered in the forest, years ago,' Rose said.

The story was well known to everyone in Lowbury. The killer had been a decorated veteran of the Great War, a hero who could never outrun the horrors he had seen. When he could no longer live among people, he had built a cabin for himself in Silverwood. There were many who pitied the poor man, leaving him food and other supplies, Rose's mother among them. But he only worsened over the years, his mind trapped in the trenches, battling the enemy night and day. Then one evening, a young boy had wandered into the forest and, mistaking him for the advancing enemy, the man had killed him. Rose hadn't really understood how it was possible to mistake a local boy for a German soldier, but as she struggled with Walter through the trees, she thought she understood a little better, now.

Telling friend from foe wasn't always easy.

It was a sturdy little place, the hermit's cabin, sunk in a hollow in the centre of a clearing. The cabin had a well in the front and a root cellar Evelyn and Rose had explored a few times, enjoying a delicious sense of danger as they climbed down the rickety ladder. The cabin had just one room, with a fire for heating and cooking, and a raised pallet that served as a bed. In the corner was an old trunk she and Evelyn had dragged in from their garden shed, back when they were still young enough to play house. It still held the last of their supplies, covered over with a thin layer of dust: matches, boiled sweets, drawing paper and a small packet of tea.

It felt strange, being here without Evelyn. Stranger still to share their secret hideaway with someone else.

Rose lowered Walter onto the pallet, wishing she had brought him a blanket and a change of clothing. Since she had neither, she built a fire, opening the window just a little as Evelyn had shown her to allow a steady supply of oxygen to the room. Soon, steam was rising from their clothes and the cabin was warm and welcoming.

When Rose turned away from the fire, she saw Walter gnawing on a piece of her bread.

'They never told us,' he said.

'What?'

'About the law you mentioned. What did you call it... the Treachery Act? For the execution of German spies.'

'Who never told you?' Rose asked.

Walter propped himself up on one elbow so that he could breathe more easily. He held a hand against his cracked ribs.

'In our training,' he said slowly, 'there were many things we were not taught. They did not teach us how to pass for English. You can tell I am German, yes?'

'Your accent is very strong,' Rose admitted.

'It was all done so quickly, you see,' Walter said. 'Hitler will invade your country very soon. You know this? And he has need of spies, on the ground. There was no time for the proper training. We learned to plant bombs, to defuse them. And we learned... what is the word? Sabotage. But there was no time to teach us to blend with the English.'

'So there are more of you?' Rose asked, startled. Somehow, this hadn't occurred to her.

'I do not know how many,' Walter replied, 'but I was not the only one to leave for England last night.'

Rose thought about this. Spies, landing all over the south coast, in preparation for Hitler's invasion. The thought made her blood run cold.

'Eat, please,' Walter said. He tore off a chunk of the bread and passed it to her. 'I think you are hungry also.'

Rose felt touched by his concern. She accepted the food and he smiled, both cheeks dimpling at the point where his beard ended.

He leaned towards her. 'You must not think I am the enemy,' he said. 'Please believe me. My sentiments are not with the Reich.'

Rose said nothing, weighing his words, and Walter sank back onto the pallet, defeated and in pain. For a while they sat in silence, listening to the trees shivering in the wind and raindrops hitting the dirty glass of the single window like sifted sand. Then Walter lifted his head to look at her again. 'Even through the rain I could tell your forest is quite beautiful,' he said. 'Beautiful, like you.'

A warmth spread through Rose that had nothing to do with the fire now crackling in the grate, its flames drawing a map across their faces.

'I'm going to make us both a cup of tea,' she said, keeping her voice steady, 'and then I think you should tell me who you are.'

SEVEN

ROSE

September 1940

Walter was born, he said, in Bischofswiesen, in the Bavarian Alps. It was a place of towering mountains, ice-cold lakes and forested trails that fired his imagination as soon as he was old enough to explore. His father had been injured in the Great War and was deeply embittered by Germany's defeat. The family lived in poverty, only getting by on the charity of their neighbours, and Walter often went to bed hungry.

But when he was seven years old, Walter's mother received an offer of help from a distant cousin, Frederick, who lived in England. Frederick had a secure income but no son of his own and he offered to take Walter for an extended holiday. So, the little boy found himself transplanted from the mountains of Bavaria to the flat expanse of the Lincolnshire countryside.

At first, he was desperately homesick, but food was plentiful and Frederick was kind. Best of all, his new guardian owned a landscape gardening business and he was often contracted to work on the region's most glorious gardens. Walter joined him at Belvoir Castle, where they designed a wildflower

garden at the request of the Duchess of Rutland, and at Grim-
sthorpe Castle, as they restored a woodland garden to its former
glory.

At seven years old, Walter developed a passion for
gardening and decided that his life's work would be the cultiva-
tion of beauty.

With good food and rigorous exercise, little Walter grew
sturdy and strong. When he had mastered English, he started to
attend the local school and joined the Wolf Cubs. He might
have been bullied as a German, but his burgeoning size made
him intimidating to others, so his schoolmates were wary of him.
Walter longed to be one of them, but he always found himself
excluded.

Despite this, the five years he spent in Lincolnshire were
the happiest of his life.

But when he was twelve years old, everything changed
again. Illness forced Frederick to retire and while Walter would
have chosen to stay and help the surrogate father he had come
to love, he received a letter from his parents instructing him to
return at once to Germany. His father had secured a job in
Munich and had risen quickly through the civic ranks of the
National Socialist German Workers' Party.

The family's financial troubles were over.

Walter returned home to a life and a country transformed
beyond recognition. For the first time he was living in a city and
he hated it. His father was fiercely proud of his new role and a
photograph of Hitler – now the self-appointed chancellor of the
Reich – hung in pride of place over the dining room table. The
streets of Munich were adorned with posters venerating the
new leader and Walter felt a sense of impending doom. He
recalled what Frederick had told him as they worked the
gardens together: that Hitler was a menace and a threat to
Europe's fragile peace.

Only his hours spent in the Jungvolk gave Walter respite

from his misery. This club for young boys reminded him of the Wolf Cubs back in Lincolnshire, only now he wasn't excluded – he was admired for his size and superior strength. With his troop, he returned to the mountains and lakes he loved, camping, hiking and swimming. In the Jungvolk he found a camaraderie he had longed for all his life – friendship with boys his own age who did not fear him, but respected him for his strength and athleticism.

Two years later, Walter graduated from the Jungvolk to the Hitlerjugend – the Hitler Youth. By that time, he had no choice.

Attendance was mandatory.

At this point in his story Walter hesitated and Rose topped up his tea with boiling water. His words thrilled her. She had never heard of the Hitler Youth but she could imagine Walter leading groups of boys through forests just like Silverwood as pennies of sunlight fell through the canopy and flickered gold against his skin.

'Go on,' she urged.

'These clubs,' Walter said, suddenly morose, 'Deutsches Jungvolk, Hitlerjugend… they are not just to make healthy boys, healthy men. They are to capture the minds of the young and at first I did not see it. I had lived outside the Fatherland, which made others suspicious of me, and I wanted to belong. It is the dream of every child. You understand?'

Rose nodded. She knew what it felt like to stand on the outside of a group, looking in.

Walter's face twisted with pain that was not physical this time and he clutched both sides of the pallet tightly as he strained forward. 'The desire to be included – it is not an excuse for what we did,' he said. 'I can say only that we were very young. Too young to understand.'

. . .

The group Walter was assigned to in the Hitler Youth was led by a boy called Otto. Blond-haired, blue-eyed and a born leader, Otto was a poster child for the German Reich. At seventeen he was barely taller than fourteen-year-old Walter, but what he lacked in size he made up for with a whip-sharp intelligence.

There was something dangerous about Otto and Walter disliked him at once. He sneered at weakness, mocked failure and ruled his group with an iron hand. He knew how to manipulate others – how to pinpoint every boy's vulnerability and work it against them. Otto was Walter's nemesis. He drew attention to the younger boy's difference at every opportunity, reminding the others that Walter had spent years of his life in England and hinting that this made his loyalty suspect.

One day, as they returned to Munich after a vigorous hike along the banks of Lake Starnberg, Otto stopped his group outside a small bakery. The boys lined up behind him in their black shorts and tan shirts, each of them wearing an armband with a diamond-shaped swastika emblem.

'This shop is run by a Jew,' Otto said to Walter. He pointed to a pile of bricks stacked along the wall and said loudly, 'I order you to smash the window.'

A current of excitement rippled through the boys.

'How can you be sure who owns the shop?' Walter asked. He looked through the large display window to rows of freshly baked bread and sugar-dusted Krapfen.

'Everyone knows,' a second boy said.

'It's true,' added a third. 'My father told me.'

'What are you waiting for?' Otto's eyes glittered, cold as ice.

Walter sensed he stood on a threshold. Refuse the challenge and everything would change. He would be an outsider in the group, a traitor in their midst to be sneered at and tormented.

He might even find himself denounced for un-German behaviour.

But how could he do such a thing? He thought of kind, gentle Frederick, who had loved and trusted him. What would he think if he could see Walter now?

'Go on,' a boy whispered behind him and the others chorused his words: 'Go on. Go on.'

Otto looked at him, his steely eyes glittering. 'What are you waiting for?' he asked.

Walter picked up a brick and the other boys cheered. He swung back his arms and aimed, but as he let go he pretended to stumble on the uneven ground and the brick landed harmlessly on the wall beside the display window. The other boys barely noticed Walter's failure, for now they were all picking up bricks of their own and hurling them at the bakery.

But Otto noticed.

The boys howled like animals as they threw their missiles and the display window shattered into a million pieces. Across the road a small crowd gathered, the adults seeming curious and bemused rather than disapproving. The boys reached through the broken glass to seize the produce, tossing loaves to the crowd and chewing on the sweet delights of Krapfen, their uniforms dusted with powdered sugar.

Otto stood apart from the others, looking at Walter with dark and knowing eyes.

A window opened above the store and a man poked his head out. He opened his mouth to shout at the boys, but then he saw their uniforms, and the crowds, and his shoulders sagged. He reached out to close the shutters and, as he did so, Otto moved with lighting speed, grabbing a brick at his feet. He swung his arm back, preparing to hurl it at the man's head.

Walter knew Otto had impeccable aim. That the brick was large and heavy enough to smash the baker's skull. He reached out and gave Otto a shove. The brick thudded to the ground and the man in the window ducked inside and closed the shutter behind him.

In the frenzy of jostling, hooting boys, no one saw what Walter did.

No one knew. Except for Otto.

Later, Walter walked home alone, demoralised and despondent. Otto now had proof that Walter did not share the Nazi Party's sentiments and he was likely to make his life a misery. It hit Walter harder than it ever had before: his future was not his to shape as he wished. He was trapped in a system that demanded total obedience and in the years to come he would be called upon to do far worse than smash the windows of a Jewish bakery.

But as luck would have it, Walter did not have Otto to worry about for long. The older boy was honoured with a spot at one of Germany's new elite academies, designed to train Nazi leaders of the future, and he disappeared from Walter's life. After three more years in the Hitler Youth, Walter was conscripted into the Wehrmacht, the Germany army. By then, there were no Jews running shops of any kind in Munich and Germany was at war.

And that was where Walter's life took an unexpected turn.

He was considered a promising recruit due to his size and his athleticism. Basic training was gruelling, but nothing he couldn't handle. He rose before dawn with the other recruits and his days were filled with an endless series of drills, with long lectures on the ideals of the German Reich that were delivered while the men stood to attention in the baking June sun. But one day, during a lecture on the superiority of the Aryan race, Walter was called aside and ordered to report to the commanding officer.

His heart thudded with terror. True, by day he was the perfect recruit: eager, obedient, fit in mind and body, a model soldier. But at night, the thoughts he had, the beliefs he allowed free rein under cover of darkness, would surely see him condemned. He felt certain that his superior officers had somehow learned of his contempt for the Reich. That they thought him capable of betraying the Fatherland.

When Walter reported to his commanding officer in his plush office with its dark leather chairs and mahogany desk, he expected more than punishment. He expected court martial, perhaps even execution, for a crime he had yet to identify.

He stood to attention and saluted, noting that there were two men in the room: his commanding officer, sitting rigidly behind his desk, and a second, much older man who wore civilian clothes but glared at Walter in a way that only increased his terror.

The stranger walked slowly across the room. From the cut of his clothes, his casual saunter and the way the commanding officer deferred to him, Walter could only assume this was a person of great importance – and power.

'You have lived in England,' said the stranger and his nose wrinkled as he said the word.

Walter's past was returning to haunt him, as he had always thought it would.

'Yes, sir,' he replied. 'Years ago, as a young boy.'

'Then you speak the language. You know the customs and the culture.'

'Only vaguely, sir. And I have forgotten—'

'It is no matter,' the stranger interrupted. '"Vaguely" must be good enough, for we have little time.'

He looked Walter up and down, his nose wrinkling again, as if what he saw displeased him.

'Your commanding officer speaks most highly of you,' he continued. 'We are looking to train agents for covert operations in England, in preparation for the coming invasion. You understand?'

Walter didn't. 'I-I'm not sure, sir,' he said.

The stranger ignored this.

'Your mission will be dangerous. You will find yourself alone in enemy territory. This is something you could do – for the Fatherland?'

And Walter understood.

With a surge of excitement he realised that here, at last, was a way out. Germany wished to send him to England. Well, let them do so. Frederick had died long ago, so Walter had no one in England to help him, but he recalled the country fondly enough to see in it his salvation. He would go along with whatever plans the Reich had for him until he found himself on English soil. Then, he would walk into the nearest police station and surrender. It would be better to spend the remaining months of this war in a British prison than as a pawn of the German Reich.

'I accept, sir,' Walter said. 'I accept with all my heart.'

'So you were always going to turn yourself in when you landed in England?' Rose asked. She was perched on the edge of the pallet, her knees close to Walter's chest, though she wasn't sure how she had got there – at what point in his story she had seated herself. Embarrassed by her proximity to him, she began to pull away, but Walter placed a hand on her knee to stop her. She looked at his hand, half thrilled, half alarmed to feel the warmth of his skin on hers.

'I need to know,' he said, 'and please, you must tell the truth. Do you believe me?'

Rose had never been good at lying, at deception of any kind, unlike Evelyn. She knew that in wartime, hiding truths was often a necessity – but it just wasn't something she could do.

'I don't know if I believe you,' she said hesitantly, but, seeing his stricken expression, added, 'I think I do.' His story sounded convincing enough and she wanted to trust him. But wasn't that the job of any spy – to deceive the enemy? No matter how much this man fascinated her, could she allow him to take her for a fool?

To mask her confusion, Rose changed the subject. 'These people who recruited you to spy – what do they want you to do?' she asked.

Walter shifted his position, to ease the pain in his ribs. As his hand lifted from Rose's knee she inched away, closer to the edge of the pallet. But she didn't get up.

'I do not know, not yet,' Walter said and he frowned. 'In our training we learned radio telegraphy, Morse code, how to handle explosives, to plant and defuse bombs. Our instructors had expertise in such things but we did not learn to blend in. There was not time for this.'

'Your accent would identify you as soon as you opened your mouth,' Rose said. 'And you're carrying a photo that clearly wasn't taken in England.'

She saw her mistake at once, but Walter didn't ask why she had gone through his pockets, he just pulled out the photo and handed it to her. She looked again at the smiling woman. The stern-looking father, his hand clamped down firmly on the shoulder of his son.

'You are correct, of course,' Walter said. 'In the photograph is my father and my mother. You see how I smile here, as a little boy? When we are children, we love innocently and with all our hearts, do we not? Before we learn people can be more than what they seem. My father, he would die for the German Reich. For its ideals. My mother, too. I love them, but I cannot like them now. I cherish this photograph, for in it I am young and love is not so complicated.'

When Rose remained silent, Walter said quickly, 'Is this photograph not further proof I speak the truth? I did not intend to go undetected. And since my return home would be impossible once I had surrendered to your police, I could not bear to leave this photograph behind.' He sighed as he added, 'My father – I do not think he would be proud, if he could hear me now.'

'No, I don't suppose he would,' Rose said. It occurred to her that Walter had lost his father every bit as much as she had lost hers. She handed the photograph back and Walter slipped it into the pocket of his overalls.

While they had been talking the rain had stopped and, beyond the window, the late morning sun was streaking through the glade, turning the steam-covered panes bright gold. Rose crossed to the glass, wiping it with her sleeve. Sunshine spilled across the cabin, illuminating Walter on the pallet.

'What are you thinking?' he asked her. 'On your face, there is such an expression...'

Rose felt her cheeks colour. She couldn't bring herself to answer his question because the truth was she had been considering what it would be like to paint him. She imagined the intimacy of such a moment, giving herself permission to study every part of his face, to interpret his expression, and she felt a sudden thrill. It was hot in the cabin, she realised, and she reached out to the fire, spreading the burning logs, encouraging the flames to die back.

To sidestep Walter's question, she said, 'It's terrifying to me. The thought that Hitler might invade England, as he invaded France and Belgium.'

'You are right to be afraid,' Walter replied, grimly.

'And you said there are others like you? Spies, landing all over the country, at night?' Rose thought of the barbed wire, spread out along the dunes. The street signs that had been removed in Lowbury and elsewhere, to confuse the enemy.

'I do not think our agents will succeed,' Walter said. 'There was little time to prepare us and others may think as I do. You see, many of these spies, they were prisoners, brought from Germany's conquered lands. They were offered their freedom in return for covert work in England. Many will give themselves up as I planned to do. I am certain of it.'

Conquered lands. The phrase pulled Rose up short and, despite the heat in the small cabin, she shivered. Was this how people would refer to England in the months to come, she wondered darkly – as another of Germany's 'conquered lands'?

If she was wrong to trust Walter, that meant she was aiding the enemy. Contributing to England's defeat.

But Walter was not finished. He crooked a finger at her, signalling for her to join him again by the pallet. When he continued, his voice was low, almost a whisper.

'There is one man,' he said, 'who is here already and whose job it is to lead our clandestine operations. To pave the way for Germany's invasion. He is not a prisoner, bargaining for his freedom, and he is not a simple soldier. I did not see him during our training, but I heard much talk of his exploits and his skills. Our instructors spoke of him with admiration and reverence. I do not think this man will turn himself in. I do not think so at all.'

Rose detected something new in Walter's expression as he spoke. Something she had not seen on his face until this moment, despite his pain and his predicament.

Fear.

'This man, he is small,' Walter said, 'with white-blond hair and very cold eyes. He believes in the German Reich and he believes in the Führer as a kind of god. He will not be afraid to die for his country and he will not hesitate to kill for it. This man is skilled in sabotage, in so many things. He is very dangerous and he will never turn himself in. I knew him, you see. Better than most. His name is Otto.'

'Otto?' Rose asked and her skin prickled. 'The Otto you knew when you were in the Hitler Youth?'

Walter nodded slowly. 'The same,' he said.

EIGHT

ROSE

September 1940

Rose handed Walter the poker.

'I have to go,' she said. 'I've been out all morning and my stepfather won't like it.'

'Please,' Walter said hastily, 'there is something you must do before you leave the forest, if you are willing. You must take down my parachute so we may hide it.'

Rose saw the sense in that. Few people ever entered Silverwood Vale, but planes often flew overhead and the parachute might be visible from the air.

'I'll get it now.' She hurried towards the door.

'Rose?' Walter called to her and she paused with one hand on the latch. 'There is also my pack. It was torn away from me as I fell through the trees. You will look for it?'

She nodded.

'Also, there is something I should like to say.'

She turned back to him, noticing again the softness of his full, black beard and the dark lashes that rimmed his blue eyes. Gorgeous eyes, she thought, and it occurred to her that she couldn't think of any other time in her life when she had taken so much notice of a man's face.

'I am most grateful to you for everything you are doing,' Walter said, seeming suddenly overcome with emotion. 'Most grateful indeed.'

Rose felt her cheeks burning. Before he had time to notice, she fumbled with the latch and ran out into the trees.

The rain had stopped and the leaves of the canopy shone, their tremulous branches suspended in a brilliant blue sky. She paused in the glade to breathe deeply, to enjoy the rich scent of damp and growing things. Rose had always been observant and she suspected she knew Silverwood better than anyone else alive, yet, as she walked back along the path she had travelled with Walter just hours ago, she noticed things she had never spotted before. How sunlight, caught in a spider's web, turned the skein to finest silver. How each tiny frond of moss growing along the edges of the trail was as intricate and unique as a snowflake. A green woodpecker paused to gaze at Rose as it crept up the trunk of a birch tree and its iridescent colour seemed so vivid that it took her breath away.

Rose had the urge to sing, though she barely knew how. To leap and skip along the path, though she hadn't done such things in years.

I should feel weighed down by all my troubles, she thought. *And conflicted, because hiding Walter could be the worst mistake of my life. But I don't, not right now. I feel as light as air.*

In no time at all, she was back at the Thunder Oak and she murmured a respectful greeting to the ancient tree before clambering up into the cleft between its two split halves. From there, she could easily reach the parachute, reeling it in like a fishing net and gathering it in great folds under her arms. When a portion of it snagged in the branches, she climbed higher, her body fizzing with energy.

Rose unhooked the folds of silk from the tree and discovered she had climbed further than she thought, her limbs strong and eager to move. For far too long she had felt older than her years, hemmed in by responsibility, cowed by her stepfather's bullying. Now, it occurred to her how glorious it was to be young and the decades ahead of her felt like a shining gift, not a predictable burden, though nothing had changed about her life, not really.

Exhilarated, she looked down on her forest, a dazzling green carpet unfolding to the north. She rotated slowly, gazing down on the dunes, dotted with colourful sea aster, and the waves beyond them, tumbling across the golden sands. *How gorgeous the world is*, she thought with a sense of childlike delight she had not known in years.

A light autumn wind whipped through her long hair as she clambered down from the Thunder Oak, trailing the silk folds of the parachute behind her.

Finding Walter's pack was a little harder, but as she hunted through the undergrowth the unaccustomed feeling of happiness stayed with her. She remembered how she had played hide and seek in the forest with Evelyn, years and years ago while their father was still alive, and the delight they had felt one winter when they encountered Silverwood under a blanket of snow. How every tree had taken on a new and unfamiliar shape, the snow lying heavily on the branches and banking up against the trunks. Flakes had danced through the air ahead of them and they had raced through the trees, mouths open, trying to catch them on their tongues.

Rose felt like dancing now as she searched the undergrowth for Walter's missing pack, though she couldn't say why. She parted each bush and searched carefully, knowing the fabric might be dyed for camouflage.

In the end, it wasn't on the forest floor that she found it but in the arms of an oak sapling, its willowy trunk bending under its weight. Rose always felt a surge of joy when she found a new young tree growing in the forest. Giants like the Thunder Oak made the distant past feel tangible, but it was new trees like this little one that pointed towards a hopeful future, despite the madness of war.

In fact, she thought happily, this sapling could well have come from an acorn dropped by the Thunder Oak itself.

Rose lifted Walter's pack out of the branches. It was unexpectedly heavy and she staggered under the sudden weight.

One of the shoulder straps was broken, which was why the pack had been flung free as Walter tumbled through the canopy, but Rose slung the remaining strap over her shoulder and carried it into the light. She had imagined it would hold clothes, perhaps also maps and a compass, but the pack was too heavy for that. She placed it carefully on the ground.

It would be wrong to open it, of course. Walter had asked if she trusted him and although Rose wasn't certain that she did, she wanted to. Meddling with his pack would send a clear message that she didn't trust him at all.

She lowered her face to the khaki-coloured canvas and breathed deeply. Walter's scent lingered on it, as she had hoped it would. The unmistakably foreign scent of his cologne and hair cream mingled with the smell of green and growing things, as if he lived all his life outdoors. It occurred to her suddenly that, when she had made her way back to Silverwood at dawn, her intention had been only to leave food and medical supplies with him and then leave. When had she decided otherwise?

It was as if her subconscious mind had chosen the right thing to do, even while her logical brain had resisted.

And in just the same way, Rose didn't make a conscious decision to open Walter's pack. She didn't want to pry, not really. It was her fingers that did the work for her, unfastening the buckles, pulling on the leather straps, opening the flap.

She was surprised to discover that the pack contained nothing but a small case. Compact, made of metal and leather. Her curiosity mounting now, she slid it out, snapped it open and eased off the lid.

What Rose found inside the case knocked all the joy out of her. It reminded her that she wasn't living in a fantasy, where helpless men dropped out of the sky as if by magic to fulfil a young girl's dreams. This was reality, her country was at war, and whether or not she believed Walter's backstory, he was still an enemy spy.

Inside the pack, solid, dull grey and trailing wires, was a shortwave radio.

NINE

ROSE

September 1940

When Rose emerged from Silverwood Vale that morning, she returned to a life unchanged. Yet everything felt different. *She* felt different. The Rose who walked out of the trees and headed back to her home was not the same Rose who had chased the sunset to the beach just eighteen hours earlier.

She had returned to the cabin with Walter's parachute slung in folds over one shoulder and his pack over the other, and had slid both in through the door with only a brief goodbye. The thought of the shortwave radio troubled her immensely. It was one thing to hide an injured man in the middle of the woods, but quite another to know he had the means at his disposal to make contact with the enemy.

Yet Walter did not support the ideals of the German Reich and he had intended to surrender.

She believed him, didn't she? Believed and trusted him?

Rose wanted to, more than she could say.

In a stroke of luck, Norman had slept in longer than usual after his late shift and he was unaware that she had left the house at all. He shuffled around the kitchen, his shirt untucked and his braces dangling around his waist, before settling at the table with the newspaper held up before him.

Rose watched as her mother moved unsteadily across the linoleum to her chair. It was late morning and she must have been up for hours, but she still wore her old, quilted dressing gown, the one with the crusted fabric around the hem where she had stood too close to the fire, years ago. She was breathing heavily and when she poured herself a cup of tea, her hands shook so badly that the saucer filled before the cup did.

A bad night, then.

Taking a loaf from the bread bin, Rose set about making toast. She tried not to think about Walter, to maintain a neutral expression and focus on the task at hand, but as her mother took her seat at the table, Rose knew without looking that she was following her every move with worried, questioning eyes. She recalled looking over her shoulder that morning as she ran across the garden. The sight of her mother's face at the bedroom window, looking out.

Watching her go.

And then the coughing began. Deep, hoarse, agonising coughs with barely time in between them for Rose's mother to catch her breath. Rose hurried round the table, tipped her forward in her chair and rubbed her back in circles, over and over, until the spasm passed.

'Get her a glass of water, for Pete's sake!' Norman snapped. He behaved as if his wife coughed only to irritate him, but Rose had known for a long time that her mother's cough was more than just an irritation. It was a great deal more than that.

So many things had made the atmosphere at home unbearable over the past weeks and Norman's nastiness in the face of her mother's illness was one of them. Despite how alarmed she was by the hacking cough, Rose did what she always did when her stepfather's temper flared.

She looked for an excuse to get away.

'We're out of bacon,' she said, setting a plate of toast in front of Norman. 'I'm going into town to see if there's any to be had.'

She reached into the drawer for their ration books, grabbed the shopping basket and without another word to Norman or her mother, she headed out into the late morning sun.

The unseasonably warm weather had dried most of the puddles and where deeper ones remained, they sparkled in sunshine. The day had turned lovely. It blazed, as if in final glory, for the illusion of summer would soon be gone.

Walking down the country road towards Lowbury, Rose thought about her mother. There had been a string of unexplained hospital appointments over the past two years, but these had ended abruptly in July, leaving Rose to wonder whether this meant nothing more could be done. She had tried to ask her mother what was wrong, but all her questions were met with the same grim, martyred expression.

It was clear to Rose that Norman's bullying tendencies had worsened since his promotion to sergeant, three weeks earlier. It had been so much easier to tolerate her stepfather when she had her sister for support. Evelyn had never feared him the way Rose did and her courage had bolstered them both. But now Evelyn was gone and her letters were becoming less frequent as the weeks passed. She was moving on with her life – a life that would never have Rose in it.

And beneath these familiar cares lurked a new and pressing one.

Walter.

What Rose had done was illegal – worse, she was a traitor to her country. Yet when she thought of Walter, dangling helplessly in the branches of the Thunder Oak or limping through the forest, his face twisted with pain, it was difficult to see him as an enemy spy. She recalled how his cheeks dimpled at the exact point where his beard ended, each time he smiled. She thought of the little boy in the photograph he carried, filled with hope for the future, his face shining with happiness. And she tried to feel again the unaccustomed joy that had sent her leaping through the forest after only a couple of hours in his company.

As if she wasn't simply running down the trail she knew so well, but sailing through air.

It was market day and Lowbury's town square was busier than usual. Rose queued up at the butcher's for the meagre portions of bacon their rations allowed, wondering why she even bothered when she and her mother never got to eat any of it. Then she paused next to a market stall that held a display of shiny red apples. They were from a local orchard and thinking Walter might enjoy them, she filled a paper bag, paid and tucked it down the side of her basket with a surge of pleasure.

On the corner of the street, a newspaper seller stood next to a billboard with the day's headline written in tall, bold letters: Blitz Bombing of London Continues Nightly. Rose gazed at the pile of newspapers on the stand beside the man, thinking as her eyes scanned the lead article that her problems were minor in comparison to those of others. *Total casualties on Monday night were in the range of four hundred,* she read, *the majority of fatalities occurring when an elementary school in which families were sheltering was hit and collapsed.* Evelyn worked as an ARP warden in London, saving lives as German bombers did their worst. Rose prayed her sister would be safe.

'Them poor buggers,' the newspaper seller said. Rose looked up from the stack of papers. The man was elderly, leaning heavily on a walking stick. All the men she saw these days seemed so terribly old. Conscription had whisked away the rest.

'I know Hitler's game,' the newspaper seller continued, 'and it won't work on Londoners, no matter how many bombs he drops.'

'What do you mean?' Rose asked.

'Hitler wants 'em to give up,' the man went on, banging his stick against the pavement for emphasis. 'Drop enough bombs on 'em and they'll turn against Churchill, that's what he thinks. But Londoners are made of tougher stuff. Let Hitler do his worst, they'll never give in.'

Rose glanced down at the photograph on the front page of the newspaper, next to the Blitz story. It showed a woman in curlers and a headscarf, drinking a cup of tea and smiling defiantly at the camera. She sat on a pile of rubble that had once been her home.

'I hope you're right,' Rose said.

She looked up at the sound of a sudden commotion on the other side of the street. From inside the Fox and Hound pub came banging, the smashing of glass, the roaring of a man enraged. Then the front door of the pub burst open and the elderly publican emerged, still shouting. He paused briefly to yell something at Tom, the local drunk, who loitered outside as he always did, waiting for opening hours to begin. Then he ran as fast as his elderly legs would carry him, across the marketplace and towards the police station.

From all directions, people converged on the pavement outside the pub. From the shops and the bus stop and the town square they hurried, drawn by the screams and the possibility of drama in a place where so little ever happened. Rose saw Mildred emerge from the post office, her eyes wide with excitement. She scurried over to the gathering crowd, bursting upon them, shrieking her questions.

Within seconds, more than a dozen people had gathered outside the Fox and Hound, some of them eagerly questioning Tom and others peering in through the windows.

Inside the pub, all went silent.

Then Rose heard a police whistle and Officer Radcliffe – Mildred's father – came running full tilt round the corner, truncheon swinging in his fist. The crowd parted hastily and he burst through them and into the pub. Seconds later, the elderly publican scurried after him across the marketplace, panting heavily but smiling from ear to ear, as if he was enjoying himself immensely. He pushed through the crowds without a word and re-entered his pub.

Rose crossed the road, curious. She hovered a short distance from the others.

The front door burst open once again and Officer Radcliffe emerged alongside the publican's son, a muscled, stocky young man home on leave from the army. They were dragging something – someone – between them. The figure was dwarfed by the two men and Rose caught barely a glimpse of him, but she heard the noise he made, something between a sob and a wail. She watched as the trio crossed the town square towards the police station, Officer Radcliffe and the publican's son looming large over the slight body whose feet trailed along the ground between them.

In seconds, the men had turned down the side street and disappeared from sight.

Rose realised she was no longer alone. Her old enemy, Mildred, had moved to stand beside her.

These days, Mildred worked as a junior clerk in the post office, where she was rapidly making a name for herself as the town gossip, though she told everyone who would listen that when the war was over she planned to attend beauty school in London. Over the years, Mildred had learned to treat Rose with cold civility, but Rose was under no illusions: the civility masked a festering hatred.

'What's going on?' Rose asked her.

Mildred tossed back her dirty blond hair. 'Didn't you see? I was one of the first people to get here and I saw it all!' She sniffed. 'I don't think your stepfather was on duty this morning, was he? My dad will be so proud he was the one who got to make the arrest.'

Rose ignored her snide tone. 'Who was arrested?' she asked.

At that moment the town hall clock struck twelve, signalling the start of official pub opening hours. The jangling was loud enough to halt all conversation, but in the instant the noise ceased the crowd pushed forward and into the pub. The two girls moved further along the pavement, knowing their families would not approve of them entering a public house.

Rose looked in through the window. She saw everyone gathering around the elderly publican. But he wasn't serving drinks, he was sharing a story, gesticulating wildly as he did so.

'Who was arrested?' Rose asked again.

'A German spy!' Mildred cried, gleefully.

Despite the warmth of the day, Rose felt suddenly cold.

Mildred leaned in closer. 'The spies they send must be very stupid,' she said with unexpected vehemence. 'This one waltzed into the pub and ordered a pint before opening time! There isn't an Englishman in the land wouldn't know wartime pub hours and besides, they say the man had a German accent!'

Rose thought of Walter's words, just hours ago. How spies were landing all over the south coast, under cover of darkness. That there had been no time during their training to teach them about English customs, nor to help them blend in.

'My father will be so proud he got to make the arrest,' Mildred said again, and she glared at Rose, who understood the reason for her animosity.

Just weeks ago, Constable Radcliffe had been passed over for promotion in favour of Rose's stepfather. *One more reason for her to hate me*, Rose thought. *Just one more reason, to add to all the rest.*

'Did you hear all the banging and the smashing glass?' Mildred asked. 'I bet they beat the spy up good and proper!'

'What will they do to him?' Rose asked, before she could stop herself.

Mildred leaned in closer. 'Execute him,' she said. 'Hang him, maybe. Or it could be a firing squad – why do you care?'

'I don't.' Rose felt like a traitor as she spoke the lie. But what was a traitor, anyway? Nothing seemed as simple to her, as black and white, as it had a day ago.

'Well,' Mildred said with another toss of her curls, 'I can't hang about here, bandying words. Unlike some, I've a job to go to. And I don't need to gossip anyway. Not when my father can tell me everything himself, as soon as he gets home.'

Rose watched her stride across the road towards the post office, wondering why so many people felt the need to dominate others. Hitler might be the worst culprit of them all, but you didn't have to look far to see the same need for mastery every-where you went.

An hour later, Rose set off for home and her route took her past the police station. She could see Norman's Vauxhall parked out front, which meant he had been called into work early. It wasn't every day a spy was arrested in a place like Lowbury.

Staring up at the red brick facade of the station, with its ornate datestone over the front door, she wondered whether Norman would return home unbearably pompous because a German secret agent had been captured, or enraged because he hadn't been the one to make the arrest.

Rose shifted her shopping basket from one arm to the other and her thoughts turned to the captured German. She pictured him languishing in his cell, inside this very building, waiting to meet his fate. They would come from London to interrogate him and he would be taken away and executed. His family back home might never even learn his fate.

By hiding an enemy agent, Rose mused, *I am a traitor, too.*

The thought filled her with fear, but then she pictured Walter, bound and beaten in a cell. Betraying your country in a time of war was a terrible thing, but England had millions of people to defend her, while the man she had found in the arms of the Thunder Oak had no one else but Rose.

It might be a crime to hide Walter, but wouldn't it be morally wrong to betray him, knowing that by doing so she would be sending him to his death?

TEN

ROSE

September 1940

'What happened here? Oh, Mam...'

The scullery floor was a mess of broken dishes, congealed gravy and slimy chicken bones. Rose's mother was still wearing her quilted dressing gown. She stood propped in the doorway, a broom in her hand.

Kneeling down, Rose gathered up the larger pieces of shattered porcelain with care. She knew her mother was crying from the rhythmic sniffs she could hear behind her and she understood why. The dinner set had been a wedding gift to her parents. Rose's mother had once told the girls that, at every meal they ate together using their lovely Royal Crown Derby set, she thought about their father.

That was after her early illusions about Norman had shattered and he had revealed his true nature.

'You promised you would clean up last night, when you got back,' her mother cried as Rose threw the larger pieces of china into the bin and began to gather the smaller, sharper fragments between her finger and thumb. 'You were gone so long and you forgot all the mess you'd left in the scullery. Norman was already in a bad mood this morning because of my coughing, then letters arrived from your sister and that set him off. When he saw all the unwashed dishes...' Her voice rose in pitch, ending with an anguished wail.

Rose had completely forgotten she'd left last night before cleaning up. Returning home after dark, she had been too consumed with thoughts of Walter to worry about anything else.

'I'm sorry, Mam,' she said. 'I try not to annoy him, I really do.'

'I know,' her mother said, a note of resignation in her voice. 'You're a good girl.' She might have added *unlike your sister*, for Rose knew that, while her mother did not begrudge Evelyn her newfound freedom, she understood that in leaving, her elder daughter had put her own needs before theirs.

Yes, I'm a good girl, Rose thought, with unaccustomed bitterness. *Compliant, dutiful, obedient. And I'm starting to see what becomes of girls like me.*

She threw the last of the food scraps and porcelain shards into the bin, swiped a wet cloth across the sticky floor and stood up. Her mother was leaning so heavily on the broom that Rose worried she might fall over if her prop was removed. She looped an arm through her mother's to support her weight, prised her fingers gently from the handle and walked her through to the parlour to her armchair under the window.

'What's going on in town?' her mother asked as Rose tucked the blanket over her knees. 'That awful man came for Norman, right when he was at his worst.'

Rose knew without asking that the 'awful man' was John Radcliffe, Mildred's dad. He and Norman had worked together for years and Rose's mother had never liked him. 'He'd stab you in the back as soon as look at you,' she had said once. Like father like daughter, Rose supposed.

But although Rose was happy to be her mother's eyes and ears in Lowbury most of the time, she found she was unable to talk about the German spy languishing in his cell.

'Just an arrest,' she replied.

She was about to pull away when her mother leaned forward, clamping her fingers tightly round her wrist. 'Norman is getting worse,' she said. 'You can see that, can't you?'

Rose tried to free herself, but the fingers held her tight.

'Listen to me, Rose. You don't know what he's capable of.' Her mother tugged on her arm, pulling her down beside the chair. 'In those early years,' she said, 'while you and Evelyn were playing in the forest, Norman was...' Her words trailed off, but she didn't need to say any more – her anguished expression said it all.

There are things children don't see, Rose thought. *Things you can't imagine when you are only eight years old and you're still missing your dad, and all you knew before he died was a happy home.*

'Did he hurt you?' she asked. Rose had suspected as much for years, but she found now that she was almost reluctant to have her suspicions confirmed. What she remembered, returning from the forest with Evelyn on those long-ago after-noons, was the silence. Norman would be gone and her mother in bed with one of her migraines.

Rose's mother chose not to answer her question.

'He drank a lot, back then,' she said. 'I tried to protect you and Evelyn as much as I could. That's why I let you play in the forest whenever you asked, because it kept you away from him. But after a few months, the drinking eased off and he wasn't as bad, not for years.' Her mother pulled her closer, eyes wide with fear. 'Evelyn left home even though he had forbidden it and that's got to him, Rose,' she said, ominously. 'He's drinking as much now as he ever did.'

Rose freed herself from the fingers gripping her wrist and

stood up. She looked down at her mother, weak, vulnerable, trembling, and for a second it wasn't pity she felt, pity at everything her mother had suffered back when her daughters had been too young to notice or understand.

It was resentment.

Why didn't she ever stand up to him? Rose wondered. *Why didn't she throw him out?*

How different all their lives might have been if she had.

But then she imagined herself in her mother's shoes. *Would I have dared to challenge him?* she wondered, knowing the answer and hating herself for it. *I'll end up just like Mam, if I don't learn to stand up for myself.*

Perhaps Rose's expression altered as she thought this, for her mother said quickly, 'You must be careful, do you see that? You forgot to clean up last night and look what's happened. You mustn't do anything to annoy him because when your sister left us, he—'

'Wait,' Rose said, recalling her mother's earlier words. 'Did you say there were letters from Evelyn?'

Her mother sank back into the armchair. 'On the sideboard,' she said.

Rose looked over. Two letters, propped up in front of the carriage clock. One addressed to her mother and a second addressed to her.

At last.

Rose said, 'It's been so long since she last wrote. I was starting to think something had happened. With all the bombing in London...'

She let her sentence trail off, took her letter from the mantelpiece and walked into the hallway. She wanted to be alone as she read it, in the room she had once shared with her sister.

'Where did you go, this morning?' her mother called after

her. 'I saw you through the window, running off down the garden, and you were carrying something. Where did you go?'

Maybe it's time for me to have some secrets of my own, Rose thought. Holding Evelyn's letter close to her chest and taking the steps two at a time, she ran up to her room.

Dearest Rose,

I cannot begin to tell you what life is like in London right now. The bombers come nightly, roaring across the sky. I've swapped my frocks for the overalls of an ARP warden and I stride through the pitch-black nights with a gas mask slung over one shoulder and a bag of medical supplies over the other. Hour after hour we listen for the sirens, knowing the bombs will follow. Waiting to see which buildings will be destroyed and who will need our help.

It's awful, but no one gives up, you know? Children play football in the streets, even when their homes have been blown to bits. And their mothers wait in line for a cup of tea, somehow managing to smile and chat to their neighbours, though they may have nothing left but the clothing on their backs.

I miss you terribly, my darling Rose, but I've no regrets. Charles wants me to come back to you and Mam so I'm safer, but I mean never to set eyes on Norman again. In London I get to do my part for the war effort, which makes it easier to bear each time Charles writes to say his leave has been cancelled. I'm still living with his sister, Penny, and at nights we look up together into the sky, knowing Charles might be flying over us, heading out to do battle with the Luftwaffe.

Charles writes that as soon as he can he's taking me away somewhere special. We can spend a whole week together, he says, and pretend there is no such thing as this war. I feel myself the luckiest girl ever, to be so in love.

Rose, I know you have always toed the line, so let my

parting words be ones of advice: 'Forge your own path.' That's what they used to tell us in school, wasn't it? We always thought that sort of advice was for the boys, not us, but it isn't! The war has given opportunities to women that we never had before. You must seize them, while you can. I want you to fall in love as I did – and embrace love when it finds you, no matter what.

Find the strength inside you to defy Norman, to defy everyone if you have to, and become the person you were born to be.

Your loving sister,

Evelyn

ELEVEN

ROSE

October 1940

For Rose, the days that followed were like a dream. The decision had been made, for better or for worse, and, if that meant she was a traitor to her country, there was nothing she could do about it now. There was no way to turn back time, even if she wanted to. So instead she tried not to think about it. The moment Norman left for work each morning she was gone, without a word of explanation to her mother, over the stile, down the coastal path and into Silverwood Vale. And Walter was always waiting, his smile radiant at the sight of her.

Walter relied on her for everything in those first few days when his injuries kept him confined to the cabin. Rose fetched him food each day, but with rationing and her fear of alerting Norman this was often little more than leftovers. She brought him blankets, more painkillers, even a bag of old clothes that had belonged to her father and her grandfather, which had been hidden from sight in the attic.

When Walter had no further need of essentials, Rose set out to make the cabin as comfortable as possible, since while he recovered it was his entire world. She brought him books so he might practise his English, piled his pallet high with pillows to ease the pain in his ribs and kept the log basket filled with wood, for it was now October and the nights could be cold. She spread an embroidered cloth over the old trunk she and Evelyn had hauled through the trees so long ago and on it she placed a vase, keeping it supplied with fresh flowers she rescued from the tangled mess that had once been her mother's garden.

And Walter began to recover. The pain in his head eased, his bruised body gradually mended itself and though his cracked ribs would take longer to heal, the intense pain of the first day eased back to a continual ache that only spiked to agony if he coughed. His swollen ankle was not a fracture, thankfully, but for the first few days he could bear no weight on it.

Each morning, as Rose stood outside the cabin preparing to knock on the door, she held her breath, terrified Walter might be gone. His unexpected departure no longer felt like the answer to her prayers and she wasn't sure which she feared most: that Walter would be caught and executed, or that he might prove himself a traitor to her, limping off to do his duty to the Reich as soon as he was well enough to leave.

Rose was living a different kind of life, now. One where she woke with a thrill of anticipation each morning. Where she sat in front of her mirror before breakfast, brushing her waist-length hair until it flowed over her shoulder like a bolt of black silk. This was a life where running felt like flying, the world shone and everything that weighed her down could be forgotten the instant she jumped the ditch into Silverwood Vale.

One day, perhaps a week after his arrival, Rose entered the cabin to find Walter on all fours in the corner. She had barely seen him off the pallet until that moment and she hurried over, fearing he might have fallen and injured himself further.

She had brought fresh flowers the day before, but Walter had removed these from the vase and placed them in a heap on the floor. Now, he held her little glass vase upside down in his hand. 'There is a beetle,' he said. 'For days I have watched it, but I do not think it can survive much longer inside the cabin.'

Quick as lightning, he dropped the vase over a tiny running creature, slid his hand across the top to prevent its escape and showed it to Rose.

The beetle ran in circles in the bottom of the vase, as shiny and black as Rose's hair, its tail curling like a scorpion's.

'I have seen these before,' Walter said, 'in the Allacher Forest, near my home. They are beautiful and strange, don't you think?'

'We call him "the devil's coach horse",' Rose said, thinking that perhaps it was the richness of forest folk tales that coloured the names of its creatures.

'I could not kill him,' Walter said, morosely. 'I do not think I could kill anything.'

Rose looked at him in astonishment. 'But you were trained as a soldier!' she said, remembering after she had spoken that in Germany, as in England, conscription left men without a choice.

'Yes. This is unfortunate, is it not?' Walter said.

Rose tried to place herself in his shoes. 'I think I would hate it too,' she said. 'Being told I might have to kill someone. In a perfect world, no one should have the right to make another person do that.'

'We do not live in a perfect world,' Walter said.

'No. We really don't.'

Rose sat back on her haunches. She said, 'Sometimes when I see a soldier on leave, walking through the town, it isn't his courage I think of first, or his sacrifice. I just wonder if he has killed someone. I know how awful that sounds.'

'Not awful at all.' Walter sat on the floor and looked at her. 'Some of those soldiers must feel as we do. They are caught between loyalty to their country and revulsion at the thought of ending another's life. But war makes killers of the best of men. What is your English saying? That is the nature of the beast.'

Rose looked around the little cabin hideout and back at the man before her, tenderly holding the glass jar with its little rescued creature. 'I can't kill so much as a spider in my bedroom,' she said.

They smiled at each other, the connection between them deepening.

'No one can make you harm anyone else if they don't know you're here,' Rose said softly. 'In this cabin, in this forest, you are a secret soldier. If you can't bear the thought of killing, a secret soldier is the best kind to be.'

'A secret soldier,' Walter said. 'I like that.' He reached down and took a flower from the pile on the floor. A tiny red one on a thin stalk, fragile, almost wilting.

'What is the name for this?' he asked.

'Rose campion,' she replied.

Walter lifted the tiny flower to her head, tucking it in behind her ear. 'A rose for Rose,' he said. 'Beautiful.' And something burst into life inside her.

'Would you?' Walter asked, handing Rose the vase.

She was glad of the chance to turn away from him and step outside, for she had felt her cheeks flush as he tucked the flower behind her ear. She crouched in the grasses that fringed the glade, tilted the vase and watched as the shiny beetle scurried away.

By the time she returned to the cabin, Rose had her emotions under control. She offered to help Walter off the floor and back onto the pallet, but she saw with surprise that he could move around the cabin by himself now. Soon he wouldn't need her, not the way he had needed her over the past few days. And what would happen then?

Live for today, she told herself, ignoring the sight of the crumpled parachute in the corner of the cabin and the short-wave radio, still in its carrying case.

The future could wait. These days were a gift and they shone brighter than any days she had ever known before.

Then came a morning when Rose arrived at the cabin as usual, only to find it empty.

She charged through the trees, calling Walter's name, pausing to listen and hearing nothing but the fearful pounding of her own heart. *Perhaps he has gone forever and I will never see him again*, she thought, and the extent of her misery shocked her.

Rose traipsed back towards the cabin, feeling a deep sense of abandonment, only to see Walter standing on the roof.

He had pulled some sort of wire through the window and attached a long branch to the side wall of the cabin. The branch reached several feet above the height of the roof and as Rose watched, he stretched upwards, balancing on his one good foot, to wind the wire round the tip.

'What are you...' she began, too startled for coherent thought. 'How did you...'

Walter smiled down at her. 'How did I get up here?' he said, finishing her sentence. 'With great difficulty. And I fear there may be greater difficulties on the way down.'

He sat on the edge of the roof, his long legs dangling, and used the strength of his powerful arms to lower himself to the ground. Rose hurried forward with the bough he had been using as a crutch and he propped it under one arm.

Walter limped in through the open door of the cabin.

'I don't know how sturdy this roof is,' she said, running after him. 'You might have fallen through...'

She fell silent, gazing around the cabin in surprise.

Walter had discarded the pretty embroidered cloth and dragged her trunk underneath the window. The shortwave radio now stood on top of it, the lid of its case thrown open to reveal the ominous device inside. Several wires ran from the back of the case to a black box that must have been some kind of battery.

She pointed to a wire that trailed from the side of the case and out through the window.

'That wire...' she said.

'It is not wire,' Walter said. 'It is an aerial.'

Rose thought she had begun to know and understand Walter. To see him not as an enemy agent but as a kind and sensitive man who loved nature as she did, seemed to wait with eagerness for her arrival each morning and shared her revulsion towards cruelty. Yet this Walter, standing before the strange contraption with its wires and its aerial, was not the man she knew.

Rose was suddenly aware of the size of him as he stood before her. A giant of a man and a German at that, too large for this small cabin and strong enough to crush her if he chose.

He took a step towards her and instinctively she moved away.

'Why are you—' she began, her hand waving in the direction of the now-activated shortwave radio.

'I must, don't you see?' Walter said, emphatically. 'What is my future, here in England, with your new treachery law? If I am to survive, I must have proof of my positive intentions so that I may demonstrate them to your government.'

'And is this how you plan to do it?' Rose asked. 'By communicating with our enemies?'

'I may learn something of great importance,' Walter said. 'Information vital to England, which I may trade for my life.'

Rose considered this. Although she hated the idea of Walter in communication with his superiors back in Germany, and although the sight of the squat, metal radio chilled her, she saw the sense in his words.

'I must find out why I am here,' he said, 'and what it is my kommandant intends for his agents. Why are so many of us being sent to England, ahead of the planned invasion? Perhaps if I learn this answer, I may not only prove my intentions to your government, but I may also save lives. Do you understand?'

Rose had to admit that she did. But she didn't like it, not one bit.

When she spent time with Walter, she didn't want to be reminded of where he came from. She didn't want to think about who he was.

The day Walter installed his shortwave radio was a difficult one for Rose, but the equilibrium between the two of them was swiftly restored and as he regained his mobility, they began to take strolls together in the forest. He relied heavily on his crutch at first, persevering through the pain, but each day he was able to walk a little further.

For a time, there was no other reminder of the outside world than the shortwave radio, which stayed open on the lid of the trunk, underneath the window in the cabin.

And the radio remained silent.

Then came a morning that was warmer than all the rest. This would be the last day when they could cling to the memory of summer. It was early October and the signs of autumn were all around. The russet colours of the trees, the soft and spongy leaves on the forest trail, the red squirrels gathering their berries and nuts in an ever-increasing frenzy.

Cold days were coming soon.

She and Walter walked deeper into Silverwood Vale than they had ever managed before. When a bird began to sing with gusto in a nearby bush, Rose placed a restraining hand on his arm so they might pause to listen.

'I love robins,' she told him. 'Even in the midst of winter, when so many other birds are silent, you still hear them. Robins remind us that even if nature seems dead and you think spring will never come, life clings on.'

Walter smiled at her with what she hoped might be fondness. She lifted her hand from his arm, acutely aware that he never touched her, not for anything other than the most practical of reasons. Sometimes she agonised over this, unsure if it was because he knew how to behave like a gentleman or because he did not feel for her the way she felt for him.

'You love birds,' he said.

'I love the forest,' she replied. 'In spring, there is so much noise here, though you would hardly think it now. Blue tits and chaffinches, bullfinches and great tits, all of them flitting through the branches, singing for their mates. Woodpeckers banging, squirrels scurrying, everything alive with sound, everything in a marvellous frenzy.' She smiled.

'And I also enjoy all of nature,' Walter said softly as they walked along, side by side. 'But there is something in particular I have learned to love, something Frederick taught me, many years ago. I have a fondness for woodland plants that must be teased to life by just the right circumstances.'

Rose thought it astonishing that a man as powerful and imposing as Walter should feel an attraction to fragile things.

They had come to a clearing in the forest made by the toppling of one of its giants, decades ago. The rotting tree lay across the glade, its crown leaning on the trunk of a towering beech, high up on the far side.

'It is to Frederick that I owe my knowledge of botany,'

Walter said, 'and once I returned to Germany, I continued my study, doing it the way I did so many things, in secret. Here. Do you see this?'

He crouched down on one leg, his injured ankle splayed to the side, and parted the tangle of grasses at their feet to reveal a cluster of black berries.

'Deadly nightshade,' he said. 'Also called belladonna. It was Frederick who taught me the names. The berries have been used to make women beautiful – and to poison kings. They are deadly to us, yet rabbits and birds may eat them and do not die. That is strange, is it not?'

He struggled to his feet and reached towards the moss-covered trunk, his face suddenly animated. 'I do not believe it!' he cried. 'There are ghost orchids here, many of them. This is a beautiful flower and a rare sight.'

Rose leaned in to see. The orchids had white petals that tapered to a fine point, so they looked like tiny insects poised and frozen in mid-leap.

Walter's eyes scanned the floor of the glade. 'I would imagine,' he said, 'that here in your Silverwood Vale there hide such treasures. Species to be found in only a few spots in all this land. It is a place that is bursting with life. A treat for the senses.'

'When you notice things,' Rose said, 'you lead with your eyes, like my sister Evelyn. But I think I have always led with my ears.'

Walter looked bemused. 'What do you mean?' he asked.

'Let me show you,' Rose said. 'What can you hear?'

They listened for a few seconds together.

'Not much,' Walter admitted. 'There is a little wind, moving the trees. That is all.'

'Now close your eyes and really listen.'

He did so. Rose admired the way his features softened as he relaxed into listening and how fingers of sunlight reached through the canopy, playing across his skin. Then she closed her eyes, too.

Rose was silent a while before saying, 'Can you hear how the wind moves differently through each kind of tree? Beech, oak, ash... the leaves and the crown of each have a distinct shape and if you listen carefully, you can hear that the wind makes a different noise as it moves through each of them.'

She peeked through half-closed lids and saw a smile play across Walter's lips.

'Listen long enough,' she whispered, 'holding as still as you can, and you will learn where the dormice live. You will know which birds are flocking to fly south and where the squirrels hide their winter stores.'

'I might see those things,' Walter said, 'but I do not think I could hear them.'

'You can teach yourself to separate sounds into layers,' Rose said. 'Each of those layers tells a different story.'

She opened her eyes. Walter had moved closer. His face was now inches from her own, his breath warm on her skin.

'In wartime,' he said softly, 'there is no future, not for any of us. Not a future we can be certain of. We must live only for today.'

Rose found herself unable to speak. She nodded.

Walter leaned forward and gently brushed his lips against hers. The touch was as feather-light as an autumn leaf sighing through the forest canopy.

And then he stepped back. He took her hands, lifting them to his cheeks and holding them there. She felt the softness of his beard, as she had on the night she had first seen him, in the arms of the Thunder Oak.

'You are very beautiful,' he whispered.

Of all the images that might have risen to Rose's mind in that moment, it was her mother's face she pictured, pressed to her bedroom window, anxious and afraid. Watching as Rose left her behind and headed off towards the forest.

'I need to go,' she said. 'They will be waiting for me at home.'

'You must leave now?' Walter asked, puzzled.

Reluctantly, Rose nodded. 'I'll return tomorrow, as early as I can.'

She wanted to tell him about her mother's illness. She wanted to confess how much she feared Norman and how difficult things had become since her beloved sister had gone. But how could she burden Walter with her troubles when he already had so many of his own? Rose could barely cope with a bullying stepfather, yet the man in front of her had parachuted through the trees of an alien land, choosing exile over fighting for Hitler.

Next to his problems, her own felt inconsequential.

Rose still held her hands against his face.

'Go, if you must,' Walter said and he looped his fingers round hers, lowering her hands to her side.

Still Rose lingered a few seconds more, feeling there was something else she wanted to do. Then she turned on her heels and ran down the forest path, towards the sea.

TWELVE

ROSE

October 1940

Back in her room that afternoon, Rose replayed the kiss in her mind a hundred times. The feel of Walter's lips, soft against her own. The warmth of his cheeks against her fingers. But even more astonishing than the kiss itself was the feeling that came after. *I am worthy of love*, Rose thought, over and over, as she recalled that moment. *Someone finds me worthy of their love, and not just anyone, but this man who occupies my every thought, who is there inside my dreams when I sleep.*

What was it Walter had said? *In wartime there is no future, not for any of us.* Rose thought about this, looking out of her window across her mother's tangled garden, towards the sea. His words were not depressing, she decided, but invigorating.

If there was no future to be had, then she would live only for today, for each glorious moment life gave her.

Rose heard the heavy rattle of an engine and saw the coal merchant's lorry turn round the bend, the bed of his vehicle lined with sacks. He stopped outside their house and a young boy leapt out. He was new to the job, Rose thought, barely old enough to do the work, and he staggered as he made his way to the coal shed, a sack balanced across his shoulders. Her mother was on the doorstep at once, calling to him, always eager to chat to anyone from the world beyond their house. She heard a brief exchange between them, their voices muffled, before the boy jogged back to his lorry, leapt into the front seat and continued on his way.

Since returning from the forest, Rose had helped her mother to bathe, scrubbed the scullery floor, filled the coal scuttle and peeled potatoes for the evening meal. Now she sat with Evelyn's letter on her lap, rereading it and trying to pen a reply. The sooner she did so, the sooner she would hear from her sister again.

I am doing as you suggested, she had written in her first attempt. *I am forging my own path. Seizing opportunities, while I can.* But she had crumpled up that letter at once. How could she say such a thing to Evelyn when it would be impossible to explain what she meant?

I am going against Norman, and Mother, and the whole world, to live the life I want to lead.

That version of her letter met the same fate.

I'm eighteen years old and today I was kissed for the first time.

She smiled as she wrote that, feeling again the soft brush of Walter's lips, so gentle and tentative against her own.

No.

In the end, Rose decided she could tell Evelyn nothing at all. She couldn't entrust her secret to anyone.

And what else could she share with her sister, if not the truth?

Then she had an idea. She reached into her bedside drawer and pulled out a photograph.

They had taken photos of one another last summer next to the Thunder Oak, using their father's old Kodak. Evelyn had given her photograph to Charles, but Rose's remained in her drawer. She hadn't really liked it at the time and she liked it even less when she looked at it now. She wore a timid expression on her face, as if it took all the courage she possessed to lift her eyes from the ground.

Rose took up a pen. She turned the image over in her hand and wrote on the back, in tiny letters: *To the one who got away, love Rose.*

She knew this would please Evelyn. The photograph would be a memory of all the happy times they had spent together in Silverwood Vale and the words on the back would remind her of the courage it had taken to leave. Evelyn liked to see herself as the bold one. The sister who knew how to seize life by the horns.

Perhaps it would be enough just to send the photograph and Evelyn would forgive her for failing to write a proper letter.

Rose placed the photo in an envelope and added her sister's London address.

Will I ever get away? she wondered, *as Evelyn did?* It was pointless even asking the question. Evelyn had only been free to leave home because Rose remained behind to care for their mother. Over the past weeks, their mother's health had worsened and she could no longer manage without help.

Rose's only option was to live in the moment, seizing happiness where she could. *My life sounds bleak when you put it like that,* she thought. But it didn't feel bleak, not at all.

She felt more like herself than she ever had before.

When she heard the creaking of a floorboard outside her room, she knew her mother was standing outside, wondering whether to knock. Feeling Rose was entitled to her privacy, but not to secrets.

'Mam?' Rose called and the door opened.

Her mother had chosen to wear her favourite summer dress, the one with its print of tiny blue forget-me-nots. The fabric hung loose off her fragile body and her thin arms were prickly with goosebumps.

Leaning against the door, she glanced quickly around the room.

'The coal merchant's lad says the butcher has pork pies,' she said. 'They won't last long. Pop down there, would you, and drop a couple off at the station for Norman?'

Rose knew her mother would do anything to ensure Norman came home in a good mood. She sealed the envelope and grabbed her purse.

'I'll go right away,' she said. 'I can post this to Evelyn while I'm in town.'

Mildred was working alone behind the counter in the post office. She had a new permanent wave, Rose noticed, as she set down her bag of pork pies and pasted a stamp on Evelyn's envelope. Perhaps she was trying out a new look, ready for beauty school. Soon she'd be gone, just like her sister. Off to start her own life.

When Rose looked up, Mildred was staring at her.

'Do you know if they've taken away the spy?' Rose asked as casually as she could, sliding a coin across the counter to pay for the stamp.

Mildred snapped up the coin and dropped it into her cash box. 'Not yet,' she said, curtly. 'There's a war on, or haven't you noticed? There's more important things for the higher-ups to be doing than executing spies, especially when they've got them locked up already.'

She leaned in towards Rose.

'But let me tell you this,' she said conspiratorially, 'your stepdad and my dad, they fixed him up good and proper.'

It took a moment for Rose to work out what she meant and when she did she felt suddenly queasy.

Mildred slid a receipt towards Rose. 'You must be very proud of your stepdad,' she said with a sniff, 'now he's made sergeant. Though there's plenty think my dad should have got it.'

And I wish he had, Rose thought, but she said nothing. She turned to leave.

'You've been spending an awful lot of time in Silverwood Vale,' Mildred said.

Rose turned back round, startled.

Mildred was sorting through a pile of official-looking forms on the counter. 'I like to keep my eyes and ears open,' she said, without looking up. 'And I see you sometimes, when I walk Mam's terrier. On the coastal path, going into the forest.'

It wasn't a secret that Rose loved Silverwood Vale – she and Evelyn had been going there for years. But now was not the time for other people to take notice. And especially not Mildred.

'I don't know if you're alone or if you go there to meet someone,' Mildred said, her tone casual, 'but you enjoy yourself in there, while you still can.'

Rose couldn't help herself. 'What do you mean?' she asked.

Mildred paused in her work and looked up with mock surprise. 'Hadn't you heard?' she said. 'It's the Church of England owns Silverwood Vale and they're selling. My dad says the RAF will buy it. They'll chop down all them trees and extend Bilby airfield.' Pasting an expression of concern onto her face, she added, 'You look a little ill, all of a sudden. Can I get you a glass of water?'

Based on their past interactions, Mildred clearly expected Rose to crumble, to leave the post office in tears, but Rose felt something flare inside her. She slammed her hands down on the counter. 'Mildred Radcliffe, you're nothing but a gossip,' she yelled. 'That's all you are and it's all you'll ever be.'

The vehemence of her own reaction startled her and when

she looked at Mildred she saw that the other woman was equally stunned by it. This was not the timid little girl who cowered from confrontation, making her an easy target for bullies. This was something new and unfamiliar to them both.

Mildred's expression hardened into dislike. Gone was the civil veneer, the pseudo-polite expression she had adopted since reaching adulthood.

What Rose saw on Mildred's face now was pure hate.

Rose left the post office as quickly as possible and walked past the red brick hospital with its pretty borders of purple flowering hydrangeas towards the police station. It was such a beautiful day, but she barely noticed that now. She wasn't thinking about Walter and the feel of his breath on her cheek as they stood together, their eyes closed, only hours ago. She was filled with horror as she imagined Silverwood Vale all gone. The ancient trees, the birds, the devil's coach horse beetles, the red campion – all of it lost forever, replaced by a concrete airstrip. Such things had happened elsewhere.

And she was thinking of her response to Mildred.

What had come over her?

'May I help you, Miss Tilburn?'

'I've brought something for my stepdad.'

Rose stood before the reception desk in the small police station. The place always seemed to smell of boiled cabbage, she thought, wrinkling up her nose. It was an old building, badly in need of repair. Plaster was peeling from the walls, black mould bloomed in the corners and the floor tiles beneath her feet were cracked and stained.

Mildred's father stood behind the desk, his greasy hair plastered across his crown to hide the fact that he was prematurely balding. Radcliffe was known to be an unpleasant, mean-spirited man and he seemed unable to hide behind the deceptive warmth of a smile as his daughter did. Rose knew he was young enough to be called up, but he had failed his medical exam. A heart murmur, Norman had said. It wasn't difficult to get such a diagnosis, if you knew the right doctor and had money to sweeten the deal.

Radcliffe reached out to take the pork pies. 'Wait here,' he said. 'I'll see if the sergeant's got a message for your mother.'

There was something about the way he said that – *the sergeant* – that made Rose think he resented her stepfather's promotion every bit as much as Mildred did.

Rose waited until Radcliffe had disappeared through a door leading to the police station's main office, then she turned to look down the corridor that ran to her left. She knew where this led. To the small cells were Lowbury kept its petty criminals, or, more often, people like old Tom, who had drunk too much at the Fox and Hound and needed time to sober up.

Certainly, these cells had never before been used to detain a German agent.

Rose recalled what Mildred had said about the spy: *Your stepdad and my dad, they fixed him up good and proper.*

A chill ran down her spine.

It could have been Walter in there, she thought, and before she knew it, before she could make a conscious decision, Rose was turning away from the desk and walking down the narrow corridor with its bright, fluorescent lights towards the barred doors at the end.

The cell on the left was empty, the grey woollen blanket folded neatly on its cot and when she turned to her right, she thought that cell was empty, too. There was no blanket at all, no mattress, just the rusty frame of a narrow bed, a stinking slop bucket and, in the corner, a pile of rags.

No. Not rags. A person, curled into a ball.

The man wore a thin shirt that looked like it had been slashed down the back by something sharp and trousers several sizes too big. No socks and no pullover, though it was bitterly cold at the back of the building, despite the warmth of the day.

And as Rose stood there looking in, the man stiffened, as if he sensed he was being watched.

Then he turned, his movements painfully slow, and looked right at her.

He was cradling one arm against his chest. The wrist was swollen and twisted awkwardly, probably fractured. Blood crusted along his neck and on the collar of his shirt.

But it was his face that horrified Rose the most. His lip was cut open, revealing the white of his teeth. One cheek was badly bruised, the skin mottled purple, and his left eye was swollen almost shut.

Rose heard a noise from down the corridor and turned to see Radcliffe watching her, a cruel sneer on his face. *You did this*, she wanted to say to him, *you and Norman. Is this what justice means in a time of war?*

But she said nothing, just pushed past him and ran out into the street.

THIRTEEN

ROSE

October 1940

'Well, the spy's gone,' Norman said the next morning as he entered the kitchen. Rose stood in front of the range, frying his bacon and eggs, while her mother set the table, her every movement painfully slow. 'They came for him late yesterday and good riddance to him.'

Norman came up behind Rose and she could smell on his breath the rankness of tobacco and stale beer. He had been late home last night. Out drinking with Radcliffe, no doubt.

Shoving Rose aside, Norman grabbed a fork and speared a rasher of bacon as it sizzled in the pan. Dripping fat onto the floor, he returned with it to the table.

'What will they do to him?' Rose asked, throwing the words over her shoulder as casually as she could.

'I don't know,' Norman said, through a mouthful of food, 'and I don't much care. Interrogate him. Torture him, maybe. Then set him before a firing squad.'

Rose fetched a plate from the dresser and piled it high with bacon and eggs. She could feel the fury growing inside her. Not just resentment, not just frustration at her own lack of power, but fury.

Something of her rising anger must have been visible, perhaps in the set of her shoulders, her rigid body, for when she turned round her mother was staring at her, a warning in her eyes.

Rose carried Norman's plate over to him and set it down with a bang.

'What's rattled your cage?' he said, before tucking into his breakfast.

Rose's mother gazed at her. 'Steady...' she whispered under her breath as she had to Evelyn on so many occasions, warning her to keep her anger in check before Norman noticed. Before it was too late.

Somehow, this only emboldened Rose. *I can be as strong as my sister*, she thought.

Norman said, 'You should have seen the Nazi, by the time we were done with him,' and Rose felt it boiling inside of her, the fury, bubbling up, refusing to be contained. She had barely ever felt such a thing before, had never stood on the edge of a precipice like this, about to leap off.

It wasn't terrifying, as she had always supposed it to be each time she had watched Evelyn lose control.

It was exhilarating.

'He was a simpering wreck,' Norman went on, stabbing a fried egg with his fork and holding it there, halfway to his mouth. 'A little girl. Blubbering in Radcliffe's arms while I gave him what for.'

'You're a brute!'

The words were out of Rose's mouth before she had time to think, but after they were spoken she didn't regret them, not at all. And she was learning for herself something that Evelyn had often tried to explain.

Once you found the courage to stand up to someone, it was difficult to stop.

'You're nothing but an ignorant bully and a brute!' she screamed, her voice so loud now that her mother quivered in her seat. 'People should treat each other with dignity, even in a time of war!'

Norman's eyes widened with shock.

Rose's mother sat very still, her eyes closed, gripping the table. Witnessing her timidity, Rose was filled with contempt. *You never stood up for yourself*, she thought, *and you didn't stand up for Evelyn, not once. What will happen if Norman turns on me now? You won't stand up for me, either.*

Suddenly, Rose felt the hopelessness of it all and her eyes stung with tears. She pushed away from the table. Before Norman had time to respond to her outburst, to punish her insolence, she scooped up her bag and ran for the door, for the coastal path.

For Silverwood Vale.

Rose had tried to avoid telling Walter about the captured spy, knowing he would picture himself in the same predicament and it would only cause him pain, but now, as she sat down heavily on the pallet beside him, she could hold nothing back.

'My stepfather is the sergeant in charge,' she said, 'and he acts like Lowbury is his own little empire. He beat him, Walter. He beat that poor man black and blue. And he wasn't the only one.'

'Appalling,' Walter said.

'I didn't know I could feel like this,' Rose cried. 'So very angry and jaded. People are not good. There's a cruelty inside everyone and war gives it free rein.'

They sat in silence for a while, Walter processing everything she had told him and Rose fighting to get her emotions under control. Then Walter heaved himself off the pallet. He set a pan of water to boil over the fire and spooned tea leaves into a tin mug that had once belonged to Rose's father.

'I think tea will help,' he said, gently. 'Isn't that what the English do for one another?' He added a spoonful of his precious sugar to the mug.

Where would Walter go, Rose wondered, once his ankle was fully healed? He was always saying that in a time of war you could only live in the present, but decisions would need to be made. If Silverwood Vale became a part of Bilby airfield, they'd chop down all the trees. It was a devastating thought. The ancient woodland gone, the rare flowers uprooted, thousands of species left without food or a home. Rose pictured birds, rising in panicked flocks as the trees toppled. Hundreds of them, circling a devastated land.

And like all the other living creatures, Walter would have nowhere left to hide.

But was his fate really any more tenuous than everyone else's? All their futures rested on the outcome of the war. If the Germans invaded in the next few days, Walter would have nothing more to worry about. It would be Rose, her mother and everyone she knew whose lives might hang in the balance.

Walter poured boiling water into the mug and handed it to her.

'I should find us a teapot,' she said, watching the leaves in the water swirl and settle.

Too late, Rose realised she hadn't said 'you'. She had said 'us'.

'You sound better already,' Walter said, smiling as she sipped the hot tea.

Rose looked around the cabin. She saw Walter's food supplies, ranged on a shelf he had built along the back wall. The little stool he had made from the Thunder Oak's fallen bough, once he no longer needed it as a crutch. The pillows, propped up against the back of the pallet, so it looked more like a comfortable sofa than an improvised bed.

The cabin had an air of permanence now. It felt like a home. Only the parachute, crumpled in the corner, seemed incongruous and the shortwave radio, standing on the trunk beneath the window. She had learned to ignore the radio, though she did not like to see it there, silent and waiting.

Rose looked down at her canvas bag, which she had tossed carelessly on the floor as she stormed into the cabin.

'Your paper,' Walter said, following her gaze, 'and your art pencils.' He picked up the bag and handed it to her.

'I haven't painted anything for ages,' Rose said. 'Not a single thing. And I haven't drawn anything, either.'

She pulled out her sketchpad, a gift from Evelyn the previous Christmas, and opened it to the first blank page.

Walter perched on his home-made stool, waiting. He didn't ask her to draw him and she didn't offer. But somehow that was what the moment required.

Rose looked at him. Really looked.

There was something quite intimate about this, she thought, just as she had imagined. How he was giving her permission to study him so closely, and for so long. And Walter wasn't the only one making himself vulnerable. She would attempt to create his likeness on the paper and afterwards he would look at it and know exactly how she saw him.

She began with a rough outline, taking time over his beard. Next, she sketched his lips the way she loved to see them, not quite smiling but turned up at the edges, as if he could see the humour in something that was too difficult to put it into words. She tried to capture the kindness and intelligence in his eyes and that was even harder. Eyes were always difficult and it was almost impossible to do justice to the warmth in Walter's.

'You see?' he whispered, trying not to disturb a moment between them that had become special, and significant. 'When you draw or paint, you are yourself again. The anger is gone. You are lovely, and you are at peace.'

He was right, Rose thought. Only moments ago, she had been raging and frustrated, her mind buzzing with worries. Now she felt relaxed, all her attention on the drawing. On Walter.

She had always known she needed art to be happy but no one else in her life had ever recognised it. No one else had ever valued that part of who she was, nor seen it as something that mattered.

And it was as she was lost in her drawing, focusing on Walter's eyes, that something happened to destroy everything. To yank her out of her reverie. To burst the lovely silence that had settled between the two of them and to shatter the magic of the moment.

Walter's radio burst into life.

FOURTEEN

EMMA

June 1990

Emma stood back and watched as Tristan gathered the bones up in the parachute and tossed them back down into the root cellar.

'They're really old,' he said. 'So is the parachute, for that matter. Maybe from the Second World War. It's not like we discovered a recent crime scene or anything.' He glanced at Emma to gauge her reaction before returning his gaze to the cellar. 'There's no one alive will remember whoever this was. Maybe he wasn't even English. There could be a German warplane rusting somewhere in the forest.'

His words made sense, though Emma doubted if hiding the bones was the right thing to do.

Tristan rearranged the broken planks over the hole and covered them with fallen branches until the cellar was no longer visible. It was unlikely anyone would come back here, Emma thought, and if they did, the hole, and the bones inside it, would seem like a new discovery to them, undisturbed for decades.

'I should be getting back,' she said.

'Your taxi's on the main road?' Tristan asked. 'Come on, follow me.'

She didn't need a guide, but nevertheless she let him lead the way through the trees. As she followed, mud squelching in her ruined High Tops and her arm throbbing under the makeshift bandage, Emma thought about what they had done.

From her own perspective, returning the bones and the parachute to their hiding place was the most sensible course of action. She wanted to sell Silverwood Vale, and fast. A police investigation would slow everything down.

'This can stay between the two of us.' Tristan threw the words over his shoulder as he loped along the trail ahead of her. 'Best that way, don't you think?'

Emma thought, *I've barely been in England three hours and here I am, doing something that's almost certainly against the law. Choosing not to report the discovery of human remains.*

But Tristan was right, she told herself. The bones were old. Involving the police would benefit no one.

He stopped when the road came into sight.

'My taxi,' Emma said, pointing. She was relieved to see the driver hadn't given up on her. 'Can I drop you off somewhere?'

Tristan shook his head.

It was only after he had disappeared back into the trees and the taxi was on its way to Lowbury that Emma puzzled over Tristan's motives. He had been eager to place the bones and the parachute back in the root cellar, even covering the hole with branches and bracken, so it would be noticed.

Emma had clear reasons for wanting to hide their discovery, but what about Tristan?

Why was he so eager that the bones remain a secret?

· · ·

'Good heavens, will you look at the state of you!' declared the stout woman who stood in the open doorway of Rosebud House Bed and Breakfast. She wiped her hands on an apron already encrusted with food and looked Emma up and down, bemused.

Emma knew how terrible she looked. Her jeans and High Tops were splattered with half-dried mud, her chestnut hair hung in damp ringlets and the tie-dyed bandana Tristan had fastened round her arm was slowly leaking blood.

'Well, don't just stand there, come on in!'

The woman moved aside and Emma stepped into a dark and narrow hallway. Both walls were lined with shelves full of knick-knacks: porcelain ornaments of smiling children in summer frocks, an assortment of brass bells and thimbles, small animals made of seashells. After her own stylishly decorated condo, the tiny house seemed to Emma unbelievably cluttered.

Dragging her suitcase along the thick-pile carpet, she followed the woman into an equally cramped kitchen.

'I'm Mrs Foster,' she said, surveying Emma from head to toe. 'I'm guessing you must be my Canadian guest. I was expecting you hours ago!'

Mrs Foster turned to fill an old-fashioned brass kettle, the water thundering hollowly. She set it to boil on the gas hob.

Emma felt suddenly exhausted. Jet-lagged, overwhelmed and sad. She left her suitcase by the door and shuffled towards an oval pine table that stood in one corner of the kitchen. Dragging out a chair, she sat down heavily.

'I'm sorry,' she said. She wasn't sure what she was sorry for, exactly: her late arrival, looking such a mess or traipsing mud into Mrs Foster's home. Perhaps the things she felt sorry for had nothing to do with Mrs Foster at all. She was sorry for her stupidity in the forest, sorry for her broken marriage and sorry that she had made the impulsive decision to fly to England when really all she wanted was to be in Toronto with Mike, somehow fixing their broken lives.

Get a grip, she told herself, blinking tears of self-pity from her eyes.

'What you need is a nice cup of tea,' Mrs Foster said. 'Am I right?'

Emma preferred coffee, but she couldn't trust herself to reply, so she nodded bleakly.

'And a slice of my ginger cake? Would that do the trick?'

Emma nodded again, though she felt too choked to eat anything. With each word of kindness from Mrs Foster, her sense of desolation grew. It had been ages since anyone had fussed over her in this motherly way. And now, with Mike gone for good, she would have no one left to fuss over her at all.

'This house used to be a tea shop once – can you believe it?' Mrs Foster chattered on as she prepared the hot drinks and the cake. 'I'm not much of a baker, but my ginger cake's not half bad and I can manage a good cuppa.'

She must have noticed at that moment just how upset her guest was. Through her tears, Emma watched as the older woman turned her chair round to face her. She perched on the edge of the seat and took Emma's hands in her own.

'You've been through something, lovey,' she said and those few words of kindness were all it took for Emma's last shreds of self-control to fall away. Her tears flowed freely as Mrs Foster filled a bowl with warm water and gently removed the bandana from her arm.

'That's a nasty cut, to be sure,' she said, politely ignoring Emma's tears, 'but it's not deep enough to need stitches, thank heavens.' She dabbed at the wound to clean it, then fetched a first aid kit from the kitchen cupboard and dressed the cut with a square of gauze, which she held in place with medical tape.

Slowly, as Mrs Foster tended to her arm, Emma regained control of her emotions. 'I'm not usually like this,' she said.

Moments later, they were sitting across the table from one

another, hot cups of tea and slices of iced ginger cake between them.

'Do you want to tell me how you got yourself in such a state?' Mrs Foster asked.

Emma didn't. In fact, she didn't want to talk about Silverwood Vale at all. Instead, she said, 'My Great-Aunt Rose grew up in Lowbury, during the war. That's one of the reasons I've come to England. I'd like to find out what happened to her, if I can.'

Mrs Foster leaned across the table. She studied Emma's face intently.

'It wouldn't be Rose Tilburn you're meaning, would it?' she asked. 'Goodness, I don't know why I bother asking – I've seen pictures and you're the spitting image of her!' She leaned back in her chair, as if to study Emma from a different angle. 'Not the hair, of course,' she added. 'But you've got her eyes.'

Astonished, Emma said, 'You've heard of my great-aunt? What happened to her? Do you know?'

'That I couldn't tell you,' she said, 'but there's not a person in Lowbury hasn't seen photos of her as a girl. She was quite the local celebrity after she disappeared and every once in a while to this day the *Lowbury Chronicle* will run a feature on her, rehash the story, reprint her photo. Everyone likes an unsolved mystery.'

She closed the first aid kit and stood up, leaning against the table for support.

'I did catch a glimpse of her, once or twice, after she came back,' she said, 'outside the post office and suchlike. Of course, Rose was much older then. I'm sure people asked for her side of the story but, as far as I know, she never told it.' Mrs Foster gazed past Emma and through the kitchen window to her small square of garden beyond. 'I can't tell you much more,' she said. 'I only moved to Lowbury in the seventies, after my Christopher died.'

Emma felt a rush of pity for her. For anyone who'd had to spend two decades without someone to love.

Would that be her own fate, now?

Mrs Foster returned her first aid kit to the cupboard, closing the door with a slam. Emma pictured Mike wincing. She thought of how he hated unnecessary noise. How difficult he had found it, living with Emma's clumsiness.

Maybe what had happened between them was unavoidable and for the best.

'There's folks in town could answer your questions better than me,' Mrs Foster said. 'I only know what I've heard.' She straightened the kitchen towels on the rack in front of the cooker and returned to the table.

'Rose grew up in a house outside of Lowbury. It's gone now. Pulled down when they built the new housing estate. Then one day, during the war, she just disappeared, taking almost nothing with her. A bomb had fallen in town, so maybe that had something to do with it. And folks said she wasn't the same after her sister left to work in London.'

That was my grandmother, Evelyn, Emma thought.

'Eat your cake, dear,' Mrs Foster said, kindly. 'It'll do you good.' She nudged Emma's plate closer.

With the lump gone from her throat, Emma felt suddenly ravenous. She picked up her dessert fork.

Mrs Foster broke off a large chunk of her own cake and popped it in her mouth. 'Rose was gone for years,' she said, 'though some people claimed to have seen her, from time to time. On the beach and along the coastal path.' She paused to take a sip of her tea. 'Put plenty of sugar in yours,' she said. 'It's good for shock.' She indicated a porcelain sugar bowl filled with cubes.

Rose didn't think she had ever had sugar cubes in her tea before. She used a tiny pair of stainless steel tongs to pick up two lumps and drop them into her cup.

'By the time I came to Lowbury and bought this place,' Mrs Foster went on, 'there was one thing everyone agreed on: your great-aunt was back. There was a full-page spread in the *Chronicle* when someone found out she was the owner of Silverwood Vale and she was living inside the forest, all alone. Another chapter in the mystery.'

Emma stirred her tea and took a sip. It was strong and very sweet. She felt its warmth flow through her.

'So why did my great-aunt choose to live like a hermit for her whole life?' she asked. 'I mean, it's bizarre, isn't it? Something big must have happened to make her do that. And how did she get the money to buy a forest? How did she pay for food and other essentials for years and years, if she didn't have a job?'

'I've heard stories,' Mrs Foster said slowly, 'but there's people in Lowbury could answer those questions better than me.'

Emma was intrigued. She wondered, for the first time, if she could make something of her great-aunt's story as a journalist. The mystery of a missing girl who turned up years later, living as a recluse in a tract of ancient woodland, just a short walk from her childhood home.

'When you've cleaned yourself up and had a good night's sleep,' Mrs Foster said, 'you should take a walk into town. Go see the woman who works in the post office. If anyone can tell you about Rose, it's Mildred Radcliffe. Old Miss Radcliffe's worked behind that counter for almost fifty years – can you believe it? It boggles the mind.'

Mrs Foster held up the tie-dyed bandana she had removed from Emma's arm. 'Where's this from?' she asked. 'I may not have known you long, but it doesn't seem like something you'd own.'

Emma took it from her. 'It belongs to the man who helped me when I fell,' she said, deciding half-truths would be best. 'He said his name was Tristan.'

'Tristan?' Mrs Foster chuckled as she stacked their plates and carried them to the sink. 'So you've been over to Silverwood Vale already, have you?'

Emma was astonished. 'How do you know that?' she asked.

Scraping crumbs into the bin, Mrs Foster said, 'Tristan's a bit of a strange one and no mistake. There's people speak about him like he's a lost soul, but I'm a good judge of character and let me tell you, there's more to him than they think.'

'But how did you know I saw him in Silverwood?' Emma asked.

'Because that's where he lives! He's got a caravan in there, just off the coastal path.' Mrs Foster straightened up, looking squarely at Emma. 'What you need right now is a hot bath,' she said. 'Let me show you to your room and then I'll turn on the immersion heater. Follow me.'

Emma watched as Mrs Foster dragged her suitcase through the hall. She heard a rhythmic *thud, thud, thud* as the older woman hauled it up the stairs.

So Tristan lived in Silverwood Vale. That was why he hadn't accepted when she asked if he wanted dropping off somewhere. It was why he had headed back into the trees instead. *He's trespassing*, she thought, aware that she was being peevish, but feeling too tired, too jet-lagged to care. *He's trespassing on my land.*

Emma glanced down at the bandana in her hand, recalling how it had looked, tied round Tristan's neck. His skin below it, suntanned and leathery, as if he lived his whole life outdoors. Mike had worn a similar one on their last camping trip together, only dark green, not brightly tie-dyed like this one. Emma had a strange urge to lift the bandana to her nose and breathe in its scent. To hold it against her cheek.

How long had Tristan lived on her land? she wondered. Had he met her Great-Aunt Rose?

Emma knew what she needed to do. Right now, she would

enjoy a hot bath, as Mrs Foster suggested, before calling her solicitor in London to let him know she had arrived. After that, she planned to give in to jet lag and go to bed.

But tomorrow morning she would head back to Silverwood Vale on the pretext of returning Tristan's bandana.

Emma would ask him about her Great-Aunt Rose and find out what he knew.

FIFTEEN

EMMA

June 1990

Despite her exhaustion, Emma tossed and turned for hours that night in the little bedroom at the back of Mrs Foster's home. The room felt like a padded cell, so overheated and over-furnished it was difficult to breathe. The single bed was piled high with hand-embroidered cushions, the shelves stuffed with plush teddy bears. A huge ceramic Dobermann sat beside the door, as if to guard it, and the embossed wallpaper burst with a profusion of English wildflowers in every shade of purple and pink. Emma longed for the stylish simplicity of her bedroom back home, for this room felt not only overstuffed, but heavy with absence. She thought of Mike, so quiet and yet always so reassuringly present. Like a radio tuned to your favourite station and playing softly in the background.

Most alarming of all, Emma thought as she lay in the darkness of the unfamiliar room, was the lack of noise beyond the heavy, floral curtains. No horns blared, no sirens sounded. There were no yells from late-night revellers, no blast of music from all-night clubs. It was as if the world she knew and loved had disappeared forever.

As the endless hours wore on, Emma's thoughts returned to the bones in their pit behind the cabin. To banish from her mind the terror she had felt as she tumbled down into the cellar, the horror when she had learned what had been hidden there, Emma tried to view the whole incident through the lens of a journalist. She imagined the story she might write one day, if she was ever free to do so. The mystery she might set out to solve.

Finally, just before dawn, she fell into a restless sleep. But even in her dreams she was back in the dank root cellar, standing on the lumpy mounds of silk, smelling the rotten vegetation. Her dream-self peeled back the folds of the parachute, but it wasn't bones she found inside, speckled with age. It was the body of her Great-Aunt Rose.

Emma jolted awake. The nightmare had seemed so real that she had to tell herself over and over that the ancient bones had not belonged to her great-aunt. Rose had died only months earlier, of a heart attack in Lowbury's town square, and she was buried in the graveyard on the other side of town.

But had Rose known about the parachute and the secret it contained? Was her sudden disappearance during the war connected in some way to a death that had remained hidden from the world for half a century?

After the nightmare, sleep was impossible. Emma rose from her bed and washed Tristan's bandana, using the tiny sink in the corner of her bedroom. She wrung it out as best she could and draped it over the ugly ceramic dog to dry. Then she sat by the window, staring out into the darkness, listening for any hint of noise in the silence and longing for home.

· · ·

Emma set off straight after breakfast. Following Mrs Foster's directions, she walked through the huge housing estate that had replaced acres of farmland to the south of town, heading towards the coastal road. Tristan's bandana was stuffed in her pocket, still damp and badly crumpled but no longer stained with blood.

Was this the housing estate that had been built on top of her great-aunt's and grandmother's childhood home? Emma wondered. The estate was an endless maze of streets, but the houses were pretty, each with a tiny garden out front and a glass conservatory at the back. It occurred to her that if homes were built on Silverwood Vale, the new estate would stretch almost to meet this one, with only a field or two in between.

It was a beautiful morning. Emma had worn her lemon-coloured raincoat just in case, but it flapped open as she walked, the grey drizzle of the previous afternoon having given way to blue sky and puffy clouds. She hesitated at a signpost that pointed through a farm towards the sea, before climbing over a stile and skirting the edge of a field. From there she emerged onto a coastal path that ran parallel to the beach. Between the path and the sea ranged low, tumbling dunes, the sand knitted together with clumps of grasses and hardy spring flowers. Beyond that, waves lapped gently at the shore.

Grass, dunes, a beach and sunlight playing on the sea. Emma fought the urge to pull off her socks and boots, roll up her jeans and run into the breakers, eager to feel sand and seawater between her toes. There were more than a thousand kilometres between Toronto and the ocean, and she had only ever been to the coast a couple of times, on Caribbean holidays as a child. But now here she was, beside a real sea, with real waves.

Emma breathed deeply, tamping down the unaccustomed swell of joy, and forced herself to turn away. She saw behind her the distant roofs of the housing estate and ahead a line of trees that marked the western boundary of Silverwood Vale.

She wasn't certain she would find Tristan, despite Mrs Foster's directions, but to her surprise it wasn't difficult at all. Just after the trees began, she saw a narrow track that led off the coastal path and into the forest, just wide enough for a vehicle to pass. Some sort of logging road from long ago, she supposed, when the coastal path had also been a road of sorts. Perhaps there had been a time when someone else had intended to chop down the trees, though clearly that had never happened. Branches hung low over the track and wildflowers grew in a riotous tangle along the two tyre ruts, showing that these days it was rarely used.

Emma walked on for a few minutes until she came to a small clearing, much smaller than the one she had stumbled on the previous afternoon – and there she found him.

Mrs Foster had said Tristan was living in a caravan and this had confused Emma, until she remembered 'caravan' was the word that British people used for an RV. But Tristan's caravan was nothing like the luxury RV Emma had pictured. It was tiny, shaped like a bullet, and a dull silver in colour. From the end of the track she could see just one side of it, which had a single, circular window set in it, like the porthole of a ship.

Emma didn't call out. Instead, she stepped gingerly round the side of the caravan. It had obviously been there a long time, for tall stalks of grass had grown up around the hitch. The caravan was barely wide enough for a bed and certainly not long enough for much else.

She emerged on the other side and saw an oval-shaped door, another tiny porthole and the treeline a few feet in front. Between the caravan and the forest was a cookfire, the flames red and orange in the shadowed glade.

Beside the fire sat Tristan.

He was wearing the same flannel shirt as the day before, mud-crusted and dried across the chest. His sleeves were rolled up and she noticed again the tattoos that ran the length of his arms. A lotus flower, the yin/yang symbol, the tree of life.

Tristan looked up as she moved towards him, but he didn't appear surprised to see her. Emma held the bandana out before her, like a flag.

'I brought this back,' she said awkwardly.

Tristan nodded, but he didn't move to take it from her, so Emma stepped closer. He was sitting on a half-rotten bough, his long legs stretched out towards the fire. She draped the bandana over the end of the bough.

'Would you like some tea?' Tristan asked.

'Please.'

Emma wondered if this was what all British people did: offer a stranger tea the minute they turned up.

Tristan hung a pot of water over the fire to boil, much as Mike had done on their many camping trips. Then he reached into a canvas bag between his feet and pulled out some sort of plant with long, feather-like leaves. 'Yarrow,' he said, dropping the leaves into the water. 'Tastes better than PG Tips and it's good for you, too. Sit.'

Emma glanced around for a proper seat, recalling the folding stool she had insisted on taking along when she and Mike went camping, but there was nothing but the fallen bough, furred with moss. She lowered herself down onto it, feeling too close to Tristan for comfort. She could smell the wildness of him. Woodsmoke, damp wool and growing things. It was the scent of Mike.

She suppressed the urge to pat her unruly curls into place, but Tristan didn't look at her.

A long silence followed. Tristan made no effort to converse and Emma grew increasingly irritated. She listened to the logs crackling in the fire and thought, petulantly, *He's burning my wood*.

The water in the pot began to boil.

'My great-aunt lived in the cabin,' Emma said when the silence became too oppressive. 'The one we saw yesterday. That's why I was there.'

She felt irritated with herself for needing to explain her actions, especially when she had every right to be in the forest and Tristan did not.

'You're related to Rose?' Tristan asked. He turned towards her, his expression suddenly animated.

Emma nodded.

'You look a lot like her,' he said and added, 'I didn't know she had any family left.'

'She didn't, not in England. I live in Canada.' Tristan said nothing to that, so Emma added, 'Did you ever meet her? What was she like?'

Leaning forward, Tristan lifted the pot of boiling water from the fire. He produced a chipped mug and poured the steaming liquid into it, complete with balls of sodden leaf. Yarrow, he had called it. Emma stared at the greenish liquid with distaste as he handed the mug to her. He didn't pour tea for himself and it occurred to her that he probably only owned the one mug.

'She was wonderful,' Tristan said, wistfully. 'Rose was wonderful.' Emma thought it was a strange adjective to use and she waited for him to go on.

'I only met her a few times,' he said. 'A mate towed my caravan here when I'd nowhere else to go. I'm not from the south and when I found this place I thought, I can live quietly on this little bit of the Earth and no one will ever know or care. But within the hour, Rose walked out of those trees.' He pointed to a narrow trail, winding into the forest on the other side of the fire. 'She said this was her land, but I could stay here so long as I kept well away from her cabin. So that's what I did.'

Emma breathed in the steam from her mug. The yarrow tea smelled better than it looked.

Tristan said, 'Your great-aunt had a way about her. She was old, but so lithe and graceful. She always looked like she was floating. I know that sounds silly, but it's true. And her hair! Grey, of course, but so long. Thick, and tumbling nearly to her knees.'

Emma thought of the picture she still carried. The young girl with the long, dark hair.

'I only saw Rose a few times,' Tristan said, 'but you know what she used to say?'

Emma waited for him to go on.

'She said, there's no such thing as silence in nature. There are layers of noise, layers of life and you have to learn to listen for them.'

Emma looked over at the dark tangle of trees where the glade ended. The branches grew so thickly entwined that the forest seemed almost impenetrable. She imagined the trees holding layers of sound, speaking a language she couldn't understand. The thought was discomforting.

'My taxi driver was wary of Silverwood Vale,' she said. 'Like he believed it might be haunted or something.' She spoke scornfully, expecting Tristan would think this silly.

'It is,' he said, matter-of-factly. 'Haunted, I mean. By something.'

Emma laughed; she couldn't stop herself. The laughter sounded harsh, even unkind.

Tristan ignored her. 'Ancient things have an aura of mystery,' he said. 'They hold time inside of them. This forest's really old, you know? Not much woodland is left in Britain as ancient as this. There's an oak tree, just beyond this clearing, split in two by a storm that might have happened before... '. He looked at her. 'Before any Europeans set foot in the Americas,' he said.

Emma thought about that.

Tristan stirred the fire. 'I've seen things in the forest that I can't explain,' he said, nodding towards the dark treeline. 'Lights, dancing in the night. And I hear things sometimes, too. Once, I thought I saw a face in the moonlight, luminous and ghostlike, peering out from behind a trunk. But you don't have to believe a word I say.'

Emma didn't. She thought, *This is what you turn into if you choose to live in a forest, like an animal.* But she said nothing.

'Do you always reject things you don't understand?' Tristan asked. As he spoke, he shifted his weight and the bough they were sitting on tipped without warning. Emma leaned sideways to compensate, felt the sharp jab of a branch under her and leapt to her feet, spilling the hot tea. Tristan reached in to rescue the mug as it rolled towards the fire.

'I'm drenched!' Emma cried. She watched the damp stain spread across the top of her jeans, the spilled water flecked with sodden shreds of leaf. Her skin hurt where the boiling liquid had splashed the front of her shirt.

Suddenly, she felt furious, and at more than just Tristan.

'Do you always make judgements about people you don't know?' she cried. 'I don't reject things I can't understand – and I'm certain I understand a good many things you never will.' Her words sounded silly, which annoyed her even more. It was true that she understood how to survive in an urban jungle, but that meant nothing here.

'This is my land now,' she added, 'inherited from my Great-Aunt Rose.' She stopped short of telling him he was trespassing, though she wanted to.

Tristan looked at her, his face impassive. 'Nature belongs only to itself,' he said.

That wasn't only enigmatic, Emma thought, it was ridiculous. 'Thank you for the tea,' she said curtly. 'I need to go.' She had hoped to talk about the bones, to ask him why he had wanted them kept secret and maybe to confess that what they had done made her uncomfortable. But instead, she said, 'Perhaps I'll see you in Lowbury, sometime.'

She strode back round the caravan and onto the track.

Emma wasn't sure why she felt so upset. It wasn't just Tristan, she decided, and the shock of the boiling water on her skin. It was the dense forest, which reminded her of all those terrible camping trips. It was the strangeness of everything, exhaustion because she hadn't slept and missing Mike. It was the thought that she resembled her great-aunt, whose life choices seemed inconceivable to her.

Emma wanted to be in the open air, to hear the waves crash on the beach and walk back through the housing estate with its neat and modern homes towards the town – which was as different from Toronto as it was possible to be, but still felt closer to civilisation than this.

She was walking too fast on the uneven track and, without warning, her foot snagged in a tangle of grasses, pitching her sideways into the undergrowth. She reached out with both hands to steady her fall and cried out in pain as something bit her.

Not one bite, Emma realised, pulling back her hands in shock. Several bites on both her palms. She squatted in the dirt, cradling her hands against her chest.

Tristan must have heard her cry, for in seconds he was beside her.

'Nettles,' he said, examining the white bumps rising on her hands. 'You stumbled into a clump of stinging nettles. Hang on.'

He walked along the edge of the track a short distance, peering at the bushes growing along its edge, and returned with a large, furred leaf. He held it against Emma's palms, rubbing gently.

'Dock leaves,' he said. 'Nature's solution. Wherever there's stinging nettles, you'll always find dock leaves nearby.'

Emma had heard of neither. 'In Ontario, it's deer flies, horse flies, ticks,' she said, miserably. 'And mosquitoes, thick clouds of them, biting and sucking. Then there's poison ivy, and leeches in the shallows that suck your blood. Why does nature have to be so malevolent?'

Tristan squatted beside her, holding her sore hands in his, and Emma bit back her shame, thinking that he had come to her aid twice now in as many days. Above them, a grey cloud sailed in, blotting out the sun. Was English weather as unpredictable, as malevolent as its forests?

Emma thought of Tristan's prediction, the day before. *It's going to rain any minute now*, he had said. She waited for him to say something similar now, but he remained silent, only rubbing the dock leaf against her palms in a steady, circular motion.

Then, through the trees, they heard something. A low wail, like an animal caught in a trap. There was a brief pause and the sound returned, hollow and drawn out, like a fading echo of itself. It was a sound as filled with pain as it was otherworldly.

Tristan let go of her hand. He turned his head in the direction of the noise. 'Now do you see what I mean?' he whispered.

Emma scrambled to her feet. She didn't believe in ghosts. She had no idea what the wailing might be and she wasn't sticking around to find out.

'I have to go,' she said. 'Thanks for the...' She looked at the remnants of the huge leaf, which had dropped to the ground as she pulled away.

'Dock leaf,' Tristan said.

'Dock leaf. Right.'

She turned to go.

'Emma?' Tristan called after her as she picked her way

along the track, more carefully this time. She turned to look at him, a tall shadow standing in the gloom.

'There's more to this forest than stinging nettles,' he said. 'Come back here tonight, just before the sun sets. Let me show you what I mean.'

Emma didn't reply. She turned round and headed out of Silverwood Vale, towards the coastal path and the road back to town.

SIXTEEN

ROSE

October 1940

The shortwave radio under the window burst into life and just like that, their brief period of bliss was over.

Walter snatched the sketch from Rose, not even glancing at the almost-finished drawing of his face, and turned it blank side up. Easing the pencil from her grasp, he bent over the radio, while Rose hovered behind.

The receiver tapped out a message in Morse code and Walter listened, scribbling down a nonsensical stream of letters on the back of Rose's sketch. Then he took from his pocket a thin book and Rose leaned in closer, squinting to read the words on the front cover.

Bomben auf Monte Carlo.

It was the same book she had seen in the pocket of Walter's jumpsuit, the night she found him dangling from the branches of the Thunder Oak.

Walter flicked through the book, pausing on what appeared

to be random pages, and bit by bit he jotted down a second line of letters underneath the first.

The letters formed themselves into a legible sequence before Rose's eyes, though the words themselves were incomprehensible.

German.

'This novel is a cypher,' Walter muttered for her benefit. 'Without the book, it would be impossible to break the code.'

The receiver tap-tapped a final short sequence and fell silent.

Walter leaned over the machine. He took hold of a small key on the right-hand side, rocking it back and forth between his finger and thumb, which resulted in a sequence of muted thuds. Rose watched in astonishment. It was almost inconceivable that hundreds of miles away someone in Germany's secret intelligence was listening to a series of taps as she had done, writing down the corresponding letters so that they might decode them.

But Walter's message must have been no more than a prearranged signal, an acknowledgement, for it was very short. When he was done, he stepped back, tossing Rose's sketch onto the trunk beside the radio as if it meant nothing to him now.

He turned around to look at her.

'I have received a message from our kommandant,' he said. 'It is the message for which I was instructed to wait.' He hesitated, then continued, 'I am to intercept a supply drop.'

Rose thought of the Messerschmitt she had seen, flying over the Channel and towards the south coast, almost three weeks earlier. It had discharged its load into the night sky, circled round and disappeared again, all within the space of a moment or two and all without being detected.

'Where?' she asked. 'Where do you have to go?'

Walter said, 'The rendezvous will take place on the beach, at the point where Silverwood Vale meets Lowbury Plain. It will happen tonight, at one.'

'So soon?'

Everything was happening too quickly. Everything unravelling before her eyes.

Walter looked past her, gazing through the window of the cabin as if night had already fallen. 'They have chosen this evening for a reason,' he said. 'The weather conditions are perfect at last. And there will be no moon.'

Rose felt suddenly so afraid for Walter. Terrified of what might happen to him.

'You can't do this!' she cried. 'Your life is already on the line. You will never be able to convince the authorities that your sentiments are not with Germany – not once you have followed their orders! And besides, if you've been honest with me, why would you even want—'

'Stop.'

Rose could feel her heart thumping in her chest as Walter raised his hand for silence. The gesture irritated her, but she let it pass. There were more important things to focus on now.

'I must do this,' Walter said, a hardness to his voice that Rose had never heard before. He limped over to the small stool he had made, sitting down upon it so heavily that it almost collapsed beneath him.

'I don't see why!' Rose cried. She felt so agitated that it was impossible for her to stay still and she paced the cabin, back and forth, as she spoke. 'You can turn this information over to the police. Offer it in exchange for your life!' An idea occurred to her. 'I could notify the Home Guard about the supply drop,' she said. 'My stepfather, even. Write an anonymous letter, so the police rendezvous with the plane instead of you. Walter, you need to stay hidden, here in the forest, where no one can find you.'

This plan made total sense to her, but Walter shook his head. He was holding his injured ankle, massaging it absentmindedly as he spoke.

'I cannot do as you suggest,' he said. 'I do not know the contents of this drop. I do not know what it is my country intends for us to do. These are things I must discover. If we tell your authorities now, we may never learn what is planned, not until it is too late.'

Rose opened her mouth to object, but Walter made the infuriating motion with his hand again, to silence her. She wondered if it was a gesture he had learned from his father. The father who had adored the German Reich so completely that he had placed a portrait of Hitler above the dining room table.

And all at once, Walter didn't seem familiar any more. He wasn't the peace-loving boy who cultivated gardens, nor the gentle adolescent, caught in a system that demanded absolute obedience. He was no longer the man she dreamed of each night, thought of in her every waking moment.

He was an enemy agent.

A German spy.

'I can't believe this!' Rose cried. 'Do you want Hitler to invade Britain? Is that what you want?'

'No!'

The rage in Walter's voice cut through Rose's distress.

'Please,' he said. 'You must put aside your emotions and you must listen.'

Rose fell silent. She stopped her pacing, leaned against the wooden siding of the cabin and glared at him.

'You must try to see the logic in what I say,' Walter said. 'If we alert your Home Guard, or your police, before we discover the contents of the drop, what will we have to share with them? Coordinates, nothing more. And because I will not know what has been sent, my communication with our superiors will no longer be effective. I must retrieve the supplies myself and discover their contents. This way... how do you say it...? my cover will not be blown. Our commanding officer will continue to trust in my loyalty and I will learn what it is they intend to do. When we have real information, that is the time to notify your authorities.'

Rose breathed deeply. She needed to keep her emotions in check for Walter to take her seriously.

'So you believe you have to find out what it is your... superiors want you to do?'

'That is correct,' Walter said. 'My kommandant must continue to believe I am loyal to the Reich until we know what is contained in the drop and what is planned. Then I may be in a position to help your country. Perhaps even to save lives.'

'And that's when we involve the authorities?' Rose asked.

'That is when we involve the authorities.'

It occurred to Rose that with such concrete information Walter would be in a better position to bargain for his life. His loyalty to England would be beyond doubt.

'So you need to know what the Germans send over tonight,' she said, 'but you won't have any use for whatever it is.'

'Perhaps...' Walter replied, cautiously.

'Then rendezvous with the drop and afterwards hand over whatever it is you receive.'

'What?'

Surprising herself with her absolute conviction, Rose said, 'This is what we are going to do, Walter. You intercept the supplies, so you can continue communicating with... with your kommandant. We'll hide whatever they send and I will write an anonymous note to my stepfather, leading the police to the location. If we do this, as long as no one sees you at the site of the drop, there will be nothing to incriminate you. And if you are ever captured, you can refer to the letter as a way to prove you were never loyal to the Reich.'

Walter hesitated. 'If you insist,' he said finally.

'I do.'

And this way, thought Rose, *I will also have proof of your allegiance. If you let me write my anonymous note, I will know you haven't been taking me for a fool.*

Walter struggled to his feet. He limped across the cabin to the radio and took up the sketch Rose had completed so lovingly. He moved with it towards the fire and she saw the sequence of coded letters on the back of the paper, scribbled hastily, with the neat translation underneath.

'I will rendezvous with the plane at 0100 hours,' Walter said. 'I will hide the supplies and tomorrow you may come and write your anonymous note.'

'No.' *I need to know for sure I can trust you.* Rose squeezed all emotion from her voice, matching the firmness of her tone to his, and said, 'I will meet you tonight, just after midnight, at the western edge of Silverwood Vale where the trees meet the coastal path. We'll rendezvous with the plane together.'

Walter hesitated, but he must have seen from the unaccustomed steeliness in Rose's expression that she wouldn't be swayed.

'Very well,' he conceded.

Walter crouched down and dropped the sheet of paper into the grate. He struck a match, holding the flame to one corner.

They watched together as the paper burned. Walter's secret message on the one side and on the other the portrait Rose had lovingly made of him. All of it curling, blackening, burning, until only a small pile of ash remained.

SEVENTEEN

ROSE

October 1940

As Walter had said, there was no moon that night.

Rose stood by her bedroom window as the grandfather clock in the hallway chimed twelve times. She was wearing a thick pullover of dark-brown wool that her mother had once used for gardening and her long hair was gathered into a whorl at the back of her neck.

I am not made for such things as this, she thought, marvelling at how quickly everything had spoiled. Just a few hours earlier she had trusted Walter, cared for him. Now, she wondered if she had ever known him at all and whether she was caught up in events beyond her control. Rose had wanted to help the war effort, she had wanted it with all her heart, and for so long – but that was because friend and foe, good and evil, had once felt so clear-cut. Now, she no longer felt sure of anything.

If Walter turns out to be no more than an enemy spy, Rose thought, *would I be capable of turning him in?*

Allowing a German agent to go free would be a traitorous act, even more so if she discovered proof that he was loyal to the

Reich. That his actions were helping pave the way for an invasion.

But Walter wasn't a stranger any longer – he was someone she had learned to care for. Could she knowingly do anything that would lead to his execution?

I hope I never have to find out.

Rose held her breath and listened. All she could hear in the darkness was Norman's thunderous snores, drowning out even the loud tick of the grandfather clock down in the hall.

It was time.

She had watched her sister climb out of their bedroom window on an endless string of Saturday nights, her high heels clutched in her hands, and Evelyn had always made it look so easy. But now, as Rose sat on the windowsill, one leg inside the room and the other out, her courage almost deserted her.

She hooked a foot in the trellis that hung against the wall, held on to the window frame and swung the rest of her body out of the window. Then she stayed where she was for several minutes, clinging tight to the wooden frame, feeling the cool nip of the night air before she worked up the courage to reach down with one leg.

Her toes connected with the roof of the porch.

From there, it wasn't difficult to shimmy down the supporting pole and into her mother's hydrangeas. She waited a while, breathing heavily. Listening.

And as she did so, Rose's fear turned to exhilaration.

Starting something was the hardest part. Swinging her foot out of the window, committing to the act. After that, it was easier than she had expected. She thought of the night when Evelyn had begged her to sneak out with her, to join her at the dance. Rose had sensed that their lives together were coming to an end and soon Evelyn would be gone.

I wish I had gone with her that last Saturday night, I really do, Rose thought, sadly.

And here she was, climbing out of the window, alone and for a very different reason.

She padded softly across the garden, jumped the stile and ran through the wheat field towards the coastal path.

It was so dark without a moon, with blackout curtains drawn across every window in the town behind her, that Rose could barely see a hand held in front of her face. It was years since she had run like this, through the dark fields at night, towards the sea.

In fact, she could remember only one other time in her life that she had done so.

It was the night they first met Norman. Neither Evelyn nor Rose had liked him, not even at that first meal when he had sat across the table from them both, on his best behaviour. 'I am going to marry your mother,' Norman had said and the two girls had gazed over at him, eyes wide with astonishment.

Their mother should have been the one to tell them, Evelyn said, but Norman hadn't given her the chance, blurting it out like that. And Evelyn also felt sure their mother didn't love him, that she just wanted to be taken care of.

She told Rose all this an hour later, down on the beach.

There had been an awful row after Norman had gone. Evelyn had accused their mother of betraying their father's memory and then she had grabbed Rose's little hand, dragging her out into the darkness, ignoring their mother's feeble cries that they should return at once and apologise.

Rose hadn't understood much of anything, not at the time. She had been too young. Evelyn had almost pulled her off her feet as they ran for the beach and that was where they had spent that terrible night, curled up together in the dunes, sobbing with helplessness and grief for their father.

Perhaps it was that night when Evelyn first determined to be her own person, Rose thought, as she hurried through the darkness towards Walter. To seize her life and make of it whatever she chose, no matter who she had to defy in the process.

It had taken Rose much longer than that.

Standing at the place where Lowbury Plain ended and Silverwood Vale began, she wondered if 'seizing her life' was what she was doing right now, or if she had simply allowed Walter to manipulate her, the same way Norman always had.

She would know for sure, soon enough.

The world was a blank, ahead of her and behind. An endless darkness, as if she stood with her eyes clamped shut. But then she listened, hearing the shiver of trees along the edge of the forest. The gentle sigh of waves against the sand.

And as she sorted out the noises to her left and to her right, the world pulled back into focus, known and familiar.

'Rose?'

She jumped at the sound of her name.

Walter stood on the path, right beside her. She could smell the appealing woodiness of him, as if he was a part of the natural world, not a human being with all the contradictions that came with that.

'Do you know the time?' he asked.

'It must be almost one,' Rose said.

Above the sea, the clouds parted to reveal a narrow band of stars and the light spangled across the surface of the water, faint and beautiful. She could see Walter, now – a vague shape, dark grey against the deep black of the forest.

There had been an ease between them for weeks now. The conversation always flowed and even when neither of them spoke they still felt close, as if they could almost hear each other's thoughts. But as they stood side by side on the coastal path, the connection was missing and the silence that stretched between them was fraught with tension.

When at last they heard the plane, Rose felt almost relieved. It began as just the hint of a noise, growing louder as it crossed the Channel in their direction. She shrank down, behind the dunes, listening to its path across the sky.

'A Junkers Ju 86,' Walter muttered. 'Kampfgeschwader 200.'

The words meant nothing to Rose, but Walter's voice, speaking German, reminded her of Hitler on the wireless in the moments before BBC newscasters broke through to translate and she felt suddenly fearful.

What was she doing out here?

But it was too late to question the choices she had made. Before she knew it, the plane was overhead and Walter was switching on a little torch, flashing it into the sky, signalling. Rose saw the movement of something in starlight, an object swinging through the air on the end of a parachute. It was visible for only seconds. As they tracked it with their eyes the plane was already banking, turning, heading back across the sea, its engine fading to silence.

The falling object had disappeared from sight.

'Where did it go?' Rose breathed.

Walter licked his finger and held it up, testing the direction of the wind. 'Over there.' He pointed down the coastal path, in the direction of Lowbury.

They heard a faint thud as the object came to land somewhere ahead.

Walter moved quickly, the uneven sound of his footfall revealing that his ankle had not yet healed completely, that he still limped. Rose followed behind, struggling to keep up, until Walter stopped so suddenly that she almost crashed into him.

The object lay before them both on the path. It was a parcel of some kind, wrapped in layers of protective packaging and encased in a canvas sack.

They crouched down beside it. Walter produced a knife, cutting through the straps that bound the package to its parachute, and slicing with care through the protective layers.

Rose looked up, shivering. She saw the deep grey of the sea, heaving and roiling, the white foam of the breakers crashing on the beach. Blackout curtains had obliterated all sign of the town. She and Walter might have been the last people left alive.

Walter pushed up his sleeves and she saw the white skin of his arms, almost luminescent in the darkness. He separated the layers of padding, reaching down so that his hands, his arms, disappeared into the package.

He held them there, inside the layers of canvas, saying nothing.

'What is it?' Rose breathed at last and her voice sounded alarmingly loud in the silence, the stillness of night. 'What's inside?'

Walter withdrew his hand and sat down on the coastal path, not replying. Thinking.

Behind them, on Lowbury Plain, an owl hooted. Rose heard the sudden, frenetic beat of wings aloft in the darkness and the high-pitched scream of prey. She pictured the owl, its talons deep in the body of a rabbit. Its head slowly turning, on the lookout for predators, before it settled down to its meal.

'Well?' she asked again. 'What's inside the package? What did they send?'

'Hexogen,' Walter said.

'What?'

'Explosives,' he explained.

They buried the stash on the dunes, right next to the broken fence post, working in silence. As they dug with their hands in sand still warm from the day, more clouds parted, starlight illuminating them both so clearly that Rose feared for their safety, wondering how she would explain her actions in this moment if anyone should happen to see them.

But there was no one to notice what they were doing, no

one walking on the coastal path in the early hours of the morning, and before long all that remained to mark the spot where the explosives had been buried was the broken fence post, laid sideways over the newly turned sand.

Rose sat back among the dune grasses as Walter finished the job. She watched starlight dancing on the water and imagined again the warships that could be gathering, even now, somewhere on the coast of Normandy as Hitler put in place his final plans for the invasion of Britain.

'Now I know the contents of this drop,' Walter said to her, 'I must learn the intended purpose.'

He pushed something towards her and Rose looked down.

Art paper and a packet of pencils, taken from her stash in the old trunk.

'It is time to write your letter,' he said.

Rose tried to read Walter's expression, but all she could see was the pale outline of his face in the darkness.

'There is a great deal of hexogen here,' he said, patting the dunes with his hand. 'When I think of the damage such an amount could cause, I am alarmed. I am very alarmed.'

'But the explosives will never be used now,' Rose said. 'They will never blow up anything.' She wondered what the intended target might have been. A railway line, perhaps? She had heard about such things on the Continent, the Germans blowing up supply lines as they advanced across Europe. Or the airstrip, in Bilby? This was where Charles had been stationed when Evelyn first met him and it was very close by, just the opposite side of Silverwood Vale.

She took up the paper and a pencil, wondering what to write. Then something occurred to her and she slid the paper back towards Walter.

'You must write the note,' she told him. 'No one will recognise your handwriting. And if you are ever captured, the letter will be evidence in your favour.'

He took the paper from her. 'That is wise,' he conceded. 'You must dictate. And try to use phrases that do not sound like you.'

Rose was silent for a while, wondering how to begin. *Less is more*, she thought. She would describe the location of the buried explosives and how they came to be there.

Only in her final sentence did she allow herself the luxury of a poetic flourish. 'The Nazis must have intended these explosives to cause maximum loss of life,' she wrote, 'for that is the nature of the beast.'

'Nature of the beast,' Walter repeated, copying down her phrase. 'Those were my exact words to you, were they not?'

'Yes,' Rose replied. 'In the cabin, as we rescued the devil's coach horse. You said that soldiers follow orders. That people always do, even if they don't agree with what is being asked of them. You said, "That is the nature of the beast".'

'I did,' Walter replied. 'But perhaps it is not the nature of every beast.'

A faint glow was spreading across the horizon now, lighter to the east, where the dense treeline met the coastal path and the beach.

'I should go,' Rose said. 'It will be dawn soon.'

She stood up, taking the note from Walter and folding it. 'How will you find your way back to the cabin, in the darkness?' she asked.

Walter looked at the white glow, separating sea and sky. 'I will wait for sunrise,' he said. 'It won't be long now.'

Surprising herself, Rose leaned forward and brushed her lips across his cheek. 'Stay safe,' she whispered.

And then she was off, running down the coastal path towards home, the note clutched in her hand, her mind racing, her heart fit to burst.

Walter was every bit the person he had claimed to be. Not an enemy spy who longed for the invasion and would do anything to pave its way, but a man who would betray his country for the sake of England, who would hand over a package of explosives sent by his superiors in Germany rather than see them put to use.

A man worthy of the love she could no longer hide.

Rose was at the stile before she knew it, sailing on air as she had that very first morning, just before discovering the short-wave radio. She crossed the country lane and ran silently up the garden path. But she didn't climb back to her bedroom, mimicking the route Evelyn had taken up and over the porch roof on so many occasions, while Rose watched her anxiously from the bedroom window.

Or at least, she didn't do that right away.

Keeping to the shadows, Rose moved round to the side of the house, where Norman's Vauxhall 12 sat in the driveway.

She looked at the anonymous note one more time, reading it through carefully to ensure it contained nothing that might be traced back to her.

Then she lifted one of Norman's windscreen wipers and slipped the note underneath.

EIGHTEEN

ROSE

October 1940

After unearthing the cache of explosives buried in the dunes, Norman was insufferable, as Rose had known he would be.

The police investigation had rivalled the arrest of the German spy for its excitement and now, the morning after, the three of them sat round the kitchen table, Rose and her mother in silence, Norman full of his customary bluster.

'Radcliffe took a call from the chief superintendent,' he said, his mouth full of black pudding. 'It seems he'll be paying us a visit over the next few days. Wants to congratulate me himself, I shouldn't wonder.'

Anyone would think he'd shot down the plane, Rose thought, *not just dug up a package on the dunes.*

She smiled to herself, thinking of Walter that night. The shape of him in the darkness and how she had startled herself by leaning forward to kiss his cheek.

He's not an enemy, she repeated to herself for the umpteenth time, bursting with joy. *He is a good man, and worthy of my love.*

It was now more than twenty-four hours since she had seen him. Her stepfather had kept her busy all the previous day, running errands.

And she missed him more than she could have guessed.

'What's the matter with you, girl?' Norman leaned across the table towards Rose and her mother stiffened.

'Me?' Rose asked.

'You're smiling like an idiot.'

She tried to paste a blank expression onto her face, but somehow she couldn't do it, not with the thought of Walter still fresh in her mind.

Norman picked up his knife, stabbing the air with it as he spoke.

'You should smarten yourself up,' he said. 'You're an embarrassment to me, that's what you are. Chop off that hair of yours. Get yourself a permanent wave, like Radcliffe's girl. What's her name? Mildred. There's a daughter to make a father proud.'

He shoved his empty plate across the table towards her, but Rose ignored it. 'You're not my father,' she said.

Norman's face began to colour, the way it did when he got mad, though it had always been Evelyn who challenged him in the past, never Rose. The colour spread from his cheeks to his ears, turning their tips crimson, as he lifted himself slowly from his chair.

'Are you giving me lip?' he bellowed.

'Norman...' said Rose's mother, feebly.

'Shut it,' he told her, before turning back to Rose. He waved his hand over his dirty plate. 'Get this lot cleared,' he commanded.

'No.'

Rose felt entirely calm. She had watched Evelyn defy Norman so many times and always she had wondered at the fear she must feel, but it wasn't like that at all. Rose wasn't afraid. Norman and his bullying just didn't matter any more, not set against her feelings for Walter and her sense of triumph when she thought of what they had done. Of the hexogen, which might have caused a catastrophic loss of life, but was now safely in the hands of the police.

'You're just like your sister,' Norman spat. 'I should have known it.' His hands moved down to his waist. 'You won't defy me like she did,' he said, unfastening his belt, the one with the hard, steel buckle.

Rose's mother gave a tiny, involuntary squeal.

Rose watched the belt unwind. She watched Norman's hands tighten round the buckle and she saw the glint in his eye, the one that signalled the pleasure he took in dominating others. She thought how her mother had known that glint for so many years, when she and Evelyn had been too young to understand, and how her mother must have known the belt, too, and more besides. But as Norman prepared to strike her, Rose felt no fear. All she felt was a deep sadness, that the world could not be other than the way it was.

And in that moment, the doorbell rang.

Without even looking at Rose's mother, Norman said to her, 'You. Get it.' She struggled to make it out of her chair, her movements painfully slow despite her best efforts.

The doorbell rang again.

'Oh, for Pete's sake, woman.' Norman stabbed a finger at Rose. 'Go see who it is and be quick about it.'

Rose moved slowly to annoy him, through to the hall as the bell rang again, three times in quick succession.

She opened the door. On the front step stood Mildred, her face red with exertion, her bicycle propped against her hip.

'Dad says can your stepdad come right away, please? The chief superintendent rang our house this morning. He will be here in' – she glanced past Rose, at the grandfather clock – 'in fifteen minutes,' she finished. 'Good morning, sir.'

Rose turned to see Norman behind her, fastening his belt again, reaching for his coat.

'You need to get a telephone,' Mildred hissed at Rose, as if she was to blame for her hurried bike ride across the town. 'My father had one installed ages ago.'

Norman pushed past them both and out to the car. Mildred mounted her bicycle and followed him onto the road towards Lowbury.

Rose turned back to the kitchen, but her mother wasn't there. She was standing in the dining room at the window, watching Norman's car disappear round the corner. From the set of her shoulders, Rose could tell she was crying.

'Why did you do it?' she sobbed, without turning round. 'Why did you defy him? It's like your sister, all over again...'

Rose knew she should apologise for upsetting her mother, for antagonising Norman. But she couldn't.

'What choice did Evelyn have?' she cried. 'What choice do I have? You never stood up to Norman, not once. Not even when he drove Evelyn away! You've spent your whole life being afraid of him.'

Now she had started, Rose found she couldn't stop. 'What would you do if he turned on me, Mam?' she yelled. 'What would you do if he had taken his belt to me, just now? Nothing, that's what. You wouldn't stand up for me any more than you stood up for Evelyn.'

When Rose had finished there was a long silence and still her mother didn't turn round. When at last she spoke, her voice was little more than a whisper.

'I may not have stood up for you,' her mother said, 'but I've been making your excuses every day these past few weeks when you disappear for hours on end.' She turned round to face her. 'Where is it you go to, Rose?' she pleaded.

Rose said nothing.

'Are you courting? Is that what this is?'

Still Rose didn't answer, though she felt her cheeks redden.

Her mother shook her head, so overcome with emotion that for a moment she was unable to speak.

'Norman's forbidden it,' she said at last. 'If he should find out...'

'Why shouldn't I have a little happiness?' Rose cried, unmoved by her mother's tears, exasperated by her timidity. 'It's normal for girls my age to have a beau. Why shouldn't I?'

'Then it's true...' her mother said.

Rose neither denied nor admitted it. If her mother thought she was sneaking out to meet a soldier home on leave, why not go along with it?

'There's something you need to see,' her mother said. Her voice was flat now, void of emotion. She crossed the dining room to the sideboard and opened it.

Rose watched as her mother pulled something out and set it on the table between them.

It was a bottle of Glenfiddich.

So what if Norman is drinking? Rose thought. *It's not like that's news to anyone.* It was surprising that he'd been able to find a single malt Scotch when there was a war on, but Norman was sergeant now. She suspected he could get his hands on anything, if he had a mind to.

'So?' Rose said.

Her mother was trembling with emotion, but her voice remained toneless as she said, 'In the early days when you girls were small, Norman was at his most dangerous when he bought Glenfiddich. If I saw this on the kitchen table when he came home, I'd know there was about to be trouble. That he would work himself up to violence. That's when I'd say to you and Evelyn, "Run along to the forest and have some fun. Forget your chores and go!"'

As her mother mimicked the words she had spoken so many times all those years ago, Rose remembered. She recalled how her mother had chivvied them both out of the door on so many occasions, a smile plastered on her face, while Norman hovered behind.

She had never wondered at the truth behind her mother's smile.

Until now.

'Oh, Mam...' she said. Her mother's eyes were red and swollen, but her cheeks had the pale and waxy pallor that Rose had come to associate with her illness.

'There hasn't been a bottle of Glenfiddich in the house for years,' her mother went on. 'But now he's buying it again. It's not a good sign, Rose. If you ever see him drinking Glenfiddich, you need to leave. See your beau, spend a few hours in the woods, whatever. Just stay out of his way.'

Her mother paused to catch her breath, shoulders heaving as she looked down at the bottle. Rose thought she was trying to make her mind up about something.

Then she returned to the sideboard. This time she crouched down awkwardly, rummaging right in the back.

She pulled out a small glass bottle. It was about the size of her little finger, opaque, with a rubber stopper.

The bottle had no label.

Rose's mother unscrewed the top, revealing a thin glass pipette. When she spoke again, it was hurriedly, as if she thought Rose might shut her down before she had time to say her piece.

'This is a sleeping draught,' she said. 'After your father died, I got it from the doctor. A single drop, he said, to calm the mind, and five for a deep sleep. Whenever I sensed there was trouble coming, that there was no other way to stop him getting violent, I'd add a few drops to Norman's Scotch. It might save me a beating and he'd never know. I'm telling you this, Rose, in case there's a time when you need to do the same. I'll put it here...'

Her mother returned the glass bottle to the sideboard, but

this time she didn't hide it in the back; she slipped it underneath the placemats.

Rose felt indignation boil up inside her. Fury that her mother should feel that the only way to keep yourself safe from a person was to drug them.

'I won't live my life in fear of him, Mam,' she said. 'Not as you did.'

'But if that's the only—'

'No. I won't do it.'

Rose had seen enough. She strode through to the hall, grabbed her coat and made for the door, without so much as a goodbye. Moments later, she was running for the coastal path, trying to banish from her mind the image of her mother, propped up against the sideboard, her eyes red from crying and her face as pale as a ghost.

But when Rose reached the point where the old track veered off towards the Thunder Oak and the cabin, she paused.

Something about her mam's words had troubled her and it was only now that she realised what it was.

Her mother had spoken as if she wouldn't be around much longer to see what became of Rose. As if Rose would need to learn how to handle her stepfather on her own.

Despite everything, Rose and Walter had a lovely morning. They wandered together through Silverwood, Walter pointing out with ever-increasing delight the rare flowers that grew in tenuous clumps among the trees. When they grew hungry, they feasted on beech nuts and wild plums. When they felt thirsty, they located a crystal-clear brook, chattering over mossy stones, an enchanted place if ever there was one. They cupped their hands and drank, Walter declaring it the most delicious water he had ever tasted.

They returned to the cabin in the early afternoon. Walter

dragged a fallen log into a shaft of afternoon sunshine as it spilled through the clearing and they sat side by side, next to the old well. Despite the sunny weather, there was a distinct chill in the air and it was only now when they were sitting, a silence falling between them, that Rose's worries came crowding back.

She thought about her mother, alone and unwell, and she felt guilty for leaving her. She pined for her sister and she wondered whether Norman truly was as dangerous as her mother feared. And then, looking around the sun-splashed glade, she wondered whether Mildred had spoken the truth when she said that Silverwood Vale was at risk of destruction.

I have so many troubles, Rose thought, looking at Walter, *and I can't share any of them with you.*

Walter had enough to worry about, since he faced an impossible situation. He couldn't return to Germany, not if he wished to escape becoming a pawn of the Nazis again, but by remaining in England he would always be a fugitive. A non-person, forever at risk of arrest and execution.

'What is it you English say?' he murmured. 'A penny for your thoughts?' He laid a hand over hers.

'I'm sorry,' Rose said. 'I just have a lot on my mind.' *Why do you even care about me?* she wondered, gazing down at his hand on hers. *Why would anyone?* She wasn't vivacious and daring like Evelyn, nor beautiful and stylish like Mildred. She was nothing, really.

Walter said, softly, 'Perhaps you are concerned that by protecting me you have also committed treason and now there is no going back.'

Rose added that worry to all the others. She thought of the radio, behind them in the cabin. Its malevolent presence.

Before the war, her life and her future had seemed predictable. Now, she had no idea what even the next day would bring.

'What are we going to do?' she asked Walter.

His certainty was a surprise to her.

'We will continue to do what we have done already,' he said, 'live day by day and let the future take care of itself. I will decode messages and we will learn what it is my kommandant has planned. When we have the information we need, you will write another anonymous letter to the authorities, so that no harm may come to anyone.'

No harm may come to anyone. Rose liked that. Walter might be German and she English, but they shared more than their love of nature. They shared a belief that life was sacred and must be protected at all costs.

'I should get back,' she said. 'My mother was not feeling well this morning. Perhaps she needs me.'

'You have many troubles,' Walter said, 'and yet you do not tell me what they are.' An awkward silence followed and Rose knew he was waiting for her to do exactly that – to tell him. But she couldn't find the words. And when she said nothing, Rose wondered how he interpreted her silence. Was he worried that she still didn't trust him?

But perhaps she was reading too much into his expression, for in the next instant Walter slid an arm round her, pulling her close. He kissed her gently, but as the kiss ignited passion between them he drew back, always the gentleman. He stroked her hair away from her face, letting the long strands run through his fingers. 'You are so lovely,' he breathed. 'Lovely, and brave, and compassionate. Perhaps it is also part of your charm that you do not know this. You do not know it at all.'

Rose thought, *I have a great deal to rejoice about. I am in love with a wonderful man who cares for me. I am learning to be more like Evelyn. And I have a chance to make a difference in this war.*

There was so much to give her life meaning. But she couldn't help feeling, no matter how hard she tried, that she was in over her head.

NINETEEN

ROSE

October 1940

It was mid-afternoon when Rose returned home. She should have found her mother in her favourite armchair by the window, a pile of tissues in her lap and the wireless on, playing the cloyingly sentimental music she loved so much. But even before Rose entered the house, she could tell that something was wrong.

She peered into the scullery, at all the unwashed dishes. Her mother hadn't even tried to clean up after breakfast, which meant this was one of her bad days. *No harm done*, Rose thought. *I'm back in time to make everything spick and span before Norman gets home.*

The kitchen was exactly as she had left it, too.

'Mam?' Rose called.

There was no answer.

In the dining room, the bottle of Glenfiddich was gone from the table, but otherwise the room looked the same as when she had left, five hours earlier. Except, it was also empty.

'Mam?' Her voice was louder now, pitched higher.

Rose hurried through to the parlour. Her mother's armchair under the window stood empty. The room looked the same as when Rose had last seen it, with a couple of alarming exceptions.

The crumpled tissues, scattered across the carpet. Her mother's shawl, in a heap in the middle of the room.

Rose ran into the hall and up the stairs.

The bathroom, empty.

The bedrooms, empty.

And as she screamed for her mother, her heart pounding with fear, Rose heard a car pull up outside.

She looked through the tiny window at the end of the landing.

Norman.

Rose took the stairs two at a time and leapt into the hall just as he opened the front door.

'Where is my mother?' she screamed.

Norman looked at her, steely-eyed, as he peeled off his jacket.

'What's happened?' Rose asked.

'If you had been here,' Norman said, 'you would know.' He walked past her and into the kitchen. 'Get me a beer,' he called over his shoulder.

'Where is she?' Rose cried from the doorway.

Norman scraped a chair out from under the table and sat down. 'I came back here for my sandwiches,' he said, 'after the chief had left. Found her collapsed on the carpet, in the parlour. She's down St Margaret's. Now get me that beer.'

Rose didn't move. 'You left her there?' she asked. 'In the hospital, by herself?'

'I hardly think you're the one to talk. Now get me—'

'What's wrong with her? What's the matter?'

Norman let out what sounded like a low growl. He stood up, pushed past Rose and went into the scullery. She heard the tinkling of bottles in their crate behind the scullery door and he returned with a beer in each hand. But he stopped when he reached Rose.

'She's dying, did you know that?' Norman said. 'Your mother's been dying for a while, though she wouldn't have you knowing. Didn't want to be a burden.' His tone was full of mockery as he spoke the last few words and he moved closer, backing Rose into the doorframe. She felt his body, pressed hard against hers. His sour breath on her cheek.

'Your mother will be gone soon,' Norman whispered. 'And then it'll be just you and me.'

St Margaret's Hospital in Lowbury was a squat, stone building that occupied one side of the town square. The blank windows and stark exterior always put Rose in mind of a prison, or an asylum, despite the cheery hydrangea bushes bordering the path to the main doors. The hospital had expanded in recent years, but the newer wing had been cleared of patients ready to start its new life as a convalescent home for the war wounded.

Rose's mother's ward was located at the very front of the hospital, just inside the main doors. An older nurse with kindly eyes sat behind the reception desk, tight grey curls escaping from beneath her cap. Behind her stretched dozens of metal beds, each covered with starched white sheets.

Every one of the beds was occupied. Rose scanned the ward, but she couldn't see her mother.

'Are you here to see Mrs Spencer?' asked the nurse.

Norman's surname. Rose had never thought of her mother as Mrs Spencer.

'Yes,' she said.

The nurse's smile was full of empathy, but under the circumstances Rose wasn't certain that was a good sign.

'She was admitted only a short time ago,' the nurse said.

'Visiting hours begin in a few moments.' She was playing with her pen, moving it from one hand to the other as she spoke. 'I admitted her myself. She's a lovely woman, your mam. Always was.'

Rose blinked at the nurse, trying to place her.

'Oh, you wouldn't remember me,' she said. 'My name's Gertrude Buxton. I used to run the Rosebud Tea Shop in Lowbury, back when you and Evelyn were small. The four of you would come in every Saturday afternoon, you and your sister sandwiched between your mam and dad. Always smiling, you were, the four of you. And every week, your parents would let you choose a cream cake. You liked my eclairs the best.'

'I remember now,' Rose said, her eyes filling with tears.

It wasn't the tea shop she remembered, it was her mother and father each holding one of her hands, swinging her down the street, while Evelyn skipped along beside.

Nurse Buxton laid down her pen. She said softly, 'Your mother asked us to ring the warden post where your sister is stationed, but there was no answer. Do you know how we can reach her?'

Rose shook her head. 'She's staying with her fiancé's sister,' she said, 'but they don't have a telephone.' She choked back her tears. 'It must be serious,' she said, 'if Mam wants my sister to come.'

Nurse Buxton's expression was grave. 'Rose, do you know your mother is consumptive?' she asked.

Rose nodded, not trusting herself to speak. No one had said as much, least of all her mother. But although Rose hadn't allowed herself to think about it, she supposed on a subconscious level she had known.

'She has been consumptive for quite some time,' Nurse Buxton added.

Rose still said nothing and perhaps the kindly nurse took this to mean she failed to understand the gravity of the situation, for she leaned across the desk towards Rose and said gently, 'I'm so sorry to tell you this, but your mother doesn't have very long.'

Rose sat by her mother's bed and watched her sleep. Each breath she took was a struggle, accompanied by hisses and wheezing. Rose gripped the arms of her chair tightly, listening to the sounds and dreading the moment when they would stop.

All along the ward, patients sat up in bed, chatting with their visitors. Only Rose's mother remained still, silent and fast asleep.

Rose took her hand. 'I'm sorry,' she whispered, thinking of all the times she had left her mother alone in the past weeks. Even the final words she had spoken to her that morning had been words of contempt.

You were always so alone, Rose thought. *Not just these last three weeks, but for years.* She recalled how she and Evelyn would disappear to their room, closing the door behind them, the minute Norman entered the house. How they would run off to Silverwood Vale, to breathe in the fresh air, to pretend they lived together in the little cabin, away from everything that was harmful about the world.

It had all been self-preservation, of course. Children find ways to survive. But every time they found a way to escape, their mother had been left behind.

Rose gazed down at her mother. Her eyes were scrunched tight as if she was in pain, though surely that wasn't possible, not if she was asleep? Her body seemed to occupy so little space under the sheets that it was as if she had already faded away. Rose thought, *A decade married to Norman would do that to a person.*

She could hardly bear her remorse. She wanted her mother to wake up, to look at her so she could say, *I love you, and I'm so sorry I left you alone.* But alongside her need to apologise, Rose couldn't ignore the resentment she felt, even now. The little voice that whispered, *You were the one to marry him, Mother. You made your own bed and we all had to lie in it.*

Rose left the hospital an hour later with the other visitors, emerging into bright sunshine. In her misery she wanted rain, endless sheets of it, drowning the world. But the sky was a clear, bright blue.

Hearing engines idling along the side of the hospital, Rose turned to see a line of army trucks and field ambulances. A cluster of nurses stood waiting and, as the rear doors of each vehicle opened, soldiers in uniform emerged. Some of them were in wheelchairs, others walked with the aid of crutches. One held out his arms in front of him and both his hands were swathed in bandages. As the ambulances disgorged the wounded soldiers, nurses rushed forward to help, ushering the servicemen into the hospital's new convalescent wing.

These were the lucky ones, back from the front and home to stay. No one would ask them to fight any more. No one would ask them to kill.

Rose tore her gaze away from them.

Across the marketplace, Mildred was leaving the post office, the elderly postmaster by her side. They were closing up for the day. And, as Rose watched them, Mildred turned round and looked straight at her.

Everyone knew that Rose's mother was very ill, so it must have been obvious to Mildred why she stood outside St Margaret's, alone. Yet there was no empathy in Mildred's expression. None at all.

Rose thought of how Mr Radcliffe had helped Norman to beat up the spy, even though he was in custody and could do no harm. She wondered if Mildred was capable of such malevolence.

It was three days before Rose found the time to return to Walter. Three days spent watching over her mother, praying for her to regain consciousness, though she never did. Three days worrying about Evelyn, who could not be reached, though Rose rang her warden post time and again, even sending letters to the address where Evelyn was staying.

Three full days until she finally carved an hour from her schedule, running through pouring rain in the early evening, along the coastal path, into Silverwood Vale, past the Thunder Oak and towards the cabin.

Rose didn't knock as she usually did. She burst through the door, drenched from head to toe, breathing heavily.

Walter stood by the radio, under the window. He turned round and looked at her as she entered, his expression hurt and resentful. He waited for her to give a reason for her long absence, but Rose was startled by the coldness in his eyes and suddenly she didn't know where to begin.

When she said nothing, it was Walter who broke the tense silence.

'I have received another message,' he said.

TWENTY

EMMA

June 1990

As Emma left Tristan behind and walked back along the coastal path towards Lowbury, she wondered at his strange words. *There's more to this forest than stinging nettles,* Tristan had said. *Come back here tonight, just before the sun sets. Let me show you what I mean.*

Emma had no intention of returning to the forest. Tristan could live alone in his poky caravan until the land was sold, for all she cared – but she doubted he would be allowed to stay once the area had been cleared for development.

It occurred to her that she could make some sort of provision for Tristan, if she wanted to. Take his tiny portion of the forest out of the deed of sale, so he could remain as long as he wanted. But when she pictured his caravan marooned in a sea of houses, she couldn't imagine him wanting to be there.

When the sun emerged from behind a wall of cloud, Emma clambered over the dunes and walked along the beach. She wondered if Rose had ever done the same thing, using the beach as a short cut between the forest and town, and knew she must have. Even with the little she had learned about her great-aunt, Emma felt certain the beach and the dunes would have been special to her, perhaps almost as much as the forest itself.

But something had happened to Rose during the war and Emma still had no idea what it was – only that it had been monumental enough for her to run away. Where had she lived after leaving home? And why had she returned to Silverwood Vale, so close to where she had grown up, living alone in the cabin for decades, like a hermit?

Even more perplexing, how was Rose connected to the human remains they had found, wrapped in the old parachute in the root cellar?

Emma's grandmother – Evelyn – had spent years searching for Rose. Even after starting her new life in Canada, she had never forgotten her little sister. Emma had been young when her grandmother died, but she could recall an expression that passed over her face sometimes. A sadness; a sudden pain that creased the corners of her eyes. Had she been thinking of her lost sister in those moments?

When a single-propeller plane puttered across the sky, Emma paused to watch it, wondering what kind of planes Rose might have seen from this very spot during the war. As the Nazis conquered great swathes of Europe, she must have feared England would be next.

And that was when she made up her mind. Emma wouldn't head straight back to her bed and breakfast, with its stuffy rooms and well-meaning but overbearing hostess. She would walk into Lowbury, right now. What was it Mrs Foster had said? There was a woman who had worked in the post office for nearly fifty years.

Well, if that was the case, she might have known Rose.

Emma turned away from the beach, crossed the coastal path and set off at a brisk pace across the farmer's field, to Lowbury.

. . .

It was a small town, old and pretty in an unassuming sort of way. Emma supposed there were hundreds of places in England just like it: not quaint enough to be popular with the tourists, but still interesting, especially for someone new to the country.

It was a weekday and the streets were mostly deserted. She paused to marvel at a tiny, red brick police station with a carved datestone above the entrance. *1767*, she read.

There wasn't a single building in Ontario that old.

Emma passed a little pub called the Fox and Hound. When the door opened to admit an elderly man, she heard a sudden burst of chatter from inside. She considered stopping for a bite to eat, but the thought of so many strangers gave her pause. Instead she walked onwards, into a spacious square that might once have been the heart of the community. Here, the buildings looked much newer, with several of them clearly built since the war.

On one side of the town square was a pretty parkette, with rows of beech trees and brightly painted benches, and in front of the parkette stood a memorial plaque, surrounded by an ornamental fence. Emma leaned over to read the words engraved upon the marble and outlined in gold leaf:

> *On this site stood St Margaret's Hospital,*
> *destroyed by a Luftwaffe bombing raid*
> *on the night of 12ᵗʰ October 1940.*
> *Eleven people lost their lives.*

It was alarming to think that the war had caused such devastation even in this sleepy town.

Emma looked up from the plaque and across the town square. Tucked in between a modern-looking insurance brokers and a bank made entirely of glass and steel she saw a narrow stone building every bit as old as the police station and in front of it, a traditional red pillar box.

The sign over the building read: Post Office.

The building may have been old on the outside, but the interior was entirely modern. Bright strip-lighting ran the length of the shop and there was a row of glassed-in counters along the far wall. Display shelves to the left held stationery items and a high counter to the right provided a convenient area for people to complete forms or address their letters.

Emma was the only customer. She wandered through the post office, browsing the stationery, feeling conspicuous, until she reached the glassed-in portion at the end. Just one of the counters was occupied and it held a female postal worker, but Emma did not think this could be the woman she needed to talk with. *Mildred*, Mrs Foster had said her name was. Anyone who had worked in the post office for as long as Mildred would be well into their later years, but as this clerk bent low over a form, bright, blond curls spilled across her face.

'Can I help you?' the clerk asked sharply, without looking up.

'It's okay, thank you, I'm just browsing,' Emma replied and she began to turn away.

Perhaps it was surprise at hearing a Canadian accent, but the woman looked up at once.

Her appearance was startling. Bleached-blond hair framed a ravaged face that must once have been beautiful. Emma recalled how her grandmother had referred to her own wrinkles as 'laughter lines', but the wrinkles on this woman's face could never be described that way. Her mouth was pulled downwards and the lines across her forehead and between her brows gave the impression of a scowl, etched deeply into her face by years of irritability.

Sour. That was the word that came to mind as Emma looked at her.

The brass name plate on her grey blouse read: MILDRED.

'Can I do something for you?' Mildred snapped. And when Emma hesitated, unsure how to respond, she spun round and disappeared into the office at the back of the shop.

Emma was wondering whether to leave, unsure how she would ever start a productive conversation with this woman, when Mildred re-emerged from the office carrying a large cardboard box. She used a key to let herself out of the sealed-in portion of the post office and entered the shop. Mildred heaved her box onto the counter intended for customer use, lifted out a stack of postcards and started arranging them in a display box on the wall.

Emma moved tentatively towards her. 'Could I...' she began. 'Do you have a moment...'

Mildred abruptly stopped what she was doing and turned round.

'Yes?' she snapped.

She has to be close to seventy, Emma thought, wondering why the old lady hadn't retired. Why she had gone on working in the same place for half a century. Mildred moved with the agility of a much younger woman, which made her features all the more startling. Even her dyed curls, seen close up, reminded Emma of the brittle, straw-like hair she had once seen on a mummy in the Royal Ontario Museum.

Mildred glared at Emma, her veined hands hovering over the pile of postcards, and waited for her to speak.

'I beg your pardon,' Emma said, 'but I'm trying to find out a little about Rose Tilburn. I'm told you knew her.'

Mildred's face seemed to sink into itself at the mention of Rose. 'For years people have been coming here, asking their questions,' she said, sounding strangely distressed. 'Questions, and more questions. First, because she was missing, then because she was back, and always because of who she was and what she did. But Rose is dead now. Am I never to be rid of her?'

Emma felt so flustered at Mildred's speech that words eluded her.

'Who are you anyway?' the old woman asked, sharpness returning to her voice. 'A journalist?'

'Yes, but...'

'So many journalists poking around here, year after year.'

Mildred returned to her task, yanking dozens of postcards from her box and hitting them hard against the counter to align their corners. Emma looked at the postcards. Each of them had the same image on the front: a ruined castle on a promontory – so ruined that the walls looked as if they were slipped into the sea. *Browminster Castle* read the text across the front. Emma wondered if the castle was a local landmark.

'I have nothing else to tell any of you, so be on your way.' Mildred threw the words over her shoulder as she worked.

'It's true that I'm a journalist,' Emma said quickly, 'but that's not why I'm here. I live in Canada, but my family comes from Lowbury. Rose Tilburn was my great-aunt.'

This had a profound impact on the old woman. She was holding in her hand another stack of postcards, but she didn't knock them hard against the counter to align their edges; she placed them down gently and turned to Emma.

'You look like her,' she said.

Emma tried to read her expression, the tone of her voice, but she couldn't.

'I never knew my great-aunt,' Emma said. 'I never got to meet her.'

There was a pause and Mildred's chiselled features hard-ened again. 'Well,' she said, 'you weren't missing much.'

The words startled Emma and even more so the venom behind them.

'Your great-aunt as good as abandoned her dying mother in her time of need,' Mildred said. The words spilled from her, thick and fast, as if now she had decided what to tell Emma there was no stopping her. 'She had a fancy man, did you know that?'

A fancy man. The term seemed ridiculously old-fashioned.

'Rose got what was coming to her,' Mildred said. 'But she escaped, and after that it was a long time before any of us saw her again. She kept tongues wagging in Lowbury for years.'

And your tongue more than the rest, Emma guessed. But she said nothing.

Mildred turned away again. She pushed the scattered leaflets with her fingers, aligning them on the counter, but slowly, as if her thoughts were elsewhere.

Out of the blue, she cried, 'There's no justice in this world.'

Puzzled, Emma said, 'I beg your pardon?'

'Everything goes to those that don't deserve it.'

Emma waited for Mildred to say more, but she didn't. 'When was the last time you saw Rose?' she prompted.

'Oh, I saw her all the time,' Mildred replied. 'Right up until the day she died.' Her head was bent, her eyes on her task. In the absence of an expression to read, Emma tried to make sense of her tone. Was it regret? Envy, even? 'She came in here to post her parcels,' Mildred said.

'Parcels?' Emma asked. Here at last was new information.

'That's right,' Mildred said. 'Every month or so, for decades. She sent them to banks and government offices. Company head-quarters in London and Manchester. Even private residences in Mayfair, Knightsbridge and suchlike. I was the first to know she was back when she waltzed in here one morning, a smile on her face and a huge package under one arm, like she'd never been away.'

You were the gossip who spread rumours about Rose, Emma thought. *You don't like people asking questions about her, but it was you who kept her story alive.*

'What was inside all the parcels?' Emma asked.

Mildred's hands stilled.

She knows, but she isn't going to say.

'I have work to do,' Mildred said. 'Take your questions else-where. But if you really want to find Rose, go look in the museum.'

Go look in the museum. Not the cemetery on the edge of town, where Rose had been buried.

The museum.

Emma followed the tourist signs through Lowbury, under a midday sun that carried the promise of summer, and as she walked, she thought about everything Mildred had told her. One statement in particular had seemed strange: *Rose got what was coming to her*, Mildred had said, *but she escaped.*

If Rose had *escaped*, what was she escaping from?

Emma thought about Mildred. She had spent her entire adult life in one place, never moving on. *Could this be my fate?* she wondered. *To keep doing the same thing, year after year, until I'm old?* If you didn't want your life to stagnate, you had to take risks. Big risks sometimes, like leaving behind a city you loved, as Mike had asked her to do.

For the first time, it occurred to Emma that perhaps it wasn't moving away from Toronto that she was resisting.

Perhaps it was change itself.

The museum was nothing more than three rooms at the back of the town hall. Curious to learn what Mildred had meant, Emma dropped a handful of coins into the donation box by the entrance and wandered inside.

The first room was given over to the ancient history of the

area. Emma was mildly interested to learn that a range of cliffs just outside Lowbury had crumbled during a storm a few years earlier, revealing so many fragments of dinosaur bones that the discoveries were reported internationally. And during construction of the housing estate Emma had walked through earlier that day, a mechanical excavator had uncovered remains of an Iron Age settlement. Sadly, there had not been time to grant an injunction and the site had been obliterated by the new homes.

Emma wondered how many places in England told the same story: history wiped out in the name of progress. And no one would ever know how much had been lost, because that was the nature of loss, really.

From there she passed into the second room, stopping short at the door. This room was bathed in greenish light, filled with nature displays and accompanied by a soundtrack of bird calls.

The entire room was a celebration of Silverwood Vale.

I own all this, Emma thought in amazement as she wandered between the exhibits. On one wall, naturalists had created a display that gathered together the wonders of Silverwood Vale in a single glass cabinet, or so the sign said. Emma learned that her land was home to more than a thousand kinds of fungi as well as polecats, badgers, dormice and water shrews. The forest boasted a rare colony of barbastelle bats and more than half the species of butterflies to be found in the British Isles.

She hurried through the exhibit, hardly knowing why. In the 1960s there had been an effort to raise money to purchase Silverwood Vale for the Woodland Trust, she learned, but fundraisers had been unable to secure the vast sum of money required, *so the forest remains unprotected and privately owned.*

Emma moved towards the exit door. Silverwood Vale, proclaimed a final sign, was a woodland treasure so ancient it was even mentioned in the Domesday Book. Reading on, Emma learned that the Domesday Book was a survey of England completed in 1086.

She turned away from the sign and stepped through into the third and final room.

This portion of the museum was a celebration of famous people born in Lowbury. The two side walls were filled with black and white photographs, each accompanied by long blocks of text. But it was the far wall that grabbed Emma's attention.

She stared in amazement, walking slowly down the long room.

A single oil painting occupied almost the entire rear wall. On the canvas, huge flames shot up from a half-collapsed building, rising in nightmarish swirls towards a blue-black sky. Along the bottom of the canvas, bodies lay twisted across rubble, or held in the arms of survivors whose faces burned with anguish. A child sat in one corner, a little boy holding a blanket, and three soldiers stood behind him, their army uniforms covered in soot. One leaned on a crutch, another had his eyes swathed in gauze and a third reached out bandaged hands towards the child.

The painting was wild with action and fury, with vibrant colour and texture, realistic and yet in a style all of its own.

It had a title: *The Bombing of St Margaret's Hospital, 12th October 1940.*

In the very middle of the canvas, in the centre of the broken building, a young woman stood alone, both arms raised to the skies. She had black hair that reached past her waist and she was staring upwards, like Joan of Arc burning on her stake, only this girl wasn't gazing at the face of God, she was looking up at a German Messerschmitt.

It was the young woman's expression that shocked Emma as she stood in front of the enormous canvas. Not the bodies, nor the flames, but the expression of the girl, who was so clearly her Great-Aunt Rose. It contained anger, but there was something questioning about it, too, as if she felt puzzled by the actions of the German pilot. Puzzled, saddened and betrayed.

How was that possible? Emma wondered. How could Rose have felt anything other than revulsion for the bombing of a hospital – for anything the Nazis did?

She stepped closer to read the artist's signature, knowing even before she did so what she would see.

The artist was her Great-Aunt Rose.

How talented she had been, Emma thought with a rush of pride. Yet no one in her family had ever known.

The painting solved one mystery, at least. If her great-aunt was an artist, mailing her work to collectors all over the country, she would have had no problem supporting herself financially as she lived out her life alone in the forest. But would an artist – even a successful one – have made enough money to purchase an entire forest in the first place?

The more she learned about Great-Aunt Rose, the more of a mystery she became.

TWENTY-ONE

EMMA

June 1990

It was mid-afternoon when the telephone rang. Emma was back at her bed and breakfast, lying in a nest of embroidered cushions in Mrs Foster's back bedroom. She was wondering where Rose had been on the night the hospital was bombed. What had been running through her great-aunt's mind as she painted herself in the centre of the rubble and flames?

The phone rang several times before Emma heard Mrs Foster thud down the stairs from her own room. A few murmured words followed and then she called from the hallway, 'It's for you, dear! A gentleman from London. A solicitor, no less!'

Emma hurried down to take the call.

'I have the most wonderful news,' said Richard Barrow. He had a clipped, upper-class accent and to Emma, who had little experience of such things, he sounded like Prince Charles. 'I understand this is coming a great deal sooner than you expected,' he continued, 'and before you have even begun formal arrangements for the sale of your land, but it seems I may have found you a buyer.' There was a brief pause on the line, as if Mr Barrow expected some sort of response. When Emma said nothing, he went on, 'Last week, British Rail announced plans to increase the number of daily trains serving your portion of the south coast. This increases Lowbury's viability as a commuter town for homebuyers working in London and I have been approached personally by a developer interested in acquiring Silverwood Vale.'

Emma only half listened as her solicitor went into further detail, explaining at length how the developer had come to hear about her land. She hadn't expected this to happen so quickly, hadn't expected to be approached by a potential buyer before she had even put her property on the market. When Mr Barrow named the sum that the corporation was willing to pay, Emma could barely believe she was hearing correctly. It was an enormous amount – larger than she could have possibly imagined.

'The interested party happens to be a chum of mine,' Mr Barrow said with a chuckle. Emma wondered if the situation was as irregular as it sounded, or if this was how such things worked in England. 'The truth is,' the solicitor continued, 'you'd be well advised to offload your land swiftly and privately, while you have the opportunity to do so. There is bound to be an environmental assessment and the usual outcry whenever there's a few trees for the chop. Best handled by a corporation with clout. Don't you agree?'

Emma thought of the bones wrapped in their tattered parachute in the old root cellar. Once a real estate agent started poking around back there, the discovery could delay the sale by weeks. Months, even. Mr Barrow was right: there was a great deal to be said for offloading her land as quickly as possible.

'Could you make it to the city, first thing in the morning?' Mr Barrow asked.

Emma said that she could.

After ending the call, she stood for a while beside Mrs

Foster's telephone table in the hall, trying to make sense of what had just taken place.

It was the best possible outcome, wasn't it? No doubt she would make even more money from the sale of her land if she waited to advertise it properly, but still, the developer was offering her an enormous sum – enough to buy her Toronto condo outright, with plenty of funds to spare. And what could be more convenient? She'd leave Lowbury early the next morning, spend a day or two in London finalising things and be back in Toronto by the end of the week. She might even have a chance to see Mike before he moved out.

Yes. This really was the perfect solution.

So why didn't she feel more thrilled?

Mrs Foster emerged from the kitchen. 'Are you feeling all right?' she asked. 'You haven't had some bad news, have you, dear?'

Emma forced a smile. 'Not at all,' she said, the cheery tone in her voice sounding forced, even to her. 'Terrific news in fact, Mrs Foster. It's just that I may need to leave Lowbury much sooner than I thought. Tomorrow morning, to be exact.'

Emma returned to the little bedroom, closed the door behind her and looked around. She hadn't even had time to unpack. No time to visit her great-aunt's grave, nor to say goodbye to Tristan. But did any of that matter? She could return next month, next year, whenever she chose.

It was late afternoon. The heavy curtains were drawn back, but from behind the net curtains Emma could hear nothing. Just as it had the night before, the silence unnerved her. She thought about Tristan's first meeting with Rose and how Rose had told him that silence wasn't always that. It contained layers of sound, especially in nature, if only you took the time to listen.

Emma stepped closer to the window and closed her eyes.

For a moment she could hear nothing at all, not even Mrs Foster moving around in the kitchen below. But she held her breath, scrunched her eyes tight shut and waited.

The wind had risen and, out in the back garden, leaves rustled softly as the breeze shook their branches. A sparrow chirped and fell silent. She heard a repetitive clicking noise, perhaps the claws of a squirrel as he scrambled across the gutter. And then suddenly, a songbird, loud and glorious, the melody rising and falling as if everything else had been a prelude to this.

Hearing the bird, Emma remembered something. A similar bird, bright with song on a cool April morning, during her last camping trip. They had set out early by canoe because Mike wanted to photograph otters. Emma couldn't figure out how to steer no matter how hard she tried, so he sat in the stern, his telephoto lens tucked between his knees, and they drifted slowly through bog. She felt miserable and resentful, as she always did on their trips, her nose assaulted by the stench of rotting vegetation newly released from the winter ice. She was shivering and her feet were already damp in their boots.

This was what she usually recalled when she thought about that morning, but now, listening to the songbird through Mrs Foster's window, Emma remembered more.

They hadn't seen otters, but what they had found was even better. The canoe rounded a snag, the dead trees ghoulish in the low light, and emerged into a still pond. Mist rose from water still tinkling with broken ice and just ahead of them they saw a moose. She stood up to her knobbly knees in the water, her long nose lifted to smell the air, but the two of them were upwind of her so she had yet to detect their presence. The canoe drifted and Emma knew Mike had set down his paddle because he would need both hands for his camera.

And then it happened. Something moved behind the moose and under her belly a tiny face appeared, wide-eyed and alert, the long muzzle quivering. A baby. Newborn, perhaps opening its eyes on its very first morning. The calf stood with legs splayed and blinked at them both, while in the snag behind them a songbird began its joyous melody, as if to welcome the little creature to the world.

Why had I forgotten that moment? Emma wondered. *Why did I only recall being cold and wet?* Perhaps she had trained herself to view nature negatively, because wilderness was Mike's thing and she needed to be her own person, distinct from him.

Truth be told, since my parents died I've hardly known myself.

Who was she? Someone who avoided new experiences by always focusing on the negative? She recalled Tristan's words: *there's more to this forest than stinging nettles.*

Well, in a few hours Emma would be gone and she would never see Tristan again.

She pushed aside one corner of the net curtain. The sun was low in the sky, but sunset was still a long way off. Tristan had said there was something he wanted to show her. If she had only a few hours left in Lowbury, why not make the most of her time? That was what Mike would have done.

Emma grabbed her raincoat and hurried back down the stairs. Calling a brief goodbye to Mrs Foster, she ran out of the front door and turned left, towards the new housing estate, the coastal path and Silverwood Vale.

TWENTY-TWO

ROSE

October 1940

When Rose said nothing, only stood in the doorway with her mouth agape, Walter repeated himself. 'We have received another message,' he said.

It was cool in the cabin, the forest in autumn's tight grip now, and a small fire burned in the grate. Rose crossed to it, bending over the flames, warming her hands, and Walter watched her.

There was something cold about his gaze, something accusing. Rose thought, *he wants to know why I stayed away so long. Whether I've stopped caring for him, stopped trusting him.* Perhaps he also worried that she had stopped believing in his loyalty; that she might have betrayed him to the police.

Rose knew all this and she wanted to ease his doubts, but again she couldn't find the words. So many things terrified her. The thought of her mother, dying slowly in the hospital. Evelyn, who still hadn't contacted them, and might have been killed in the Blitz for all she knew. Then there was Norman, who had always been a bully but was even more dangerous now he had started drinking heavily again.

How could she begin to explain all of that?

'Well?' Walter prompted. When she still did nothing to break the tension between them, he said abruptly, 'I need to know something. Where is your Browminster Castle?'

The question came out of the blue. 'What?' Rose asked, perplexed.

'This place – I need to know where it is.'

'You want to know about Browminster Castle?'

'Yes.'

'It's... it's near Bilby airfield, on the other side of Silverwood,' she said. 'There's not much left of it, just a few walls on the edge of a cliff. Why?'

Walter said, 'I have orders to rendezvous there with another agent.'

His tone was guarded and she couldn't blame him. She imagined what it must have been like for him, waiting here alone, wondering if she would ever return.

'I brought you food,' she said softly, indicating the bag she had set down just inside the door. 'Walter, this has been a very difficult—'

She would have told him, then. Would have found the words to explain why she had stayed away. That her mother was dying and perhaps her sister was already dead.

'I must meet with another agent,' Walter interrupted. 'Did you hear me say this? Do you understand?'

And this time, she did. Rose had known there were others, that Walter was a cog in a much bigger machine, but still his words came as a shock.

'I will attend this rendezvous,' Walter said. He was pacing now, up and down between the door and fireplace, as if his energy could not be contained by the four walls of the little cabin. 'I will discover for what purpose the explosives were sent.

After that, we can involve your police and' – he flicked a hand over to the radio – 'we will have no further need of this.'

Rose considered Walter's words. He was about to meet with another German spy, someone who believed in the coming invasion and would stop at nothing to make it happen. But he was also giving her hope. He would not need to play this game for much longer, the end was in sight.

She studied Walter's expression, but he didn't seem as hopeful as he should have. In fact, she read on his face an emotion she had never seen there before.

Fear.

'Something's wrong,' Rose whispered. Everything was wrong, of course. The war, her life, Walter's situation, the whole idea that he planned to make contact with an enemy agent, even if he was telling the truth and his goal was to sabotage Germany's mission.

But Walter knew what she meant.

'This agent I am to meet,' he said slowly, 'he is my superior. Experienced in subterfuge and in the handling of explosives, more so than I. He has his orders and I am to follow his lead.' He stopped pacing and looked at her. 'Rose, this is not good. I know this man. I knew him, many years ago. His name is Otto.'

Rose frowned. 'Otto from your time in the Hitler Youth?' she asked.

'The same.' Walter sat down heavily on the pallet. If he had noticed how troubled Rose had looked when she arrived, his mind was now entirely on other things.

'When I was taken from the Wehrmacht,' he said, 'the men who trained us for our mission in England, they held him up to us as an ideal. He was the best, they said, as they taught us to plant and defuse bombs. Rose, I believe he would be assigned only to the most vital of missions. Something critical to the coming invasion.'

Rose moved back to lean against the wall. *Yes*, she decided as she looked over at him, *Walter is afraid.*

'I knew Otto as a boy – and since then, I have heard stories,' Walter continued.

'What kind of stories?' Rose asked, disturbed.

'Otto attended the same training facility I did, in the months before I arrived,' he said. 'During his time there, it was discovered that communists were hiding out on a farm nearby. The kommandant ordered his trainees to pay them a visit. Otto was among the group, their self-appointed leader. It was a test, I believe. They were instructed to capture the communists, but Otto did more than that, Rose. He lined them up against the wall of a barn and shot them all.'

Rose said, 'That's terrible...'

'I cannot say for certain this story is true,' Walter said, 'only that I believe Otto to be capable of such a thing.'

'So you think whatever mission he is in charge of,' Rose said, 'it's something big...'

'I am afraid so,' he replied. 'Something very big. An operation that requires his special kind of ruthlessness. But I will meet with him, Rose. I will find out what his orders are and I will stop him.'

Rose glanced out of the window. She had taken a risk, coming to see Walter so late in the day. It was nearly dark and Norman would be home within the hour. But she had needed to do it. She had wanted him to hold her, to take away her worries, if only for a few minutes.

She hadn't expected this.

'Can't you just let me tell the police, so they can take care of it?' she asked, without conviction. She knew what his answer would be.

Walter shook his head.

'Otto is faithful only to the Fatherland,' he said. 'If he was captured, he would not betray the Reich. He would not talk. And his arrest would serve for nothing, because the planned mission would proceed anyway, with a different agent at the helm. So there is no other way. I must meet with Otto and discover the plan, so that I may sabotage it. I must take a risk, handing over the explosives so that I may learn what is intended for them—'

Walter stopped short. He saw his mistake at once and the colour drained from his face.

Rose pushed away from the wall and took a step towards him. 'But Walter,' she said, 'you don't have the explosives, not any longer.'

He looked down at the floor.

'Walter?' Rose asked, a coldness creeping into her voice. 'Where are the explosives?'

He looked up at her, regretful, remorseful – and unwavering.

'I could not leave them for your police,' he said. 'I thought perhaps I might have need of them and I was correct, Rose. I was correct! The explosives will seem to Otto proof of my loyalty. Without them, I could never—'

'But my stepfather,' Rose said, spluttering with disbelief. 'He found the package we buried together, in the dunes...'

Walter sighed. 'He found a very small part of it,' he said.

Disbelief gave way to rising anger as Rose understood the truth.

Walter had betrayed her. She had trusted him, believed in him entirely since the night of the supply drop, and he had betrayed her.

'What did you do with the rest?' she asked, coldly.

Walter hesitated. 'It is hidden,' he said, vaguely.

'You lied to me!' Rose felt the enormity of her words as she spoke them. The enormity of what he had done. 'I trusted you when I shouldn't have and you lied to me!'

Walter stood up. 'I intended to hand over all of the hexogen,' he said quickly, 'I truly did. But after you left that night, I was sitting on the dunes, thinking, and I realised that—'

Rose didn't need his explanations. She needed to give voice to her rage.

'You asked me to trust you,' she cried. 'When that first message came through, I thought, maybe you're using me. Maybe you don't care for me, you're pretending, feeding me the words I need to hear—'

'Rose...'

'No. You'll listen to me, Walter!'

She was angry. Perhaps angrier than she had been in all her life. Angry at him, and angry at a world filled with lies.

'When you did exactly what we had agreed,' Rose said, 'when you hid the explosives, and you let me write that note, I was so happy, because it was the proof I needed. Proof that I could trust you...' She felt tears prick her eyes, but she blinked them away, furiously. When she spoke again, her voice was level and cold. 'Now I find out that you lied. That you have been keeping secrets from me all along.'

Walter looked at her steadily. 'I don't think I'm the only one keeping secrets,' he said.

Rose thought of her mother, how sick she was. Evelyn, who could be lying dead under a collapsed building. She thought of Silverwood Vale, swept away to make way for a new airfield. The animals and birds gone, the wildflowers withered and dead, the rare beauty of the ancient forest replaced by asphalt and all because of the stupid war.

Her anger ebbed away and was replaced by abject misery.

'I am not an enemy to England,' Walter said, 'quite the opposite. But I am afraid of what may happen next. It was the only thing I could do, keeping back the hexogen. Otto is dangerous and I must earn his trust so that I may learn what is planned. Many lives could depend on this.'

'You're going to give the explosives to Otto,' Rose stated, in disbelief.

'If he does not receive them from me, he will get them elsewhere,' Walter said. 'It is not difficult for our kommandant to send whatever is required – you have seen that for yourself. He will secure the explosives he needs, by any means, and the plan will go ahead. What matters is that Otto must trust me. That way, I will learn the details of the mission and I will put a stop to it.'

His features softened and he looked at her with what seemed to be tenderness, but Rose wouldn't be taken for a fool again.

'Where did you hide the explosives?' she asked.

Walter did not reply.

'We don't trust each other,' she whispered, miserably.

'It seems not.'

A long silence stretched between them. It was as if they were retreating from one another, Rose thought. Erecting a barrier.

And nothing would ever be the same again.

'When are you meeting Otto?' she asked.

Walter hesitated, as if considering whether to tell her. Then he said, 'Tomorrow night, at one. In the ruins of your Browminster Castle.'

Rose moved towards the door. There was nothing else for her to say. Walter had explosives in his possession and he was about to rendezvous with a ruthless Nazi, an enemy to England.

'Rose.'

She turned round at the desperation in his voice.

'You will not say anything?' he asked, and then, 'You will not alert your police.'

She thought this was a question – but what if it wasn't? What if it was a command? A threat, even?

'I don't know,' she replied.

'You cannot want me dead.'

Here at last was a question she could answer. 'I don't want you dead, Walter,' she said. *I love you.* She thought the words she would never speak and as she did so, she felt as if her heart was breaking.

One hand on the latch of the door, she paused. 'I don't know what to believe,' she said. 'You're planning to hand explosives over to a German agent – a man who is loyal to Hitler and a threat to my country. If you are who you say you are, and you want to save lives, then you are taking an enormous risk. Maybe an irresponsible one. And how do I know your real intention isn't to help Otto?'

Walter stepped towards her and Rose held on tighter to the latch, ready to run out into the forest if she needed to.

'I have had days to think about this,' he said. 'Days alone in our little cabin, when you did not come. Handing the explosives to Otto is a risk, you are correct. But I do not believe there is any other way. If I do this, he will think me loyal and I will be in a position to prevent a catastrophe.'

Walter took another step towards her.

'If we involve your police now,' he said, 'Otto will be arrested, perhaps executed, and I will share his fate. The hexogen will be confiscated. But the catastrophe will only be delayed, not prevented. There will be other agents and more explosives, because the Reich will not accept failure. That is why I must meet Otto and learn for myself what is planned so that I may sabotage the mission.' He leaned towards her. 'You must trust me, Rose,' he said.

'Why must I?' she asked, flatly.

'Because I care for you.' Walter's voice dropped to a whisper. 'Because I love you.'

Until moments ago, Rose would have given anything to hear those words. Now, as he spoke them, she felt only pain.

'You would still say that, even if you were loyal to

Germany,' she replied. 'You would say it because you'd want to keep me quiet.'

Walter said, 'Then hear this. I cannot be sure you will not betray me, not in this moment. So, if my loyalty was to the Fatherland, I could not let you leave this cabin alive.'

Tendrils of fear slid down Rose's throat.

Walter inclined his head towards the door. 'Go,' he said. 'Try to leave.'

Rose hesitated.

She opened the door. Glanced back.

Walter did nothing.

She stepped out into the darkness.

Still nothing.

Rose turned and ran. She stumbled through the trees, hardly caring when branches tore at her long hair, when roots caught at her feet. She wasn't sure if she hated Walter or loved him and sorrow fought with rage inside her. She didn't know who she was any more, or what she wanted. Ever since finding Walter's radio, she had felt herself to be in over her head, a part of events too big for her to handle, and never had she felt this more so than now.

Rose felt angry, hurt and betrayed, but, even as conflicting emotions fought for her attention, she knew she had a decision to make.

She could say nothing to anyone and tomorrow night explosives would change hands between two enemy agents, at least one of whom meant to wreak havoc with them. Or she could tell the police and the first and only man she had ever loved – someone who might still be everything he claimed to be – would face execution.

Rose's mind whirled as she ran through the darkness of the forest and out onto the coastal path. She stopped by the dunes, in the place where she and Walter had buried the explosives, noting the huge hole the police had made as they dug.

She breathed deeply.

The evening was crisp, a hint of winter in the air. A lone star flickered over the surface of the water like a firefly and even this late, curlews moved in the shallows, their eerie wails piercing the night.

Rose couldn't go home. She couldn't bear the thought of Norman, of the bottle of Glenfiddich in the sideboard and what might happen when he opened it.

And she couldn't go to her mother. Visiting hours wouldn't start again until the following day.

She wanted to be with Walter, but that wasn't possible, not now and most likely never again.

Crouching in the dunes, Rose shuffled around until the soft sand moulded itself to her spine. Then she ignored the cold against her back and tried to still her mind.

She gazed at the blue-black of the foam-tipped breakers as they washed up on the sand. The curlews, scuttling crablike across the beach, until darkness drove them away. The stars, appearing one by one until a swarm of fireflies danced on the water. Slowly, her worries ceased whirling. Her racing mind calmed. The waves and the stars soothed her.

Rose closed her eyes. She separated the sounds into their layers. The trees rustling at her back, the sand sifting and falling on the dunes, the soft shush of the waves.

And then, as a sliver of moon rose over the water, pale and luminescent, she slept.

TWENTY-THREE

ROSE

October 1940

Even before she opened her eyes, Rose knew that something was wrong. She was sure there had been a noise, long and terrible, in the seconds before she clawed her way out of sleep.

Before she was awake enough to know what it was.

She rubbed her eyes. Sand pressed in all around her and she felt a jolt of terror to think she might have been buried alive. But she was only curled in on herself, the cold sand encasing her body like a cast.

Rose wriggled free, shivering. She hugged her knees and gazed out over the water, trying to make sense of her certainty that something terrible had just taken place. Then she heard another noise, which she knew to be different from the first. Less terrible, though bad enough.

A single Messerschmitt high above her, visible in the grey of early dawn. It was approaching from inland, heading back towards the sea.

Rose stood up.

The water was so still it might have been a pool of ink. A

faint golden line was spreading across the horizon, a precursor to the dawn.

She turned round, feelings of dread twisting in her gut, and looked past the coastal path, over the fields in the direction of Lowbury.

The sky was red. Whorls and waves of colour twisted and turned, spreading outwards.

A sunrise?

No. Not a sunrise.

Fire.

Rose scrambled over the dunes and onto the coastal path as she realised what the sound was that had awoken her, tugging her from sleep.

It was an explosion.

A bomb, falling on Lowbury.

She broke into a run. Over the fields she charged, past her home, which stood dark and silent in the early morning, and onwards in the direction of the town.

Lurid, scarlet waves spread across the sky, obliterated for a while by the houses on both sides of her as she ran down side streets, towards the centre, towards the spiralling smoke. People staggered from their houses, still wearing nightdresses and pyjamas, clutching bleary-eyed children in their arms. Then the air raid siren began, too late to be any use at all, and she could smell burning, hear the clanging of fire engines which grew louder by the second as she neared the marketplace.

Rose emerged from a side street into total chaos.

Bells rang, people screamed, sirens ripped through the darkness. Thick smoke rose to meet her, choking her as she stumbled into the road in front of the post office, one hand held across her mouth and nose, trying to make sense of what she saw.

The hospital was burning.

The entire front portion of it was gone, replaced by a crater from which plumes of smoke and flames rose into the sky.

Mam. Oh no, Mam...

Rose charged towards the hydrangea bushes, all of them on fire, and up the front path to the glass doors. Except there was no front path, or no more than the first few feet of it anyway, and she couldn't even tell where the front doors of the hospital had been.

All that remained was rubble, teetering fragments of wall, and the terrible flames.

'Mam!'

She screamed the word this time, fighting through clouds of smoke, dimly aware of firemen snaking out their huge hoses, of the bells going on and on, jets of water twisting through the air and turning at once to steam.

Rose was not alone in her fight to reach the burning heart of the fire, the place where her mother's ward had stood. Many of the others trying to edge their way inside were injured servicemen from the convalescent ward. She watched the soldier whose hands were swathed in bandages follow the hissing path of a water jet into the flames and realised that his ruined hands were a sign that this was not the first fire he had known.

And then she was engulfed in smoke, choking on it, stopped short by the intense heat. She could no more have gone on than she could have placed her hands inside an oven and held them there.

And besides, someone was grabbing her, pulling her backwards.

Rose staggered, almost fell, and allowed herself to be dragged, choking, from the fire.

'My mam...' she wailed, gasping for air. 'My mam's in there...'

'Oh, Rose...'

She opened her eyes fully and saw through a blur of tears that the person who had grabbed her was Nurse Buxton, although she wasn't in her uniform now. She must have been asleep in her home somewhere close by at the time of the explosion because under her long coat she wore only a flannel nightdress.

Nurse Buxton took hold of Rose's shoulders and held on to her until her vision cleared and she could see properly. They stood very still, the two of them, while people ran and screamed all around.

'Your mother's ward took a direct hit,' Nurse Buxton said, slowly and gently, allowing Rose the time she needed to process this news. 'There's nothing left of it now. Underneath all those flames, there's nothing left but a crater.'

The words had barely time to sink in before a doctor appeared before them. He was wearing his white coat but like his face, it was streaked with ash and soot.

'The paediatric ward is safe,' he said. 'They're bringing the children out through the back doors. We could do with your help, Nurse.'

Nurse Buxton hesitated, then grabbed a tight hold of Rose's hand and the two women ran along the side wall of the hospital to the rear entrance.

From the back, the hospital looked untouched. Firemen and injured servicemen hurried out of the rear doors, leading children by the hand. The children were bewildered and crying, but unharmed.

Nurse Buxton and Rose hurried into the rear vestibule. Here, the hospital looked undamaged, only a thin line of smoke from under the swing doors hinting at the chaos and flames of the bomb site, a few walls away. A fireman emerged from the corridor, running towards them. For a brief instant as the swing doors opened, Rose could hear the flames again, along with a low and ominous rumbling.

'That's the last of the kids safe and sound,' he shouted. 'We need to get out of here, ladies. The walls in there are structurally unsafe and likely to collapse. Come on!'

He charged past them, heading for the exit, and Nurse Buxton tugged at Rose's hand.

'No.'

Rose wasn't sure how she knew someone was still inside. It was neither a feeling, nor intuition. Nothing like that. It was more that her ears had registered a sound too low for her mind to make sense of. She had heard a cry, just one. A low wail, almost inaudible.

'You heard what the fireman said,' Nurse Buxton cried. 'We have to get out of here!'

'But there's someone still inside!'

'Rose, your mother is—'

'Not my mother – I heard something!'

Knowing there was no other way, Rose yanked her hand free of Nurse Buxton's grasp, charging through the swing door and into the building.

The smoke was thicker as soon as she burst through and the only light came from emergency bulbs set at intervals along the walls, their faint glow lurid in the thick air.

'Is anyone in here?' Rose shouted.

Another wail, so faint it might have been a rescued child, out on the lawn, on the other side of the swing doors.

Except she knew that it wasn't.

Smoke stung Rose's eyes. It was impossible to see more than a few feet through the smoke, but she paused at each door she came to, squinting to read the signs.

If a child had been overlooked, where might they be?

Not on the ward at the end of the corridor, surely?

The first few doors were consulting rooms, all of them locked. Then she came to a store cupboard and a swing door leading down a flight of stairs into the basement.

Then, to the bathrooms.

Rose shoved open the door to the girls' bathroom first. There were no lights at all inside, but she knew whoever it was could cry, so she called, 'Is anyone in here?'

When there was no answer, she walked backwards out into the corridor.

Rose pushed on the second door – the boys' bathroom. This one was also pitch dark inside, but this time when she said, 'Is anyone in here?' her question was met with a faint mewling.

She grabbed a metal bin from inside the bathroom and propped open the door, letting in enough light to show her the outline of a little boy in his pyjamas, clutching a blanket and curled into a ball underneath one of the sinks.

'It's all right,' she soothed. 'It's going to be all right, but you have to come with me.' She leaned over him. 'Put your arms round my neck,' she said, 'and let's get out of here.'

There was a sudden commotion, further down the corridor. A loud rumbling and a crash, followed by the crackling of flames, closer now.

Rose glanced back at the doorway. The smoke was thicker, pouring in.

'Let me take this.' She grabbed the little boy's blanket and held it under the tap. When it was drenched, she gave him one end to press against his mouth, holding the other in front of her own face, and backed out into the corridor.

There was so much smoke now and for a moment she was disoriented, unsure whether to turn left or right. But she could hear flames somewhere close so she moved in the opposite direction, down the corridor, the little boy's thin arms wrapped tight round her neck, his bare feet pressed into her hip.

Rose hadn't felt afraid, not while she could hear the child's wails and all she had to focus on was locating the sound, but now, with the boy in her arms, inching along the smoke-filled corridor, utterly alone, she was frightened. 'Mam, help me...' she whispered under her breath, but the only response was a crash behind her as another of the hospital's interior walls collapsed.

The little boy whined and stiffened in her arms.

Step by slow step, Rose shuffled back along the corridor. The emergency lights had gone out now, but it hardly mattered because the smoke was so thick she couldn't bear to open her eyes. The little boy pressed his face into her shoulder, trembling with fear, but Rose couldn't soothe him, she could only focus her energy on making it to the end of the corridor, so disoriented that at one point she walked them both into a wall. After that, she moved with one shoulder pressed against the plaster, breathing into the blanket, shuffling along.

And then they were at the swing door, bursting out into the rear vestibule, the door closing behind them. She could hear voices shouting, Nurse Buxton's among them, and someone was leading her out into the dawn, the little boy still fastened tight to her body. She couldn't see anything, for her eyes burned from the smoke, but she could hear it all. The clanging bells, the jubilant shouts as they emerged, the running feet.

And, above the sound of it all, flames crackling.

Rose opened her eyes and blinked to clear them. Two people stood before her, Nurse Buxton and the soldier with the bandaged hands.

'How did you know he was still in there?' Nurse Buxton asked, amazed. 'I couldn't hear a thing.'

Rose wanted to say that she had always had excellent hearing, that many hours spent in the forest had taught her how to listen, but she couldn't trust her own voice after the smoke she had inhaled, so she stayed silent.

'Let me take him,' the nurse said. 'Let me check him over.' The little boy slid from her arms into those of the nurse, pulling his comfort blanket with him, and the two of them were gone.

'Drink this.'

The soldier held out a canteen between his two bandaged

hands and Rose took it from him, sipping first, then drinking deeply. The water soothed her parched throat.

'Thank you,' she managed to say.

'Come with me.' He placed a hand on her back, guiding her towards a tiny parkette behind the hospital. Through her stinging eyes, Rose saw a group of the convalescing servicemen standing together, under a beech tree.

The soldier with the injured hands led her towards his friends.

'You should get yourself checked out, too,' he said, 'but you might need to wait a while for that.'

She clutched his canteen like a lifeline, trying to still the trembling in her body.

'That was a brave thing you did in there,' he said, kindly.

Rose shook her head. She looked at his burnt and bandaged hands. Saw the other soldiers watching the two of them, smoking and chatting, their lives transformed by a war not of their choosing.

'No,' she said, 'you're the brave ones.' She was surprised to find that her voice worked, though it cracked as she spoke.

The serviceman chuckled. 'You think?' he said and Rose was unsure how to interpret his words.

'I've never been brave,' she told him. She thought of Evelyn, how courageous she had been, defying Norman, leaving home to start her own life, while Rose had been unable to pluck up the courage even to sneak out to a dance.

'But you saved that kid!' the soldier said and what Rose heard in his voice astonished her.

Respect and admiration.

For weeks she had thought of Evelyn's work as an air raid warden, how much strength and courage she must have to keep on going while the Germans bombed London, night after night. *I never thought I could be like her*, she thought, *but perhaps I can. Just a little bit.*

Recalling her sister brought back the anguish and the grief. There was a good chance Evelyn was dead and no chance at all that her mam was still alive.

Rose wanted to cry for her mother, to let out her pain in a never-ending stream of tears, but she couldn't. The last words she had spoken to her were words of condemnation and what had she done in the last weeks of her mother's life to ease her suffering? Nothing. She had left her alone, time and again, running into the forest to spend every possible moment with Walter.

No. She did not deserve to shed her tears. What she deserved was for her grief and remorse to burn inside her, for the rest of her life.

'Cigarette, love?'

One of the soldiers held out a packet to her, but Rose only looked at him. 'Why would they...' she started. She swallowed as her voice cracked again. 'Why would the Germans bomb a hospital?'

It was the man with eyes swathed in bandages who answered, leaning back on the trunk of the tree. 'I doubt the hospital was their target,' he said. 'That was a lone bomber, I'd say, on its way home. Dropping its load before heading over the Channel. It happens.'

There was a pause as Rose and the other soldiers considered his words. The man with the burnt hands broke their reverie. 'She's brave, this one,' he said to his mates, smiling kindly at Rose.

Rose shook her head, overcome with emotion, and walked away from them all.

'Are you all right, love?' he called after her, but she couldn't bring herself to speak.

· · ·

At the front of the hospital, it was still chaos. The flames raged over the bomb crater, on the exact spot where Rose had last seen her mother, only hours ago. In the marketplace, she saw a row of injured patients lying on the ground, all of them waiting for ambulances. The luckier ones leaned against the post office wall, blankets wrapped round their shoulders, gazing on as firemen fought the flames. Local residents wandered among them with cups of tea.

Rose stood apart from it all, watching. It troubled her, the nonchalance of the blinded soldier's words. *It happens.* As if such suffering as she had witnessed in the past hour was an unavoidable fact of war, not an appalling reality to be resisted. Rose thought, *All across Europe, at this very moment, people are suffering because of Hitler, because of the Germans.* And suddenly she was thinking again of Walter, his coming rendezvous with Otto. The explosives he would hand over to a man capable of causing such devastation as this.

Otto had to be stopped – but, even if Walter might be loyal to Germany after all, Rose could not send a man she loved to his death.

And suddenly, she saw what she had to do. There was a way to bring about Otto's arrest, while making certain Walter was not captured alongside him, and Rose thought she knew what it was.

'A cup of tea, dear?'

The elderly lady who stood before her was wearing a house coat, and she still had her hair in curlers, as if she had clambered out of bed, but stopped to do nothing else before putting on the kettle.

It's what we do, Rose thought, *we British. The world might burn around us, but we still put on the kettle and smile and soldier on.*

Well, today she had her own soldiering to do.

'No thank you,' Rose said to the woman, 'but do you have a pen and paper I could use?'

Moments later, she crouched against the wall of a house in a neighbouring street, writing her second anonymous note. She informed Norman of the rendezvous to take place at one in the morning, in the ruins of Browminster Castle. Rose did her best to disguise her handwriting, but when she had almost finished, she wondered how she could link this note in the mind of her stepfather to the previous anonymous note he had received, so that he would take it seriously.

'You must bring this German spy to justice or he will cause terrible harm,' she wrote, 'for that is the nature of the beast.'

She hoped her use of the same phrase in the closing line of each letter would connect them in Norman's mind and he would believe what she had written.

Folding the letter, Rose walked slowly through the early morning streets, an exhaustion settling upon her, the grief she felt for her mother now a crater in her stomach that seemed every bit as all-consuming as the crater left by the bomb.

Rose had a plan now. If she carried it out to the letter, Walter would not be there at one, when the police arrived. But he would not have time to warn Otto, either.

She found Norman's Vauxhall 12 parked at the back of the police station, as she had known she would, and slipped her note underneath the windscreen wipers, praying it would be found in time.

Then, filled with a sorrow so deep it would never find words, Rose turned and set out for home.

TWENTY-FOUR

ROSE

October 1940

Time passed so slowly for the rest of that day.

At first, Rose felt only relief when Norman did not return home. She sat on Evelyn's bed for what seemed like hours, smelling the ash and smoke on her clothes, hearing in her mind the clanging of those terrible bells and feeling the weight of the little boy in her arms. She was hungry and thirsty, her eyes and throat still burning, and she felt the raw ache of grief in the pit of her stomach. But at least she did not have to deal with Norman and his temper.

In the early afternoon she took a bath, not caring that the water was a bone-chilling cold, just sitting in the tub with her knees drawn up to her chest, her wet hair falling limply over her shoulders and trailing in the water. Then she dressed in dark clothes, ready for the ordeal to come. She made herself tea and as she moved around the house she saw her mother everywhere. Propped up against the door of the scullery, seated at the dining room table with a shawl over her shoulders, melting into her armchair in the parlour.

Rose sipped tea and forced down a slice of toast. On sudden impulse, she rushed to the front door and checked the mat in case a letter had been delivered from Evelyn. When there was nothing, she returned to her bedroom, to the spot she had occupied all that morning. She perched on the edge of her sister's bed, pining for her mother, worrying for her sister and trying not to think of the confrontation to come.

But when Norman had still not returned home by late afternoon, Rose began to worry. She knew it was possible that he wouldn't find the time to come home between policing the aftermath of the explosion and laying a trap for a German spy – but what if that wasn't the reason? What if he had gone straight from the hospital to the pub, or back to Radcliffe's house for beer, and he didn't see the note under his windscreen wipers until it was too late?

It's ironic, Rose thought, *that of all people my plan relies on Norman.*

And the hours continued to drag, to pass more slowly than ever in her life before. As she waited for the day to end and night to fall, Rose had plenty of time to question her actions, to wonder if she had made the right decision. And so much rested on timing, too. If something went wrong, within a few hours the man she loved would be arrested and facing execution.

Rose felt exactly as she had on the night she first found Walter hanging from the branches of the Thunder Oak: that she was insufficient for the task ahead. She needed someone with more life experience to tell her what to do.

But there was no one.

Her mother had been wise, yet Rose had not confided in her and now it was too late for that, as it was for so many things. Rose's mother had died believing her younger daughter saw her as weak and spineless. A victim. Thinking that, Rose felt the weight of the sadness inside her. The endless sea of tears she would drag around for the rest of her life because she did not deserve the relief of shedding them.

Emotionally and physically exhausted, she fell at last into a fitful sleep. In a dream, she saw again the gaping hole where the front door of the hospital had been, the flames spiralling upwards, the firemen, the wounded soldiers. All of the people trying to save lives; and now among them she saw Evelyn, in her ARP uniform, as brave as she'd always been, charging into the fray. And it seemed that the dream was sent by Evelyn as a kind of goodbye, so Rose would know the truth, even before the official letter arrived.

Evelyn had died in the Blitz.

She had charged into a burning building in the course of her duties and she had not made it out.

Rose's eyes snapped open. She felt a jolt of fear. The room was pitch black and outside the window it was already night.

Had she waited all day only to sleep through the whole thing?

Was it too late to save Walter?

She turned on the light, not caring that the blackout curtains were still open, and looked at the clock on the wall.

Her heart pounded.

It was ten thirty. Almost too late.

Almost, but not quite.

She could see through her window that Norman's Vauxhall 12 was not in the driveway. That he had not returned. She ran down the stairs, grabbed a torch from the utility room and hurried out into the darkness.

Now that it was too late for Walter to warn Otto, Rose would burst into the cabin and tell him what she had done. That the authorities would be there to intercept Otto at Browminster Castle, at one.

And she would do this before Walter left for the rendezvous, so that he would be safe.

Rose dreaded the coming confrontation, but she had to believe she could make Walter understand why she had acted as she had. Why she had notified the police. *If it turns out Walter truly is loyal to England,* she thought, *he will understand, even if it takes a while. And after that, we can begin again.*

Navigating the coastal path and the trail through Silverwood was so much easier with the small torch to light her way. Rose moved swiftly, stopping only once to allow the noises of the night to ease her jangled nerves. She listened to the shivering of the leaves, the distant hoot of an owl, a nightjar's eerie whistle.

And greatly calmed, she walked on.

When she reached the cabin, she hesitated a moment. Then she took a deep breath and opened the door.

The cabin was empty.

Walter had already gone.

How? It was barely eleven o clock – two full hours before the rendezvous.

Rose's heart thumped, thinking of Walter at the mercy of her stepfather. Walter in the cell down at Lowbury police station, restrained by Radcliffe while Norman rolled up his sleeves, smiling in cruel anticipation at the beating to come.

Walter, facing a firing squad.

But this made no sense! She hadn't left it too late. He should have been here.

Rose stood at the door of the cabin, scanning every inch of it with her torch. Then the beam settled on Walter's pallet and she saw the note.

She crossed to the bed and sat down. The note was written on a piece of paper torn from her sketchbook. She unfolded the paper and began to read.

Rose,

If you are reading this, it means you have betrayed me to your countrymen, intending for me to die. It breaks my heart to think this may be true.

I lied about the rendezvous with Otto tonight, because, just as you doubted my loyalty to England, so I had begun to question your trust in me.

Our meeting at the castle was arranged for eleven, not one. If you have involved your police then they will arrive two hours late. By then, our business will be concluded and I will be safe from arrest.

I plan to meet Otto as instructed, hand over the explosives and discover the use for which they are meant. Then, after our rendezvous, I will wait in the ruins until one. If your police do not arrive, I will return here and destroy this letter, knowing you loved and trusted me.

But if your police arrive at the time I falsely gave to you, I will know your distrust was so strong you were willing to give me up for execution. In that case, I will never come back to our cabin. I will lie low some other place until it is time to stop Otto. To foil whatever act of sabotage Germany has planned. Perhaps I will not survive beyond this – but my life will be the price for the lives I save.

If you are reading this, then it means you have betrayed me. That you were willing to send me to my death. We will not meet again.

I do not think you believed me yesterday when I said I loved you. But it was true. I have loved you more deeply than you will ever know and I will grieve for you, if you have betrayed me, as I have never grieved before.

Walter

Rose glanced at her watch. It was eleven o clock, exactly. Walter was meeting with Otto at this very moment.

Afterwards he would wait, hiding in the ruins or along the edge of the forest, until one.

And when the police arrived, Walter would think Rose had chosen to betray him, never knowing that she had come here to warn him, to save him from arrest.

For the rest of his days, he would think that Rose had trusted him so little, cared for him so little, that she was willing to send him to his death.

She left the cabin and ran through the forest as fast as she could, through the darkness of deep night. But when she reached the coastal path, she didn't turn right as she usually did.

Instead, she turned left, in the direction of Bilby airfield, and the castle.

TWENTY-FIVE

ROSE

October 1940

It was not often that Rose travelled this stretch of the coastal path; Silverwood Vale always lured her away before she could get as far as Browminster Castle. She ran until she was gasping for breath and still she ran, until the path widened into a gravel road. Further along, she recalled, the narrow track turned inland, continuing parallel to the eastern flank of the forest before connecting with the country lane to the north.

Just before the point where the road turned, Rose stopped. She stepped backwards into the undergrowth, crouching low.

On the other side of the road she could see a coil of wire and beyond that a beach. The tide was out and the waves sounded far off in the darkness, like a memory.

And to the left of the beach, on a low rise overlooking the sea, stood Browminster Castle.

The moon over the water seemed to pulse as small clouds travelled across it and a faint sprinkling of stars reflected on the sea. Not much remained of the castle, only a few crumbling walls outlined deep black against the dark grey of the sky.

Swirls of mist hung above the ruin.

Rose was shivering. She hadn't expected to lie low in the frigid darkness, she had only thought to run to the cabin and warn Walter before heading back home. She was wearing just a light linen jacket, not her winter coat, and the sea wind was chill and damp.

Walter would be meeting with Otto at this very moment, somewhere within these ruined walls. As soon as their meeting was concluded, Rose would burst from her hiding place, intercept Walter and tell him the truth. That the police *would* be turning up at one, but this did not mean she had betrayed him.

Even if she had doubted his loyalty – which felt somehow ludicrous to her now – she would never have sent him to his death.

It was past eleven already, but still she could see nothing in the ruined castle, no movement at all, only the decrepit walls, dark and foreboding, wearing their halo of mist. This castle had once been someone's home, she thought. A fortress, a haven where they felt safe from harm. And now there was almost nothing left of it. *You're never really safe anywhere*, she mused, thinking of the bombed hospital, the forest that would soon give way to loggers, her own unhappy home. *Safety is only ever an illusion.*

As more time passed and she shivered in the darkness, unwilling to risk the light from her small torch, Rose wondered if something might have gone wrong. No figures moved between the castle's ruined walls and she could hear nothing but the far-off tumbling of the waves.

But then, two people emerged from behind a crumbling turret, walking side by side. One was a giant of a man, his silhouette distorted by the huge package he carried in his arms.

Walter.

The other man was slender, much shorter, and his movements were fluid and sinuous.

Otto.

The meeting had taken a long time. Perhaps that was good, Rose thought. It could mean Otto was sharing his operational plans in detail. But it was close to midnight now and only a short while remained before the arrival of the police. It occurred to her that the apprehension of a German spy might be considered too great a responsibility for a small-town constabulary. It was likely that an entire fleet of police cars was on its way. They might already be here, lying in wait round the corner, their engines turned off.

Mist rolled in off the sea and the two figures between the ruined walls disappeared.

Rose squinted into the darkness. She had to keep sight of Walter, or how would she warn him after Otto left? If the police arrived early to stake out the castle, they might find him there. It was unbearable to think that he might be arrested and executed because of her actions.

That he could go to his death believing she had betrayed him.

Then the mist cleared and Walter was gone. Rose saw a lone figure, the small, slight man, now carrying the huge package. Otto clambered down the castle glacis, towards the beach. He picked his way around rocks, heading across the sand in the direction of Lowbury, and Rose watched him for a long time until she could be sure he had gone. Then she turned back to the ruin.

Still there was no sign of Walter.

He wouldn't leave, the letter had made that clear. He would hide somewhere nearby, waiting to see if the police turned up at one. And as she thought this, the fear she felt for him became unbearable.

She had to get to Walter before the police arrived.

There was still time, she was sure of it. She would run across the road, up to the castle, and she would find him.

Rose burst from her hiding spot and, in that instant, a car came hurtling round the bend. The headlights were off and the driver did not see her, not until the very last minute. She let out an involuntary squeal and did the only thing she could think of to save herself: she leapt over the road, landing heavily in the bushes on the other side.

She fell hard, smacking the side of her head, and for a moment she lay where she had fallen, dazed and shocked. She could hear not one engine but two, before each of them was silenced in turn as the drivers switched off their ignitions. Then she heard car doors slamming.

There was no time for Rose to move. She could only hope that the bushes shielded her from view.

'Bloody hell, Radcliffe. Don't stop here.'

It was her stepfather's voice.

'Someone ran out in front of the car,' Radcliffe growled.

She could hear feet crunching over the gravel.

'It must have been an animal, you fool,' Norman grunted. 'Get back in your car. There's a logging trail further down. We can hide both cars there and walk back before one.'

'It wasn't an animal,' Radcliffe mumbled and the wide beam of a powerful torch arced over the road.

Rose held her breath. She tried to make herself as small as possible and she prayed.

If Norman found her out here, heavens only knew what her punishment would be. And worse still, she wouldn't be able to intercept Walter. He would see the police from wherever he was hiding and he would go the rest of his days thinking Rose had betrayed him.

'Turn off that bloody light!' Norman snarled, but Radcliffe didn't listen.

'I saw something,' he muttered. From the way he said it, Rose thought he knew exactly what it was he had seen.

The beam swung from the road to the bushes, rolling slowly

along them until it came to rest right where Rose lay, only partially concealed in the undergrowth.

She squinted into the sudden glare.

'You!'

The word was spoken by Norman, not Radcliffe, in utter astonishment. But it was Radcliffe's meaty hands that reached down for her, hauling her out of her hiding place and tossing her onto the road.

Rose remained where she had fallen as the beam from Radcliffe's torch pinned her in its unforgiving glare.

She shielded her eyes. Squinted and looked up to see Radcliffe and Norman, neither of them in uniform, and behind them four other officers, all plainclothed, all of them Norman's own men.

'My Mildred says she's got a fancy man,' Radcliffe said to Norman as the men looked down at her. 'She meets him in Silverwood Vale.'

Norman walked slowly towards Rose. She could hear his feet on the gravel, see the huge bulk of him as he came to a standstill, towering over her.

'You are in deep trouble, my girl,' he said, his voice calm. Rose could tell he was enjoying this, that he would relish the punishment to come; and, just in case she had any doubt about what her punishment might be, Norman laid a hand meaningfully against the huge buckle on his belt. 'But I'm afraid you will have to wait your turn. I've a spy to catch, first.'

He left Rose where she was, sitting on the road, and walked with purpose back to the Vauxhall. 'Get into my car, all of you,' he snapped and his men obeyed at once.

'And you,' Norman said to Radcliffe, 'get her back to my place and guard her, you hear? I want her waiting for me when all this is over and if she isn't, I'll hold you responsible.'

'But Sergeant...' Radcliffe spluttered, clearly not wanting to miss the action. 'You said I would—'

'Just do it.' The command was laced with threat.

Norman climbed into his car and the Vauxhall inched past Radcliffe's vehicle, scraping the bushes along the side of the road on its way to the logging track, where it would be easily hidden.

Leaving Rose alone with Radcliffe.

He moved quickly, grabbing her wrist, hauling her to her feet.

Where are you, Walter? Rose thought. Was he watching all this from the castle, choosing not to intervene? Why would he risk exposing himself to the police when their presence here must seem to him a confirmation of her betrayal? And in any case, Rose had told him nothing about Norman. He had no idea how much she feared him.

She could not let Radcliffe drag her back home. She had to escape from him and now was her only chance.

'No!'

Rose screamed the word, yanking her wrist from Radcliffe's grasp. Surprise was on her side and she lunged for the trees, almost making it, but Radcliffe was quicker than she thought possible; he hooked one of his arms round her waist and hauled her towards the car.

'You just robbed me of my part in all this,' he growled, his face close to hers. He lifted a fist, swinging it towards her, but Rose ducked and his knuckles connected with the window.

Radcliffe let out a howl of pain, but for the second time he reacted with surprising speed, clamping his hands round Rose's neck.

'Just give me an excuse to knock you senseless,' he snarled. 'And don't think you can go crying to Norman. We both know who he'd believe.'

Rose was fighting to catch her breath, choking, struggling to peel away his hands. As she gasped and wriggled, Radcliffe opened the rear door of the car and shoved her inside. The engine started and she craned her neck to look out of the window, squinting at the walls of the castle, noting how void of life they were, squat and grey in the darkness, with not even a single figure moving through the gathering mist.

'Where are you, Walter?' Rose whispered in despair. Radcliffe spun the car round and she turned for a last look at the ruins, knowing that even if Walter had not already noticed the police, he would soon. He would take their presence as confirmation of her betrayal and she would never see him again.

TWENTY-SIX

ROSE

October 1940

Radcliffe drove at breakneck speed along the country road towards Lowbury. But he didn't take Rose straight home, as Norman had instructed. He drove to his own terraced house on the northern outskirts of town. When he pulled up outside his blue front gate, he stuck a hand on the horn, blasting it repeatedly, despite the hour, until a light came on in the bedroom, the outline of a person just visible behind the blackout curtains.

Seconds later, Mildred opened the front door.

'Dad?' she said.

Radcliffe wound down his window. 'Get over here,' he barked.

She ran down the garden path in her housecoat and slippers, stopping short when she caught sight of Rose in the back seat of her father's car. 'What's she doing...' Mildred asked, unable to mask her gleeful curiosity.

'Never you mind,' Radcliffe said. 'There's a phone call you've got to make.'

Mildred bent down, her head half in the window. Rose

strained to hear what Radcliffe was saying to her, but she couldn't make out a single word.

'Will do, Dad,' Mildred said, clearly eager to do whatever had been asked of her.

Radcliffe turned on the engine and drove off at the same speed with which they had arrived, leaving Mildred behind them on the pavement.

They took no more detours after that and arrived at Rose's home within minutes. Radcliffe bundled her out of the car and towards the front door, one of his thick hands clamped round her neck.

Once indoors, he dragged her up the stairs to her room, thrust her inside and slammed the door behind her.

Rose hurried over to the window. She considered climbing down the trellis and running as fast as she could for Browminster Castle, just in case Walter might still be there, but before she had time even to open the window Radcliffe appeared in the front porch below. He lit a cigarette and the tip of it flared brightly in the darkness as he gazed down towards the sea.

Then he looked up at her, smiling shrewdly.

Rose hurried into the bedroom her mother had shared with Norman, determined to find another way out, but that window would not open wide enough for her to climb through. The same was true of the bathroom window, so she ran downstairs. The only possible means of escape was the back door, but that was locked from the outside and the key was not hanging in its usual place.

She was trapped.

Rose traipsed back up to her room and it seemed with every step she took that the worries and the sadness piled up inside her until the pressure was overwhelming. Her mother would never come back, though Rose could still smell her lingering presence: lavender perfume and Pond's hand cream. Evelyn could not be reached and Rose feared that her dream had indeed been a premonition and her sister might already be dead, her body lying under rubble somewhere in London. And now, just as Rose was learning what it meant to be cherished and to love, Walter had been snatched away from her.

The grandfather clock in the corridor chimed one.

All hope was lost.

Even if Rose found a way to get past Radcliffe, by the time she made it to Browminster Castle Walter would have seen the police and disappeared into the darkness, devastated to think that the woman he loved had been willing to send him to his death. He would feel the weight of her betrayal, his love transforming itself to rage, and there was nothing Rose could do about it.

But as time passed, all other worries were eclipsed by a thick and choking fear for herself. Norman would return soon and he would be in a foul mood, not only because Rose had defied him but also because his attempts to capture the spy had been in vain. His one chance of professional glory had ended in failure, quite possibly ridicule.

And he would take his frustration out on her.

It was shortly after three when she heard the sound of his Vauxhall pulling up in the driveway. Her heart began to beat faster, the hands she held in her lap to shake uncontrollably.

Rose heard Norman and Radcliffe chatting for a moment under her window, then the front door opened and closed behind them with a bang. Footsteps sounded on the stairs and Radcliffe flung open her bedroom door.

'He wants you downstairs and quick about it,' he said.

Rose steadied herself against the frame of the bed. There was no point in defying Norman. No sense in adding fuel to his fury.

She followed Radcliffe down the stairs, holding carefully to the banister, for it seemed every ounce of the courage she had discovered over the past few days had now deserted her.

At the bottom of the stairs, Radcliffe turned to face her.

'I wouldn't want to be in your shoes right now,' he said, 'not for all the world.' And with a last, cruel smile he headed out the door to his car, leaving Rose to face her stepfather.

Norman was opening the sideboard as she walked into the dining room. She recalled her mother's words as he pulled out the bottle of Glenfiddich and poured himself a measure so generous that it almost overflowed the crystal whisky glass.

He drank deeply, watching her over the rim, then set it down on the sideboard.

'Come here,' he said.

Rose took a step closer.

'The chief superintendent turned up about a half-hour after Radcliffe left with you,' Norman said, his tone surprisingly calm. 'He told me he'd received an anonymous call, to let him know what we were about. He said I ought to know that intercepting an enemy spy was outside my jurisdiction and he'd be revoking my promotion to sergeant. There's a reprimand coming my way.'

Norman gazed at the bottle of Glenfiddich on the table. Changing the subject unexpectedly, he said, 'You've shown some pluck, these past few days.' He didn't sound angry; in fact, he sounded almost admiring. 'Talking back, staying out all hours, not coming home at all last night.'

Rose had hoped he might not have noticed her absence the previous evening, or that it would no longer matter in the light of everything that had happened since.

'I won't have it, Rose,' Norman said. He wasn't bellowing as he so often did and yet he managed to sound more dangerous than he ever had before. He waggled a finger at her.

'If you continue to show such spirit,' he said, 'I will have to break it.'

He poured himself another full glass of Scotch and gulped it down before walking round the table towards her.

Rose stepped back, but Norman's movements were so casual that she did not think to react with any kind of haste. She was fearful, of course, and she expected the worst, but not right away, not with the slow and measured pace of his speech.

Norman lunged.

He grabbed her wrists, holding them tight, sneering when she cried out in pain.

'You can forget about whoever it is you've been seeing in the forest, right now,' he whispered. He was so strong that he barely had to exert any force at all to hold her. Rose twisted and turned in his grasp, but his hands were clamped as firmly as manacles round her wrists.

'With your mother gone, I find myself in need of help,' Norman continued, the words forced out through gritted teeth.

Rose had been mistaken to think he wasn't angry. He burned inside with white-hot rage.

'You'll remain in this house,' he continued, 'until the day you die, do you hear me? You will serve my needs. My *every* need. And you'll start tonight.'

The terror Rose felt gave her a sudden surge of strength. She kicked Norman hard, twisting both hands in a swift, circular motion to break free, and then she was running for the front door, charging for it, crying out, pulling on the handle, tumbling out into the porch.

But if Rose was fast, so was Norman. In the time it took her to pull the door open he had gained all the ground he needed. He reached for her long hair, which was flying loose about her shoulders, and yanked on it, hard.

Rose screamed as she was pulled up short, her head jerking backwards.

Norman wound her hair about his arm and dragged her back into the house. He wasn't talking now, he was laughing, and there was something strange about the sound of it. Something *wrong*.

Rose staggered, her head bent back at a jarring angle, clawing to gain traction on the carpet as he pulled on her hair, hauling her towards the dining room. He was almost running at first, Rose scrabbling on all fours behind him down the hallway, sobbing for him to let go, but then he slowed and his laughter slowed, too, as if he was a motion picture film no longer playing at the right speed.

Norman stopped. He leaned for a moment against the door-frame, taking in the table and the sideboard as if he had never seen them before. He loosened his grip on Rose's hair and she pulled herself free.

'Am ruined,' he murmured.

Rose glanced over at the bottle of Glenfiddich, puzzled. He had drunk a large portion of it, and quickly, but Norman was a seasoned drinker.

Surely this couldn't be the alcohol.

He looked down, as if he was surprised to find her there, at his feet, and his eyes were glassy, struggling to focus. Rose moved out of his reach and stood up.

'Ruined. Will never...' Norman managed, his voice trailing off. He pushed away from the door, shuffled across the room to the table and flapped a hand towards the bottle of Glenfiddich.

'This...' he said, but he couldn't seem to locate the bottle with his fingers, swiping at air instead.

As Rose looked on in amazement, Norman's legs gave way. He fell to his knees and tipped face first onto the carpet.

She moved towards him, cautiously. Fearing the worst, she crouched down.

'Norman?' she whispered.

Nothing.

She held her hand up to his nose.

He was still breathing.

In fact, within seconds he was doing more than that.

He was snoring.

Rose stood up. She looked at the bottle of Glenfiddich and over to the sideboard, as a possibility formed itself in her mind.

Surely not...

She opened the sideboard and peered inside. Where had her mother put it?

Under the placemats.

Rose shoved the mats aside and looked beneath them.

There was nothing there.

She felt with her hands along the walls of the cupboard and her fingers tightened around a little glass vial, tipped onto its side behind the door.

She pulled it out and removed the stopper.

The bottle was empty.

Rose crouched down beside the sideboard, struggling to take in what had just happened, overwhelmed by the truth as it finally shaped itself in her mind.

Her mother, who had never stood up for herself, who had never defended Evelyn against Norman and who had feared for Rose's safety in the final days of her life... her mother had left Rose a parting gift. She had done the only thing she could think of to keep her younger daughter safe.

For a while at least, Norman could not hurt her.

'Thank you, Mam...' Rose whispered.

She had been given a chance and now it was up to her to make the most of it.

Rose had to be quick, for she couldn't be sure how long the sleeping draught would last. Norman might wake up hours from now, or minutes. She ran upstairs, grabbed a valise from the store cupboard and hastily packed a change of clothes and her art supplies. She added toiletries and the few letters Evelyn had sent. The case was still three parts empty but as she looked around her room, Rose couldn't think of anything else she wanted to take.

Possessions mattered so little to her.

She paused at the door to her bedroom and looked around it for the last time. This room held a lifetime of memories. Endless bedtime stories when she was little, curled up on her dad's knee. She pictured Evelyn, bouncing around beside them. Their mother, listening from the doorway, a cup of Ovaltine in her hand and a contented smile on her face.

In this room, Rose had known great happiness but it was also the place where she had grieved for her father. Here, and in Silverwood Vale.

Her childhood bedroom and her forest. After tonight, Rose would see neither of them ever again.

She headed back down to the dining room, her valise in hand. Norman remained exactly where she had left him, sprawled out on the carpet, snoring softly. A thin line of drool snaked from the side of his mouth.

Rose would need at least a little money, if she was going to get away. She crouched down beside him.

Stealing felt wrong, she thought, even from Norman. But then she recalled how he had made her give up her job at the haberdashery and how, in the two years since, she had cooked and sewed for him, running his errands, meekly following his commands, and in all that time she had not received a single penny in return.

Rose thought of where she would be right now, if not for her mother's sleeping draught. Curled in a ball on her bed, beaten black and blue.

Or worse.

So, she swallowed her scruples, reached into Norman's

blazer and pulled out his wallet. She would take enough money for a bus fare to the nearest town. Enough to get away from him and not a shilling more.

But as she returned Norman's wallet to his pocket, Rose saw something else there. An envelope. There was no return address, but she recognised the handwriting at once.

Norman was carrying a letter from Evelyn and the letter was addressed to Rose and her mother.

When had it arrived? Rose wondered. And why was Norman carrying it around, instead of leaving it propped on the sideboard as he usually did? Had he picked it up off the mat by the door, placed it in his pocket and forgotten all about it? It was possible. But more likely, Norman had decided Evelyn was not a role model he wanted Rose to have.

If she hadn't found the letter by accident in this way, Rose might never have known that her sister was still alive.

She leaned back against the leg of the table, glancing over at Norman to check that he had not regained consciousness, and allowed herself a moment of relief. Evelyn was still alive. Then she pulled the letter from its envelope and began to read:

My dearest Mother and Rose...

Rose could not help feeling a little bitter at that. If they were her dearest, why had Evelyn left them the way she did? And why had she never come home, not even for a visit? Evelyn had absented herself so completely that they hadn't even been able to reach her, when their mother was taken into the hospital.

And now their mother was dead and Evelyn didn't even know.

My dearest Mother and Rose,

I have terrible news to share, and the most glorious news, too! But you must wait to hear the happy part.

Last week, our ARP post took a direct hit. It was a stroke of luck that none of us were in the building at the time. After the all-clear sounded, I walked back in the darkness to Penny's home only to find that her house and several others had been flattened. People were wandering around in a daze, shocked to see how much damage the bombers had caused. But within moments the WVS women were there, serving hot cups of tea with plenty of sugar, and neighbours were helping one another search through what was left of their homes for anything they might salvage. The spirit of Londoners, Rose! Their cheeriness flies in the face of Hitler.

We were homeless after that, Penny and me. She decided to move to her uncle's in Brighton, but I'd no idea what I would do. Then the most marvellous thing happened – Charles came back! His leave had been cancelled so many times I thought I'd never seen him again, but he finally had a full week off and joy of joys, he made arrangements for us to be wed!

It was a hasty affair, as everything is in this dreadful war, and there was no time to tell either of you. But I'm a married woman now. Can you believe it? Charles has a friend with a cottage in Windermere and that's where we are staying as I write this letter. I'm on my honeymoon and I've never been so happy! The sun is shining and the war feels like nothing but a bad dream.

I hope you are both well. Wrap up tightly, Mam, now winter is coming. You know how easily you catch a chill.

And Rose? The same advice as always.

Love,

Evelyn

The same advice as always.

Only this time, she was about to take it.

But as Rose read the letter a second time, it occurred to her that she didn't want to be like Evelyn, not any more. Her sister had a devil-may-care attitude to life, which was how she found the courage to do the things she did. But when it came down to it, Evelyn cared about no one but herself. And this meant that, with their mother dead and Walter lost to her, Rose was utterly alone.

It would be easy to despair but her mother had given her a second chance at life and she owed it to her to make the most of it, even if she had no idea where to go and what to do.

Take things one day at a time. That's what Walter would say. All she had to do in the next few hours was get as far away as possible from Norman. After that, she would have time to think. Time to grieve the loss of both her mother and the man she loved.

Rose picked up her valise and put on her winter coat. Then she left her childhood home for the last time, closing the door softly behind her.

TWENTY-SEVEN

EMMA

June 1990

Emma walked along the coastal path in the silvered light of early evening towards the forest and Tristan's caravan. She was eager to see him again. Although the sun was low on the horizon, there was still some time to go before it was dark, but when she turned in to Silverwood Vale she was immediately plunged into shadow, as if night had already fallen.

It was a little over twenty-four hours since Emma had arrived in Lowbury and she would be gone in the morning, heading to London on the eight o'clock train. With any luck, she could finalise the sale of her land quickly and fly back to Toronto at least a week sooner than she had expected. She wondered what her condo looked like now – whether Mike had started to pack. Would it still feel like home, with the walls stripped of his photographs and all signs of him erased?

As she headed down the old logging road, the fading light and the isolation unsettled her. To bolster her confidence, she pictured the gnarled old trees replaced by rows of orderly houses, the darkness by streetlights and the dirt road by concrete and asphalt. But this time the mental image gave her no pleasure at all.

Tristan was waiting for her near the end of the track.

'How did you know I would come?' Emma asked.

'I didn't,' he said, 'but you make so much noise I heard you before you left the coastal path!'

Emma didn't believe him. She wondered if he had been pacing the length of the rutted track, eager to see if she would show up. After all, he spent his days alone in the forest. What else would he have to do?

He was wearing different clothes today. She couldn't say *clean clothes* because they weren't, not entirely. They were greyed by exposure to rain and sun, stained by green and living things. He was brave enough to live the life he was meant for, Emma thought as she looked at him, and that wasn't easy to do. But living in isolation, without anyone to love, the way Great-Aunt Rose had also done – surely that was never a choice.

Tristan seemed jittery and excitable. He shifted his weight from one foot to the other as he said, 'I've a special place to show you, just like I promised, but there's something else you need to see first. Something to do with Rose.'

With that, he turned on his heel, diving through trees onto a path so faint that it was more likely made by animals than people and leaving Emma to follow.

They walked along a warren of trails. Branches snagged at Emma's hair, mud sucked at her boots and she thought with longing of her city clothes back in Toronto, of the life she had left behind. Sipping champagne on a harbourfront patio, the soft strains of jazz in her ears and the boardwalk filled with people, all of them strolling and chatting.

But champagne on summer patios was a thing she did with Mike. Would she even want to do that any more, with him gone?

A branch reached out through the gloom to slap her in the face and she thought, *Nature always seems to get me. No matter how hard I try, it won't leave me alone.*

A moment later Tristan stopped abruptly and she moved to stand beside him. 'It's going to be night soon,' she whispered. 'We'll get caught out here in the dark.'

'Don't worry,' he said. 'I have a torch.'

'A torch?' Emma asked, confused. Then she remembered that was what British people called a flashlight.

'It's in my pocket. But we won't need it. Now, look. This is what I wanted you to see.'

The area in front of them was nothing special, so far as she could tell. A tree had toppled decades ago, coming to rest against another trunk. Its falling had created a clearing, with the dead tree propped diagonally across it. The trunk was thick with life: fungi, mosses, lichen.

We must be on the far side of the forest, Emma decided. Speckles of soft evening light filtered through the trees ahead, spilling like summer raindrops onto the fallen tree.

So many fairytales were set in ancient forests like this one. 'Hansel and Gretel', 'Snow White', 'Sleeping Beauty'. They were places of mysticism and enchantment, the domain of elves and witches, prophecies and spells. Emma shifted her weight from one foot to the other and moss sprang back beneath her feet, as if even the solidity of the ground could not be trusted.

'What's so special about this place?' she asked, nonchalantly. She stepped forward to take a closer look, but Tristan swung out an arm to block her.

'Careful,' he warned her. 'See all of this?'

And then she did.

Everywhere she looked, at her feet and all through the clearing, wildflowers. Tiny plants with delicate, quivering stems and fragile petals. Lilac, white, burgundy, yellow, blue.

Tristan crouched down, tenderly parting the leaves of a small plant to reveal a cluster of pink blooms inside.

The flowers were pretty enough, but they hardly justified a hike in near darkness.

'I've no idea what they are,' Emma said.

'That's just the point!' Tristan grabbed her arm, pulling her down beside him. 'I've lived in the countryside all my life,' he said. 'My folks were farmers and I've spent years mucking around in woods like this one, yet I've never seen any of these before. There's maybe ten or twelve different kinds of wild-flowers just in this one glade and most of them I've never come across anywhere else.'

So the flowers were rare. Maybe endangered. For some reason, Emma couldn't let herself share his excitement.

'So?' she asked.

Tristan spun on her. 'Do you have no sense of wonder?' he snapped. 'We could be the last people in England to set eyes on some of these flowers. Look how lovely they are!'

They were lovely, Emma had to concede, with the low sun spangling through the trees, raining light upon them.

'There's more.' He reached forward, carefully bending over a small plant near his feet.

Stretching around it was a tiny fence, weathered and broken.

'At some point,' Tristan said, 'someone built protective barriers round the plants, to stop rabbits from eating them. Perhaps it's why they were able to survive. Not much of the fencing and netting remains, but this was a cultivated garden, once. A garden made of flowers so rare they might not have been seen outside of Silverwood in years.'

'My Great-Aunt Rose?' Emma asked. 'You think it was her?'

'I met her, remember?' Tristan said. 'She cared about this forest in a way no one else did.' He stood up, adding, 'I've a very special plant to show you and I know what this one is.'

He sidestepped around the carpet of flowers, moving towards the fallen trunk, and Emma followed.

'Be very careful,' he said.

They reached the centre of the clearing, where the toppled tree stood at shoulder height. Tristan placed a finger on the spongy wood, right next to a tiny plant that seemed to grow out of the bark. On the top of a fragile, wavering stalk grew a white flower, its petals wispy as tendrils. Touched by a faint wind, the tendrils seemed to move by themselves.

'I've seen this in books,' he said. 'It's a ghost orchid. Very rare.'

He glanced up. There was a small gap in the canopy above, revealing a circle of sky.

'Think about it,' he said. 'Each day, a shaft of light for maybe an hour, no more. It strikes this fallen tree, this plant, giving it just what it needs to survive. Along with the moss and lichens to hold moisture, the decaying matter in this old trunk, fungi for nutrients and the exact amount of rain. Everything just right and found nowhere else but in this spot.'

Tristan seemed to be waiting for some sort of response. When Emma said nothing, he sighed, as if she had disappointed him. 'The sun will be setting soon,' he said, 'and I don't want us to be late. Follow me.'

They came to an oak tree cleaved down the middle by an ancient storm. A storm, Tristan had said, that might have happened before Columbus sailed for the Americas. 'This is the place,' he said. 'Rose called it the Thunder Oak. And now we wait.'

They crouched side by side in the undergrowth and Emma tried not to think of creepy-crawlies. She thought instead of her great-aunt and the wildflower garden. The love it took to create such a thing. Art, photography, gardens. So many people were creators. Then she recalled the bomb that had dropped on Lowbury's hospital. The developers who would come soon to fell all the trees in Silverwood.

Which was stronger – the human need to create, or to destroy?

'What are we waiting for?' she asked, but Tristan didn't reply, only holding a long, slender finger against his lips.

Time passed. Tristan seemed to have no problem remaining silent, but to Emma the silence felt oppressive. After a while, she said, 'Why did you come here, Tristan? Why do you live in a forest, away from everyone?'

If she could understand his motives, perhaps she would understand her Great-Aunt Rose's, too.

Emma thought that the world was full of people who lived their lives all alone, the person they loved lost to them forever. She felt an ache inside her, as sharp as pain. But living alone out of necessity was one thing. Choosing to do so, inside a forest, was quite another.

Beside her, Tristan stayed silent. He made no effort to answer her question. It occurred to her that maybe he thought she wouldn't be capable of understanding. And he'd be right, wouldn't he?

'Why didn't you want to tell the police about the bones we found in the root cellar?' she asked.

And this time he answered her. 'I didn't want the unwelcome attention it would bring,' he said. 'Same as you, I suppose.'

'The same as me?'

Emma had the sensation that Tristan was turning to face her in the darkness.

'Silverwood Vale is yours,' he said, 'and I'm guessing you didn't want to deal with the police, the media, all of that.' He paused, before adding, 'You'll have the place to yourself, soon. I can make arrangements to have my caravan towed somewhere else.'

Emma was sure he wanted her to protest, to say he was welcome to stay, but she couldn't. He needed to be gone before the developers moved in. She could only imagine his pain when the trees he loved so much were felled, one by one.

'You don't intend to live in Silverwood, do you?' Tristan whispered.

'No.'

'Or even close by.'

'My life is in Toronto. I'm a city girl. A writer.'

Tristan hesitated, as if choosing his words with care. 'You could stay here for a while,' he whispered. He sounded as if he was pleading with her. 'Maybe you could write a novel, based on the life of your Great-Aunt Rose.'

Emma laughed. 'I don't write novels,' she said. 'I'm a journalist.'

'A writer is a writer,' Tristan replied. 'They create things, using words as their tools.'

After that, they sat in silence for a long time as darkness fell around them. But as the minutes passed, one after the other, Emma came to realise that what she thought of as silence really wasn't silence at all. Birdsong began tentatively and swelled to a chorus somewhere far up in the treetops, an entire community signalling to one another as they settled in for the night. She heard rustles, the call of night birds, leaves shivering in the canopy, the chirping of insects. All noises she might never have heard but for her stillness. When people bumbled through a forest, she thought, something of its essence retreated, but now that she and Tristan were still, it had gathered around them like a living thing. The forest was no longer an absence of sound and light to be moved through and out of, it was an entire world, and for a brief time it had chosen to embrace them as part of itself. The thought was exhilarating.

Tristan stiffened. 'Look!' he whispered. 'This is what I wanted you to see.'

A strip of white, near the base of the old oak tree. Emma hardly dared to breathe as a long nose appeared, twirling and sniffing, testing the air for scent, and then the rest of the creature emerged, its bright white stripes almost fluorescent in the gathering darkness.

A badger.

The creature moved warily through the twilight, checking that the clearing was safe. Next came four little ones, clumsy and playful, jostling one another, thrilled with their newfound world. Their coats were grey and looked soft as rabbit fur, their striped snouts long as a moose's muzzle and glowing in the darkness.

Emma felt the warmth of Tristan in the undergrowth beside her, as still as she was, sharing the moment.

The creatures snuffled, foraging for food. One cub shoved at another and it rolled and tumbled, revealing the dark fur of its underbelly. Another bumbled towards them, coming within inches of Emma's face, and they could see the sheen of its coat, the white tips of its tiny ears. Then the mother raised her snout to test the air and caught a scent of danger. Perhaps the two of them, or something else. In seconds, she had hurried her cubs back down into their sett.

They stayed still for a long time after, neither of them speaking, as the dusk chorus in the trees changed its tune, the birds and insects of the day giving way to creatures of the night.

Emma glanced at Tristan, now no more than a grey shadow by her side. She thought of how she had told him, peevishly, *This is my land,* and she recalled his reply: *Nature belongs only to itself.* She had scorned this at the time, thinking his response new-agey and ridiculous. Now, the idea of a person owning all the wildflowers and this ancient oak tree, and the badgers who lived under it, seemed ludicrous to her.

A sudden, thunderous crack in the darkness, somewhere close. Emma shuddered.

'Don't worry,' Tristan said. 'It's just a bough breaking. The forest is old. Things die a natural death and they feed new life. It's a cycle.'

A bough breaking. Emma was sure he must be right, but it was almost pitch dark now and as she strained her ears, listening for the sound to come again, a repeat of that deep and terrible noise, there was only one thing she could think of.

Not the fall of a single bough, but the felling of all the trees, one after the other, until the entire forest and every life in it was gone.

They didn't head back right away. Emma wasn't ready to go and Tristan seemed to sense that. She had never been in a forest at night without the comfort of a roaring fire, without Mike, and it wasn't creepy and unpleasant, as she had expected. Now she had seen the badger cubs and the ghost orchid, it was magical.

Emma emerged from her hiding place to lay her hand flat against the trunk of the oak, feeling its bark, contoured like the skin of an old man. She gazed up into the branches, barely discernible against a near-black sky, and noticed that the dip between the two cleaved halves was as scooped and welcoming as a hammock.

She wondered if Great-Aunt Rose ever sat up there, dangling her legs and looking down. 'The stories this tree could tell if only it could talk,' she said.

'Trees do talk,' Tristan replied. 'They pass messages to each other through their roots. Come.'

He reached for her hand, curling his fingers round hers, and it felt like the most natural thing in the world. He led her through the forest and Emma realised the darkness no longer troubled her. Frequently Tristan stopped without warning and she would stop by his side, close enough to catch the scent of him.

'Listen,' he would say.

They stood for long moments at a time, still and silent. Almost always there was something. The flap of a barn owl's wing as it passed through the canopy. The slow passage of an unseen mammal through the undergrowth. Once, a strange whirring, clicking sound.

'What's that?' Emma breathed, thinking the noise was like something from *The Lord of the Rings*, not the real world.

'There are lots of birds that come out with the dark,' Tristan said, 'not just owls. That's a nightjar, hunting for moths.'

He walked on ahead, through the darkness, and she admired the ease with which he moved in the forest, the stillness about him that bordered on reverence. It was impossible to watch him without feeling alive. *This is what people are supposed to be*, she thought. *At home in the world, not frightened by it.*

They hadn't walked very far and Emma had supposed Tristan was leading them back to his caravan, so she was surprised when their trail came to an end at her great-aunt's cabin. They paused for a moment, in the place where Tristan had stood when she first heard him, the previous afternoon.

It felt like a lifetime ago.

Tristan placed an arm lightly on her waist. 'Come,' he said.

He crossed to the little well, lowered down the bucket and wound the crank to bring it back to the surface. When the bucket emerged, they took it in turns to cup their hands and drink. Emma thought again of mysterious cabins in fairytales, deep in forests. How they always seemed to have a well like this one, just outside.

While Tristan returned the bucket to its hook, Emma wandered down the little path, with its border of white pebbles, to the front door. She remembered how it had been locked and that her reason for going round the back was to find the second door, because how could the cabin be locked when there was no keyhole, except from the inside?

But there had been no other door, a fact that struck her as very strange now she thought about it again.

Emma placed her hand on the rusty latch, as she had the day before, and pushed.

The door swung open.

TWENTY-EIGHT

ROSE

October 1940

Rose walked down her garden path for the very last time. Her wrists were sore where Norman had grabbed them, her muscles ached, and in the grey light of early morning she felt sad and despondent.

She recalled watching from her bedroom window as Evelyn had walked away, all those months ago, her step jaunty and her suitcase swinging by her side. Her own departure was under very different circumstances. Rose was leaving with no one to miss her, or worry about her, in the gloom of pre-dawn. Unlike Evelyn, she wasn't eager to begin her new life and she didn't have a beau waiting for her at the end of the lane, ready to whisk her away to a bright future.

Rose was utterly alone and her heart was bursting with sorrow and regret, not joy.

As she traipsed along the country lane towards Lowbury, her thoughts turned to Walter. She recalled the plums they had eaten together, giggling like children as juice ran down their chins. The shaft of sunlight spiking through the trees to bathe them in light as they sat on the old log, holding hands, like the romantic stars in a movie no one else would ever see.

But Walter believed she had betrayed him, that she cared for him so little she would willingly send him to his death. He would go on thinking that, wherever he was, for the rest of their lives. Meanwhile, men would come with their saws and their machines, obliterating Silverwood Vale and every life within it, one tree at a time.

Rose had failed at everything. She hadn't even managed to stop Otto and in all likelihood Germany's sabotage operation – whatever it was – would go ahead as planned.

But she couldn't allow herself to dwell on such things, not if she hoped to find the strength to go on. She had learned over the past weeks that she could be more than timid and compliant. She could be courageous and determined, when she needed to, and she had to believe that, as she moved on into an unknown future, those qualities would show themselves again.

Until then, she would follow Walter's advice to live day by day. And all she had to do today was leave town.

It was almost light as Rose wandered down the still and silent streets of Lowbury. The bakery had already opened and she bought a teacake for her breakfast. It lacked dried fruit because of the shortages and it was made with margarine instead of butter, but she choked it down as she wandered towards the hospital.

She needed to stand in front of the place where her mother had died and say goodbye. Perhaps then she could release her tears at last.

It was fully light by the time she arrived. The ambulances and the firemen were long gone, but Rose wasn't the only person in the marketplace – there were others, too, paying their respects. A small crowd had already gathered to hold vigil, the men with caps in hand, the women holding handker-chiefs up to their faces, many of them crying as they gazed over at the charred rubble where the front of the hospital had been.

Rose stood apart from them all, not wanting to be drawn into a collective grief.

The gaping hole was as deep as it was wide and although a full day had passed since the explosion, thin plumes of smoke still spiralled up from the wreckage. Rose wondered how many people had lost their lives in the bombing.

And then she thought about her mother.

She had always resented her mother for her weakness, her inability to stand up to Norman even where her daughters' safety was concerned. But after the past few hours, and the terror she had felt as Norman dragged her through the house by her hair, Rose thought she was better able to understand. And when she recalled her mother's final gift to her, she wondered if that was what courage amounted to, in an impossible situation.

Invisible acts of defiance.

'Goodbye, Mam,' Rose whispered. She tried to recall her mother before her father's death, when she had truly been herself, but it was such a long time ago. Evelyn had those memories, but Rose had been too young. 'I hope you knew some happiness, back then,' she said. 'I think you did.'

By standing close to the place where her mother had died, Rose had hoped she might find a way to release her grief, but still the tears would not come.

She would need to forgive herself first.

Rose wandered round the back of the hospital, towards the parkette where she had seen the wounded servicemen the day before. It was empty and early morning sunshine slanted low through the trees. From the rear, the hospital looked the same way it always had, as if the small park held a magic, moving her back to a time when her mother still lived.

What should I do now? Rose thought. She couldn't picture anywhere in the world she wanted to be except Silverwood

Vale, nor could she think of a single person she wanted to be with except Walter. She supposed she would take a bus to a town further along the coast and look for work, maybe as a chambermaid in a hotel so she'd have room and board. But she could summon up no enthusiasm, neither for the journey nor for the future that awaited her.

And she felt so very tired.

She sat down on a bench, leaned back and closed her eyes. Sunshine warmed her face, her aching body, soft as a caress. She felt exhausted by the weight of her grief and remorse.

'Miss?'

Rose struggled to open her eyes. For a moment, she couldn't recall where she was. She blinked to clear her vision and looked around the little park.

A small boy, bouncing a red ball.

Two ladies, walking their dogs as if this day was just like any other.

Sunshine, not low and warm through the trees, but directly overhead.

How much time had passed?

'Do you need anything, miss?'

Rose turned her head.

Next to the bench stood the serviceman with the bandaged hands who had helped her yesterday.

Rose struggled to her feet. 'I must have dozed off,' she said, trying to form her face into a reassuring smile and failing.

'Are you all right?'

Rose felt suddenly ashamed. There he was, with his hands so badly injured he might never regain the use of them, and all she could do was wallow in self-pity.

'I'm perfectly fine,' she said, 'but thank you. You were very kind to me yesterday. I hope your... I hope everything works out for you.'

She picked up her valise and walked away.

. . .

It was the middle of the day, maybe even later. Rose had slept for hours.

She hurried through the now-busy marketplace and towards the bus station. It was an area of town she rarely had cause to visit, so she was astonished when she came upon a place she recognised. A small tea shop, long closed, with the paint on the sign now chipped and blistering, the front window so coated in grime that she could barely see inside.

She put her nose to the glass.

The circular tables were still there, minus their pretty floral cloths and porcelain teacups. A memory came flooding back: her mother, pointing to those cups as she poured their tea.

'Look, Rose, the cups have roses on them!' she liked to say. 'These roses are almost as pretty as you.'

She recalled her mother's lovely frock and her father's Sunday suit. Swinging back and forth between them, down the street. Cream cakes in the window display and the anticipation of knowing a chocolate eclair was waiting inside, just for her.

The Rosebud Tea Shop.

Recalling the memories, Rose thought she would burst with grief. The weight she carried deep inside her was too heavy and her losses too great. She didn't have the strength to keep going on until life had meaning again. She leaned against the window, not caring that it would leave a dirty mark on her coat, and wondered how she would face another day, another hour, without hope. Without love.

And it was in that very moment, when Rose felt her loss the most keenly, that she saw a lone figure walking down the empty street on the opposite pavement, his head bent, his shoulders hunched. He was a large man, so his size drew attention to him, even though that was clearly not what he wanted. And as Rose gazed on in astonishment, he strode past her to the end of the street, turned the corner and disappeared from sight.

Walter.

TWENTY-NINE

ROSE

October 1940

Rose felt an immediate jolt of relief and joy. She wanted to rush after Walter, to tell him the truth about what she had done the previous evening, and have him trust and love her again.

But something stopped her.

Where was he heading? Why was he risking his life, walking through Lowbury in broad daylight?

There could only be one reason. Walter was following Otto's instructions, preparing to meet with him in whatever place the Reich had commanded. Something heinous was planned and no matter how much she may have doubted him before, Rose now felt certain that Walter would do whatever it took to thwart those plans. To prevent the Reich from carrying out their act of terror.

Thinking of the explosives Otto now had in his possession, she was filled with dread.

She ran to the corner and peered around. Walter had stopped further along the street and he was looking to the left and right, unsure which way to go. All the street signs in

Lowbury had been removed, as they had everywhere along the south coast, to impede the enemy's advance if a land invasion should occur. As she watched, Walter pulled a slip of paper from his pocket and consulted it. Then he continued walking, turning left and out of sight.

Rose hurried after.

It wasn't difficult to keep track of a man Walter's size and, as she had lived near Lowbury all her life, it didn't take her long to figure out where he was heading.

The railway station.

How could Walter, with his German accent, buy a train ticket without drawing attention to himself? And what was Rose to do now? Making herself known to him was out of the question. Walter would have far bigger things on his mind in this moment than her. Even if he did allow her time to explain what her true intentions had been the previous evening, he'd insist she remain behind. Whatever he was involved in, if he still cared for her, he wouldn't want her anywhere near.

Rose did not often leave Lowbury. She had never been on a train – in fact, she had rarely travelled anywhere at all. Taking a bus to a neighbouring town, that was one thing. Tailing Walter to wherever Otto had ordered him to go – that was quite another. But she didn't hesitate. However frightened she might be, Walter could have need of her help. If she had no chance to prove her loyalty in words, perhaps she might do so in deeds.

When the station came into view, Rose stepped behind a parked van and watched as Walter hurried inside. She counted to twenty before running across the road towards the building. At the glass doors she hesitated, peering through to the reception area, but Walter was nowhere to be seen.

She opened the door and slipped inside.

'Miss Tilburn! It's a surprise to see you here!' bellowed the man behind the ticket counter. Rose glanced around, alarmed at how loud his greeting was, but Walter had already moved through the glass exit door on the other side and onto the platform.

'It's a surprise to see you too, Mr Houghton,' Rose said. She knew him well, since his wife owned the haberdashery where Rose had once worked. Mr Houghton had retired long ago, but as younger men were conscripted older ones stepped out of retirement to fill their jobs.

'What a dreadful thing to have happened,' Mr Houghton said, shaking his head sadly. Rose's thoughts were so full of Walter that it took her a second to realise what he meant. 'All those poor people. I am so sorry to hear about your mother.' He twisted his hands together, awkwardly.

'Thank you, Mr Houghton. You're very kind.' Rose was trying to think of a way to ask him where his previous customer was heading when the old man leaned across the counter to her, conspiratorially.

'I just sold a ticket to the oddest fellow,' he said. 'Grunted "London" at me, he did, and tossed his money on the counter, letting me count out the coins for myself! Anyone would think he weren't used to money! When I asked him if it was third class he was after, I thought he'd faint right away, he looked so stunned.'

Rose smiled. It was exactly in situations like this that she could help Walter. 'You've no cause for concern,' she said, calmly. 'I saw him come in just now. He's a cousin of Mildred Radcliffe's, here for a visit. An odd man, as you say. But harmless.' She hesitated and then, knowing how unusual it was for a man of Walter's age to be seen out of uniform, she leaned in closer. 'He hasn't been the same since Dunkirk,' she whispered.

Mr Houghton's expression changed from puzzlement to compassion and he muttered, 'Invalided out, was he? Well, that explains it.'

'If I may have a ticket to London, please,' Rose asked, as if she bought train tickets every day of her life. 'Third class.' She fished in her pocket for the money she had taken from Norman.

'Right you are.' Mr Houghton stamped a ticket and slid it across the counter towards her. 'That'll be eight shillings.'

Rose saw her mistake at once. She had been eager not to steal more than the bare minimum from Norman and she had never expected to travel to London.

She had little more than seven shillings to her name.

Rose stared at the coins in her hand. Mr Houghton was stashing away his date stamp, so he didn't notice. 'What takes you to the big city?' he asked.

'I was hoping to visit my sister,' she said, the lie coming far easier than she had expected. 'I wanted to share news of the fire in person, but I seem to have come a little unprepared.' She placed her money down on the counter.

Mr Houghton looked at the coins and sighed. 'I'll tell you what,' he said gently, 'you consider this a gift, on behalf of the missis, since she always did say you were the best worker she ever had.' And he fished inside his own pocket to make up the fare.

'Thank you, Mr Houghton,' Rose said, feeling guilty that his kindness was offered in response to a lie.

'You'd best hurry, though. The London train only runs twice on Sundays and there's one pulling in now.' Mr Houghton looked at her with kindness and concern. 'My condolences again, to you and your sister,' he said.

Rose turned her attention to the platform, watching from the ticket counter as the train pulled in. Walter was the only other passenger to join at Lowbury, so she simply waited until he chose a carriage and then ran onto the platform and climbed into an adjacent one. She stowed her valise above her seat as the railway guard slammed the door and blew his whistle.

The train pulled out of the station, gathering speed.

What am I doing here? Rose thought, her heart beating fast.

She was utterly unprepared for whatever lay ahead. What made her think she would be any use at all to Walter in the coming hours?

Except she already had been of use to him, hadn't she? Without her intervention, Mr Houghton might have been suspicious enough of Walter's behaviour to alert the police. And if he had done so, Walter would have found officers waiting for him when the train arrived in London, his attempt to thwart Otto's mission over before it had begun.

Rose looked around. Even on a train, there were signs of war everywhere. In the blackout blinds, rolled up above the windows, ready to be pulled down at dusk. In the only other occupants of her carriage: three women not much older than Rose who wore the khaki uniform of the Auxiliary Territorial Service. And in the information posters, plastered along the walls. One showed a serviceman holding a rifle, his hand reaching towards the viewer. Is Your Journey Really Necessary? read the caption. Another displayed the cartoonish image of a shady-looking character hunched over a table in a tea shop. The word 'spy' was plastered across the back of his overcoat and the caption underneath read, Enemy Number One.

Rose swallowed and looked away.

Two hours later, after numerous stops in small towns Rose had never heard of, the train approached a London transformed by war. Through the windows, she saw streets lined with sandbags, endless houses obliterated by bombs and ragged-looking children clambering through the collapsed remains of their homes. She wondered at the barrage balloons suspended above the Thames like creatures from another world. Grey clouds pressed down on an ashen-grey city and a low sun sliced through fog with all the fury of an exploding bomb.

The train pulled into Victoria station and as Rose stepped down she was engulfed at once by the crowds. She had never seen so many people in one place, perhaps not in her entire life, a crush of people jostling and chattering. It seemed that everyone around her had an urgent need to be somewhere else and a vital role to play in the war. She saw members of the Women's Land Army dressed in men's overalls, giggling ATS girls in their prim khaki skirts and fresh-faced servicemen by the hundreds, their uniforms unblemished by dirt and blood, cheeks flushed with excitement. A band played somewhere out of sight and so many people shouted and laughed that Rose found herself fighting back panic, longing for the silence and solitude of Silverwood Vale.

She had always known cities were not for her. She didn't need to visit London to have that confirmed.

It wasn't difficult to follow Walter because he stood head and shoulders above everyone else. She trailed him along the platform, through the turnstile where a preoccupied attendant snatched her ticket and onto a busy London street. Something heavy and acrid hung in the air. A stench even stronger than the one that clung to the bombed hospital in Lowbury. It was an odour made of oil, rust, ash and other substances she could not name. A cocktail of smells built up over a month of incessant bombing.

But despite the sandbags, the piles of rubble scattered here and there along the pavements and the occasional obliterated wall or roof, life around the railway station seemed to go on as normal. Hackney cabs and double-decker buses inched along the street and a mother in a headscarf and tattered woollen coat manoeuvred her pram round a small crater. A cluster of servicemen home on leave stood shoulder to shoulder on the corner, whistling as young women hurried by. Rose passed a booth that sold cigarettes and newspapers, the placard propped against its stand reading: Blitz Bombing of London Goes on All Night.

How could people stand such noise and crowds, everything in constant motion and barely a tree or a bird to be seen? Buildings towered above her on all sides like the walls of a prison cell and she longed to break free.

Walter hesitated only briefly before striding on down the street and Rose scurried after. It was a cold day, more like mid-February than mid-October, and colourless. She followed him across a road packed with buses and cars, all of them honking, and round a corner, where she found herself in front of a set of iron gates that led into a park. Even here war was evident in the line of anti-aircraft guns pointed skyward.

Walter turned in to the park and Rose trailed him at a distance, down a path lined with mulberry trees so old and gnarled-looking that she marvelled at their survival through the centuries in the midst of such a riotous city. Walter seemed less certain of himself now, pausing on a bridge to consult his instructions. Ducks paddled by and a paper-thin sheet of ice shimmered on the half-rotten leaves that clogged the water's edge.

Then Walter hurried onwards and Rose followed.

He was moving with greater purpose now and at such speed that with her shorter legs Rose found herself almost running to keep up. She was wondering again where he could be heading, and what plans Otto might have for London, when unexpectedly the path opened up to a long, straight road. Rose looked left and saw, to her astonishment, a city landmark she had come across many times in newspapers and in books.

Buckingham Palace.

Sudden fear knotted her stomach. Was this where Walter was meeting Otto? Surely the explosives were not intended for Buckingham Palace?

But Walter hurried on.

He crossed the road into parkland again and here, the grass and the flowerbeds were replaced by victory gardens, most of the vegetables picked now, the plants shrivelled by an early frost. Moments later they emerged onto a busy road and from there Walter led her through a maze of streets. The houses were several storeys high, with arched windows, painted railings and steps leading to wide front doors.

They had been walking for nearly an hour. Rose supposed there might have been other options, if a person wished to cross London for any of the usual reasons. But for Walter, walking was safest, even if he had only a vague notion of how to reach his destination.

Sunset was not far off now and she knew what that would mean. Streets so dark in the blackout that it would be impossible to navigate them. She was bound to lose Walter then. Perhaps there would be no buses, no trains running after dark – and where would she sleep? Then there were the nightly bombs that fell on London. Rose hadn't the faintest idea where to find a public shelter.

She wondered what need Otto could have of the explosives Walter had given him when the Germans had the power to wreak havoc each night simply by dropping their bombs from the sky.

Rose followed Walter round another corner, where she was met by a sight of utter devastation. Every building in the street had been flattened, obliterated, nothing remaining of the homes that had once stood there except for a towering mess of brick, plaster and wood. A small crowd had gathered reverently and smoke rose in thin spirals here and there, indicating that this was the site of a very recent bombing. Walter stood further along the pavement, also gazing at the collapsed buildings.

'I don't understand it.'

She turned to see an ARP warden beside her, his face lined with exhaustion. Rose tried to imagine Evelyn dressed in the same grey uniform this man wore, the same tin hat perched on her head.

'Pardon?' she asked, one eye still on Walter.

'A dozen families died here, last night,' he said. 'There was nothing left of 'em, no one to pull from the rubble.' His voice shook and a nerve beside his eye pulsed as he spoke.

'That's terrible,' Rose said.

'It's their own fault!' the ARP warden cried in unexpected frustration. 'Their kids should've been safe in the country, or what was the evacuation for? But the first pleading letter they send 'ome, the mothers pull 'em back. London's full of kids again. An' why were these families not down in the public shelters? They'd've been safe there. A German bomb'll never touch 'em down there.'

Rose noticed how his hands trembled and she wondered at the horrors he must have seen in the past weeks as an ARP warden. At the horrors Evelyn must have seen, too.

'There's a camaraderie in the shelters,' the ARP warden went on. 'People coming together, laughing in the face of Hitler. That's the spirit of Londoners. Once, we thought there would be no breaking it.'

He sounded close to tears.

'My sister is an ARP warden,' Rose offered, because she couldn't think of what else to say. But he didn't seem to hear her.

'Londoners are strong,' the man said, 'but there's a limit, you know? We ain't superhuman.' He turned from the wreckage to look at Rose. 'There's only so far you can push people before they give up. We have our breaking point.'

Rose gazed at the rubble, running the length of the street. She saw a little girl, clutching hold of a doll, perched on a pile of brick, sobbing. A man who scrabbled through the ruins of his home, calling a woman's name, over and over. She thought of all the people, asleep in their beds as the bombs plummeted through the darkness towards them. How they had perished in the explosion, or in the long, dust-thick silence that came after.

The ARP warden sighed, as if acknowledging that wartime horrors were beyond his comprehension. 'Get yourself off home, love,' he said. 'It'll be night soon and you don't want to be wandering these streets after dark.'

He moved on then and Rose saw that the crowd was dispersing, no doubt everyone thinking the same thing: night would come soon and with it more bombs. She saw Walter move away too, turning in to yet another street. Not for the first time, she wondered if he was lost.

Whether Walter was lost or not, Rose did not intend to be left behind, not when she had already come this far. She hurried after him in the dying light of day, but as she did so the warden's words played over and over in her head: *There's only so far you can push people before they give up.*

THIRTY

ROSE

October 1940

The sun was setting when at last Walter came to a standstill. Consulting his slip of paper one last time, he turned into a large entranceway and hurried down a flight of stairs.

Rose recognised the sign by the entrance. It was the London Underground. The words beside it: King's Cross station.

This made no sense. They had passed several tube stations in their long, meandering walk through the streets of London. If Walter wanted to travel by underground, wouldn't he have done so by now?

Following him into the station, Rose was just in time to see him push through the turnstile and disappear from sight. There had been no time for him to purchase a ticket, so she supposed he must have received one from Otto, along with his instructions.

Rose hurried over to the ticket window, where an older man glared at her from under his peaked cap.

'I'd like to purchase a ticket, please,' she said, shifting her weight from one foot to the other. Since she had no idea where Walter was heading, every second mattered.

'Ticket to where, miss?' the man asked, making it clear he had little patience with anyone unfamiliar with the system.

Rose had no idea and as she considered his question, her pulse quickening, she realised she had made a terrible mistake.

By stealing the bare minimum from Norman, she lacked sufficient funds even to pay for the train ticket to London. Now, she hadn't as much as a penny left.

'You want to be quick about it,' the ticket seller said. 'Service stops early tonight. Don't ask me how anyone knows these things, but I'd say they're expecting a bad one. Last train's in a few minutes and after that it'll be chaos down there.'

Rose had no idea what he meant, but as the man turned round to check an ornate clock hanging on the wall behind him, she saw her chance.

She ducked under the turnstile, pulled her valise through after her and ran.

Who is this woman I have become? Rose thought. *Sneaking away, lying, trailing a German spy across London, stealing—*

'Get back here!' The ticket seller's voice bounced along the tiled walls, but Rose ran on. She hesitated only briefly at a moving staircase, an *escalator*, for she had never seen such a thing, and then she stepped on, glancing around with alarm as the walls constricted and she found herself trapped in a downward tunnel, being shunted deeper into the bowels of the earth.

Rose jumped off the bottom with surprising ease. The tunnel was deserted, the lights dim and the only sound an ominous clatter and whirr from the moving staircase behind her. Up ahead the tunnel divided, heading to different platforms.

How could she know where Walter was going? What if the tunnels divided again, further along? How many platforms might there be?

Rose heard a low rumbling sound, growing louder. With a sudden jolt of fear, she thought of earthquakes, of water gushing, roaring down tunnels to fill this space that already felt to her so much like a sewer.

The noise grew louder until the walls seemed to shake. Rose longed to turn round, to run back up to the surface, to keep running until the traffic, the buildings, the endless piles of rubble – every sign of this terrible war – gave way to forest and she could sit on the rotten stump by the old well in Silverwood Vale and listen to the call of the nightjar as a natural darkness settled all around.

Except that Walter would not be there and without him her forest would never be the same.

Rose gripped the wall in terror, holding her ground. Then she realised what the rumbling, roaring sound was. Not an earthquake. Not the tunnels filling with water just ahead.

A train.

She heard a loud, metallic squeal as the train pulled into the station, on a platform somewhere to her left. Rose was about to turn in the direction of the noise, desperate to locate Walter before he jumped onto the train, when another rumbling echoed to her right, the sound growing louder and accompanied by a second squeal of brakes as this train also slowed.

Two trains on two different platforms and Rose had no idea which one was bearing Walter away.

She had come so far, only to lose him now. She would never know where he had gone, never learn if he had managed to thwart Otto's plans, never see him again, not when he still believed she had betrayed him.

Rose stood still, processing her failure, as with a squeal of grinding metal she heard both trains pull out of the station. The rumble was deafening for just an instant, echoing off the walls of the tunnel, then it faded.

Silence settled around her as she thought of Walter, facing Otto all alone.

And then, in the silence, someone screamed.

Rose barely had time to register the sound before a woman in a fashionable floral skirt and plum-coloured raincoat charged out of the left-branching tunnel, a handbag clutched to her chest. She moved with astonishing speed despite her high heels, pushing past Rose and up the escalator.

Rose turned left, her heart thumping. She moved cautiously along an even narrower tunnel, which opened onto a platform. Looking at the domed ceiling, the tube-like tunnel disappearing into darkness at both ends of the platform, she thought, *It's like standing in the barrel of a gun.*

The platform was empty, or so she thought at first, but then she saw, at the end where the lights were dimmer, two men locked in combat, their arms wound tight round each other.

Walter. Otto.

Here was absolute proof that Walter had been telling the truth all along. His plan had never been to work for the Reich, to help his country pave the way for the invasion of Britain. He had never intended to support Otto, but to stop him.

Walter was exactly who he had always claimed to be.

But Rose barely had time to think this, for the two men were fighting, and as she watched them struggle – Walter a giant of a man and Otto thin, slick, his every move sinuous – she was put in mind of a bear trying to catch an eel.

Walter was by far the stronger of the two. He must have grabbed Otto from behind as the smaller man ran, for he held him from the back, one arm wrapped round his waist and the other clutching his neck. Otto writhed, twisting this way and that in his efforts to break free, every part of his body flailing, wriggling. They stood on the very edge of the platform and as Rose watched in horror, she saw Otto lean into the empty space in front of them both, jerking his body towards the tracks. He was not strong enough to escape Walter's grip, but he was quick enough to knock him off balance. He reached out with one leg and kicked at the wall where the platform ended, sending both of them tumbling onto the tracks. They seemed to twist in mid-air as they fell, then Walter landed heavily on the rails and Otto on top of him.

Rose pressed a hand to her mouth to stifle a scream.

Walter must have been winded by the fall, for the smaller man broke free. He leapt to his feet, running along the tracks for a distance and then scrabbling spider-like back onto the platform. He regained his balance at once and charged towards Rose. Quick as lightning she sidestepped to block his escape, swinging her valise, but he was stronger than she had expected. He knocked her aside with one flick of his arm, sending her reeling back against the wall and tumbling to the floor.

Otto ran out into the tunnel towards the exit and disappeared.

Rose sat up. She scooted to the edge of the platform and looked down, anxiously checking to see if Walter was harmed. She scanned the length of the tracks, but he wasn't there.

Then she looked up.

Walter stood right beside her. He held out a hand to pull her to her feet. 'What are you doing here?' he asked, astonished. And then he added quickly, 'Are you hurt?'

Rose shook her head. 'You?'

Walter was holding on to his side, clutching the cracked rib that had not had time to heal, but he did not reply.

'I never betrayed you, Walter,' Rose breathed. 'I went to the cabin last night, to warn you. I promise, I could never do anything to hurt you.'

There was a second when Walter registered her words and the meaning behind them, she was sure of that. Then his attention switched back to Otto and he gazed over her shoulder, towards the exit.

'Otto came to King's Cross early,' he said. 'He remembered our days in the Hitlerjugend and he could not bring himself to trust me. So he arrived early and by the time I got here he had already placed the explosives and attached the detonator. He had already set the timer. I did not see him do it.' Walter's voice quivered. 'I do not know where to find the bomb.' He looked behind him to the tracks and the gaping hole of darkness where the platform ended and repeated, his voice rising in panic, 'I do not know where he placed it.'

It took a second for Rose to understand what Walter was telling her.

Otto had already planted a bomb.

But then she scanned the empty platform. She thought of the tunnels behind her, all of them silent, void of people, and the ticket seller's words: the trains would stop early tonight. Surely they had little to worry about. If the Germans hoped to cause maximum havoc and death, they had failed. No one was in danger, except for the two of them.

'We have to get out,' she said, quickly. 'We're the only people down here. The tunnels might collapse when the bomb goes off, but no one will be hurt...'

Walter was shaking his head furiously, even before she had finished.

'You don't understand,' he said, reaching out to grip her arm. 'This station is one of the largest public air raid shelters in the city, with room for thousands of people. While the Luft-waffe attacks London tonight, from the air, a bomb will also explode in here, where people feel safest. So many deaths inside, while there are also so many deaths outside. The Führer wants to break their spirit, do you see? He wishes for people to give up, as they did in France and elsewhere. Then you will see our Panzer division rumble along the Mall to Buckingham Palace, just as it did down the Champs-Élysées.'

And in that instant, the air raid siren began to sound.

THIRTY-ONE

ROSE

October 1940

People poured into the station faster than Rose would have thought possible, dozens and then hundreds of them. Women carrying babies. The elderly, supported on the arms of their neighbours. Children who should have been safe in the countryside, racing one another along the platform.

A woman in a headscarf with a print of rosebuds held a toddler already dressed for bed. The child shrieked with laughter at his older brother, who pulled along a wooden duck on a string. The duck quacked endlessly, its beak snapping open and shut.

And through it all, the air raid siren sounded, on and on.

Several ladies in the uniform of the Women's Voluntary Service carried between them a large chest, which they opened halfway down the platform to reveal a tea urn and a huge tin of biscuits. An old man sat himself on a crate, pulled out an accordion and prepared to play.

Rose watched in disbelief as hundreds of people spread blankets out on the hard floor, propped cushions against the tiled walls, opened deckchairs and readied themselves for the long night ahead.

The platform resembled a church fete more than an air raid shelter. There was so much talking, so much laughing, Rose barely noticed when the sirens stopped.

'These people don't know the danger they're in!' she cried to Walter, her heart thumping with panic. 'We have to get them out!' She spun round. 'You must leave!' she screamed into the crowds. 'There's a bomb in the tunnel! You need to evacuate!'

But no one could hear her. Already the platform was too full of people, their shouting and chattering too loud, their voices bouncing off the walls into endless echoes. Rose's words made not the slightest impression.

And as she continued to scream her warning into the crowds, there came a loud rumble and boom overhead.

A bomb, falling close by.

Along the platform, no one paid the slightest bit of attention. It was as if Londoners had trained themselves to be nothing but upbeat and positive, down in the public shelter where they believed themselves to be safe. If anything, their voices ramped up a notch to drown out the explosions.

Walter pulled at Rose's arm, dragging her back against the wall.

'Even if you could get everyone to listen,' he cried, 'do you suppose they would risk leaving the station, with a Luftwaffe raid in full swing right over their heads?' His breath was warm on her cheek, he stood so close. 'I have to look for the timing device, Rose, but I need to know you will be safe. You must leave, right now!'

Above their heads, another bomb landed on the city. Plaster sifted down from the roof, but no one seemed to notice either the sound of the explosion or the dust raining upon them. The toddler continued squealing in his mother's arms. A gang of children chased the little boy with the wooden duck, all of them quacking madly. The WVS women walked down the crowded platform calling, 'Cup of tea! Tea and biscuits!' There was raucous laughter, the gathering more like a party than a bomb shelter, and on top of it all the accordion began to play, the people around the musician singing and others catching on, until the tune passed like an endless echo down the platform, the words looping in on themselves.

'There'll always be an England...'

Rose knew the song. Everyone did. It spoke of the nation as glorious and free. But that freedom would be no more than a memory if Nazi jackboots thundered down its streets.

'I'm sorry I doubted you,' Rose said to Walter. While her confession was meant for his ears only, she was forced to yell to be heard above the din.

'I cannot bear for you to be hurt,' Walter replied. 'If I find the bomb I can defuse it, but please go.'

Rose pressed closer to him. 'I'm not going anywhere,' she said, an unaccustomed firmness to her voice. 'All I have left is you. If we die, we die together.'

Walter saw it was useless to try to convince her. He glanced down the rails to the gaping darkness at the end.

'It is a needle in a haystack,' he said, but he was already pulling her towards the edge of the platform.

They stepped over the safety barrier and into the dusty darkness of the tunnel.

There came another explosion above them, this one closer, and Rose felt the walls of the tunnel vibrate. Back on the platform, the merrymaking faltered for just an instant. A baby wailed, a child screamed, but quickly the singing resumed, louder than ever.

'There'll always be an England...'

The Londoners sang with such gusto it sent a shiver down Rose's spine. They had no idea of the danger they faced, no idea that they were living through a moment that might propel England closer to defeat.

Then the lights along the platform went out. Seconds later, emergency bulbs fizzed to life down the length of the roof, flickering faintly. Rose turned her back on the faint glimmer and inched along the tunnel into a deeper and deeper darkness. Soon, she could no longer see Walter in front of her. She could barely see anything at all.

'It's hopeless...' she heard him say, his voice a hollow echo. 'There is no light. We will not see it.'

'What are we looking for?' Rose called.

'The hexogen has been dyed black,' Walter replied, 'so it will not be visible. But there is a detonator, a timer—'

'How long do we have?' She struggled to keep the panic out of her voice.

'Otto is using a J-Feder 504,' he replied. 'It can be set for as little as fifteen minutes, so it is possible we have almost no time left at all. Look for a box, dark in colour, but big. Solid.'

Rose scoured the walls of the tunnel, but he was right, it was hopeless. The walls were grey-black and criss-crossed with pipes, pocked with crevices where something might easily be shoved out of sight.

The timing device could be anywhere, right next to them even, and they wouldn't know it.

With rising terror, Rose imagined what a bomb, going off down here in the tunnel, would mean. She and Walter would be killed instantly. The explosion would ripple along the platform, silencing the accordion, the laughing children. Hundreds of people would die within seconds. Cracks would form along the arched walls, the roof above the tracks, widening, opening like jaws, the platform bursting apart and everything shattering like bone, falling in on itself.

Anyone still breathing in that moment would be buried alive.

She could hear them down the tunnel, in the faint circle of light. The chatter of children, their pounding feet. The members of the WVS calling, 'Tea and biscuits! Get your tea and biscuits!' The strains of the accordion. And rising above it all, the singing.

'There'll always be an England...'

Rose felt the horror of it. A horror that began with all these deaths, down here in a place that should have meant safety, continued with the collapse of the Londoners' spirit and ended with invasion. German tanks rumbling through the city. Nazi troops parading down the Mall, while a defeated people looked on in wide-eyed disbelief.

'What does it sound like?' she shouted.

'What?' Walter called back from somewhere up ahead in the darkness of the tunnel. Rose knew he was doing as she was, running his hands along the ledges, the pipes, any crevices that might be a convenient place to wedge the timer, to hide the explosives.

'The timing device. Does it make a sound?' Rose was yelling now, the words tumbling from her.

Walter shouted, 'A small one, perhaps, but we would never hear it, not with all this...' She imagined his hand sweeping backwards to indicate the crowded and noisy platform.

'What kind of sound?' she asked, desperate.

'Not a tick,' he called back. 'You might hear faint clicking as the timing mechanism winds down and you would hear the striker release but by then, it will be too late.'

On the platform, a dozen or more voices erupted into raucous laughter as someone told a joke.

'Rose,' Walter cried in desperation. 'Please. Leave now—'

'Be quiet!' she yelled. 'Please!'

Rose forced her breathing to slow. Leaning back against the wall of the tunnel, she closed her eyes and thought of Silverwood Vale. How she loved to sort the sounds into layers, each one telling its own story.

She listened deeply. Really listened.

Heard a baby's high-pitched wails.

A mother's soothing voice.

The children laughing, quacking, calling as they played their game on the edge of the platform.

Tea and biscuits! Tea and biscuits!

The accordion, its strains seeming impossibly slow.

There'll always be an England...

Layer upon layer of sound. And underneath them all, so faint, yet closer than all the other noises, almost directly above her head, a steady clicking.

'Here,' she called. 'Walter. It's here.'

He shuffled back to her and reached up, almost shoving her aside. 'Give me some space,' he cried, a grey shadow in the darkness.

She could hear it clearly, now that she knew what it was.

Click. Click. Click.

And it was too much for her, all of a sudden. She couldn't stay to watch Walter as he worked, couldn't bear to think what might happen to him, to all these people, if he failed to stop the timer.

There was nothing more she could do.

Rose walked back along the narrow ledge towards the platform, holding on to the wall, her hands, her clothes, her face black from the grime of it. She gazed at the people all around and her heart swelled to think of their courage. How they bolstered one another's spirits, night after night, sleeping down here while up above them the bombs fell. All these people, laughing and singing to drown out the sound of the explosions, never knowing whose home would be gone when daybreak came.

She glanced behind her. There was no sign of Walter.

Would any of these people live to see the morning?

Rose thought of the night she had found the parachute in the forest and the days that followed. How something inside her had burst to life, as she came to know and love Walter. Then she thought of the small child Walter had once been, trailing his new mentor through the great gardens of Lincolnshire, loving things that grew, wanting only to cultivate them. All the terrible things life had done to this gentle man since then. How he had been forced to leave a place he loved, returning to a Germany transformed, to a father caught in adoration of the Führer. She thought of his years in the Hitler Youth, his Wehrmacht training, the loneliness of always hiding his true feelings. Then, his special assignment. How hopeful he must have been, intending to surrender to the British police, and how the Treachery Act had destroyed that hope. And finally here they were, the two of them, as if everything they had lived through had served only to bring them to this moment.

She loved Walter as she had never loved anyone before and now she knew he loved her, too. Even if they died together tonight, she would regret nothing.

Rose glanced back down the tunnel.

Still no Walter.

She squeezed her eyes shut. Never had she hated the idea of war as much as she did now. The pointlessness of it all. How the killing and the destruction would go on and on, if not in this war in others, because *that was the nature of the beast*. It made her want to hide away, to sink into the rich green foliage of Silverwood Vale, the ancient arms of the Thunder Oak, and never, ever come out.

Rose stepped to the edge of the tunnel, leaned over and squinted into the darkness.

Still nothing.

On the platform, the singing, the laughter continued.

I'm not made for this, she thought, and something broke

inside her that could never be mended. *Deceit, suffering, pain, meaningless death. This is not a world I want to live in. Maybe I'm supposed to die tonight. Maybe it's all for the best...*

And then he was there. Emerging unsteadily from the blackness of the tunnel, coming up to her, his whole body trembling, the whites of his eyes luminescent in his blackened face.

'It's done,' he whispered.

He moved close to her on the ledge at the point where the darkness ended and the light, the warmth of the platform began.

'You did it,' she said, hardly believing.

He was shaking so much, so overcome with the horror of what had almost happened, of what they had just managed to prevent, that he could barely speak.

'We had seconds left,' he said. 'On the timer, there were only seconds left.'

'But you did it,' she said again. The relief she felt was beyond words.

Walter shook his head, his expression suddenly so solemn that Rose thought she might have misunderstood, that somewhere behind them in the darkness the timer was still clicking down. 'There is still Otto,' he breathed. 'Otto got away...'

This seemed so ludicrous in the light of all the lives just saved that Rose almost laughed.

She reached for his hands, for the strong warmth of them, and Walter pulled her towards him on the ledge, one hand winding around her long hair.

Oblivious to the dust and grime coating both their faces, he found her lips with his own and in the dim glow from the emergency lights he kissed her, slowly and tenderly.

But this time, when passion flared between them, Walter did not pull away.

THIRTY-TWO

ROSE

October 1940

They spent the night against the wall of the platform, Rose's small body wrapped in Walter's arms, but neither of them slept, not for a long time. At first they trembled against one another, so overcome with thoughts of the devastation narrowly averted that they could not speak.

When at last they calmed, the horror inside them both subsiding, Walter said, 'There is much you have not told me.'

It was true, Rose knew it was, and now it spilled from her. As Walter held her close and the raucous singing and laughter around them gave way to lullabies and steady snores, she told him everything. She shared memories of the father she had loved and how devastated she had been when Norman replaced him. She spoke of her mother's deteriorating health, Norman's bullying and the day Evelyn had finally left, a valise identical to Rose's swinging by her side as she strolled down the garden path and into her new life, never once looking back.

'I missed her,' Rose whispered. She couldn't find words for her pain.

Then she told Walter about all that had happened in the past few days. That her mother had been taken into the hospital and this was why she had not been to visit him in the forest. That she blamed herself for making her mother's last days so miserable, for accusing her of failing to defend either herself or her daughters. 'I left her alone so much after you came,' Rose said, thinking of her mother's face in the window as she ran through the garden and towards the coastal path as soon as Norman was gone each day, eager to spend every possible moment with Walter.

And when she relived everything she had done to hurt her mother, she felt again the congealed ball of pain in the pit of her stomach, the trapped tears she would never be able to shed.

Then Rose told Walter about the explosion at the hospital and her mother's death. How that was the reason she had gone against his wishes, telling the police about Otto and the rendezvous at the castle. 'But I came to warn you,' she whispered, as all around them people snored, sniffed and shuffled. 'I would never have betrayed you.'

He held her closer when she spoke those words and said simply, 'I know that now.'

There was more she should have told him. Norman's treatment of her the previous evening, the sleeping draught in his whisky, her escape. But she couldn't find the words for any of that yet.

'You are very brave,' Walter said to her, 'and you are strong.'

Rose turned to look at him in the lurid, flickering glow from the emergency lights.

'I'm neither of those things,' she said. 'Maybe Evelyn, but not me.'

'You stand by everything you believe in,' he said. 'Time and again you have done so. That is strength, is it not? You saved my life when you hid me in your forest. You told the police about the rendezvous with Otto because, although I asked you not to, you believed that was the right thing to do. And you followed me to London, today. You stayed down here with me when you could have saved yourself. And you are the reason all these people are still alive.'

Rose was about to point out that he had been the one to defuse the bomb when she paused to consider his words.

Perhaps she had been a little brave, after all.

'I hate the way everything is,' she said. 'People hurting other people. I could never take another human life, not for anything, which makes me think I'm not made for this world.'

Walter nodded, to show her he understood. 'Man's inhumanity to man,' he murmured, and when Rose looked confused he added, 'it is from a poem Frederick taught me as I worked his gardens, when I was a boy. I do not know who wrote it, but it ends, "Man's inhumanity to man / Makes countless thousands mourn!"'

They were silent after that, each thinking their own thoughts. Rose drifted in and out of sleep, pulled down by exhaustion and then dragged up from slumber, time and again, by the endless noise along the platform. By the crying babies, the echoing snores, the children who started from nightmares with a wail. Each time she woke, she felt Walter's arms around her, holding her close, and a spark of joy flared inside her. Then she recalled his words – *man's inhumanity to man* – and thought of Otto, roaming the streets of London.

Free to hurt others, as he would have done tonight.

It was dawn before the all-clear sounded. The lights blinked back on along the platform and the people folded up their blankets, their deckchairs, picked up their sleeping children and made for the exit. Rose and Walter joined the bleary-eyed and strangely silent crowd as it inched its way towards the escalator.

They held tight to one another's hands because they would not be parted again.

Before they shuffled out into the tunnel, Rose threw a last glance over her shoulder at the platform, now deserted but for the biscuit crumbs and a single toy: a little duck on the end of a string. *No one will ever know what happened here tonight*, she thought. *Historians will tell of the bombs that fell outside, but make no mention of the bomb that was planted in here. And no one will ever know that a German secret agent was the one to defuse it.*

Walter had saved so many lives. Perhaps he had achieved even more than that, in the long run, for the spirit of the Londoners would endure.

Yet history books would make no mention of him.

They emerged into the pink light of early dawn, to buildings reduced to rubble by the Luftwaffe, and they stood side by side with the Londoners, hundreds of them, blinking in sudden sunshine, speechless at the devastation. If Rose had wished to separate the sounds she heard into their layers, she would have noted fire bells, far off and growing closer, the soft rumble of falling debris, the crackle of flames in buildings with half their walls gone, and, above all of this, a single bird, singing. A chiffchaff, somewhere close by in a tree. One small sound among all the others. A sound that called to her.

Rose tugged on Walter's arm. 'It's time to go,' she said.

They retraced their steps through London, neither of them wishing to descend into the underground again. At the Mall they paused, gazing along the length of it to Buckingham Palace, thinking of the tanks that might one day roll along it; but not today. For the time being at least, London would fight on.

In Hyde Park they sat for a while under one of the plane trees and imagined the historic moments such venerable trees might have witnessed. Perhaps Lord Nelson himself had once strolled past them, before setting off on his final naval victory, the one that ensured Napoleon would fail in his attempts to invade.

Perhaps in the weeks or months to come, Hitler would fail, too.

They took a detour, lingering a while in front of Westminster Abbey, arm in arm, gazing at the splendour of it, and they bought pasties from a street vendor, eating them by the Thames in the shadow of a barrage balloon. They might have been any couple on a day out in the big city, except that Walter limped a little and had dried blood in his hair, and they were both as black as chimney sweeps.

They ducked into a red telephone box opposite Big Ben and, with Walter's body pressed tight against her own in the cramped space, Rose made an anonymous call to the police. She gave the location of the explosives and then returned the handset to its cradle before the officer had time to ask for her name.

In the bathrooms at Victoria station, they cleaned up as best they could. Purchasing train tickets was easier this time: Otto had given Walter plenty of money and Rose lined up to buy them while he hovered silently nearby.

'Your London may be beautiful,' he whispered to her as their train pulled out of the station, 'but I do not think I like cities very much at all.'

Rose thought of Evelyn, how clear it was from her brief letters that an urban life was the right one for her. But Rose knew now that she was not her sister. She had her own kind of strength, but she was not Evelyn.

'I don't belong here, either,' she said.

She breathed deeply, relieved, as densely packed housing gave way to countryside. She had been in London for less than twenty-four hours and something told her she would never return.

It was already night when they reached the outskirts of Silverwood Vale and they took one another's hands, walking together into the rich darkness of a world they both loved. They wandered through the trees, savouring the anticipation, moving slowly towards the four walls of their cabin, with its narrow bed and embroidered cushions. Warmth, comfort and solitude, ready to receive them. When they reached their glade, Walter opened the door to let Rose inside, closing it softly behind her. She waited in the darkness as he lit a small lantern.

'I have nowhere else to go,' she whispered, thinking of Norman and the danger he posed.

'This is where you belong,' he said. 'We belong together.'

He built a fire and brewed tea, and they drank it slowly, Walter on his stool, Rose seated on the pallet. The love between them and the desire they felt burned as fiercely as the flames that flared on their faces.

Walter smiled, his cheeks dimpling at the point where his beard ended. He placed his tin mug on the floor and moved to sit next to her on the bed, their bodies touching.

Rose let him kiss her, knowing where it would take them both. She knew, and it was all she wanted, the world outside their four walls receding until it barely existed, the world inside their cabin all that was left, all she would ever need. But in the moment when tenderness flared into passion, she was filled with a sudden sense of hopelessness.

Life was so dark, so filled with pointless violence that their love felt out of place within it.

Walter seemed to read her thoughts, for he fell still beside her. 'Think of the Londoners, Rose,' he whispered. 'How they kept up their spirits all last night and through these past weeks. There is always hope.'

She pulled away from him, perching on the edge of the pallet, overcome with sadness. 'Don't tell me we should just live for today,' she said, 'because that isn't always enough, is it? I can't stop worrying about the future and how there isn't one, not for either of us. Otto knows you betrayed your country, so you can never go back, Walter. Never set foot in Germany again. And in England you don't exist. By aiding the enemy, I'm a traitor, as well. If they ever find us, they will—'

'Then we will stay here, together,' he said, tenderly. 'Inside our forest.'

Rose's eyes filled with tears. She hadn't told him. How could she, when there had been so much else to focus on, so many more pressing problems?

'Silverwood Vale is going to be sold,' she said. 'The RAF may buy it, to extend Bilby airfield. Then all of this will be gone.'

Walter sat very still beside her on the pallet. For a long time, they said nothing to each other.

'There is so much here that should be protected,' he whispered at last, his voice heavy with emotion. Rose knew he was thinking of the ghost orchid, growing on the fallen trunk. All the wildflowers thriving in their forest and almost nowhere else. The nightjar that sang each evening at dusk and the devil's coach horse, with a tail like a scorpion and a name from a fairytale. Trees like the Thunder Oak, which had endured for centuries, only to face the axe.

Sometimes there wasn't any tomorrow to hope for. Others had accepted as much, since the start of the war. Now it was their turn.

'You can say it,' she told him.

'Say what?'

'The thing you always say: that sometimes all we can think about is now.'

'It is true,' Walter said, softly. 'I have seen it, all through my life. Moments of joy must be treasured, even when you know they will soon be gone. *Especially* when you know that.'

His arm slid round her neck and he pulled her down onto the pallet beside him, her back against the wall, her stomach pressed against his own.

'We may have no tomorrow,' Walter said, stroking hair away from her face, 'but we do have tonight.'

Rose leaned into him with a sigh, giving in to the moment, allowing herself to feel joy in what they had, even if it could not last. She felt the warmth of his breath on her face, the softness of his lips as they met hers.

And in that instant, the door burst open.

THIRTY-THREE

ROSE

October 1940

Otto.

His face was a ghoulish white, except for a jagged scar that ran from beneath his eye to the side of his mouth. His hair was so blond, so close to white that it shone in the lantern's faint glow. As they both struggled to sit upright on the pallet he leered down at them, revealing perfect, pearl-white teeth.

In his hand he held a pistol.

'I have orders to kill you,' Otto said, looking at Walter. He spoke in broken English, so Rose knew the words were for her benefit, too. 'I would like to tell you I regret this order but, alas, to say such a thing would be a lie. Killing a traitor to the Fatherland will give me great pleasure and afterwards...' His gaze shifted to Rose and she shivered as he ran his tongue slowly over his lips. 'Afterwards I shall enjoy the pleasures of your woman before she joins you in death.'

Otto hoisted a backpack from his shoulder and placed it on the makeshift table under the window, next to the shortwave radio. Then he turned to face Walter again.

'You think you can stop the invasion,' he said, his voice calm, his tone level, 'but no such thing will be possible. Germany will force all her enemies to their knees. The English will cower before the might of the Reich, a moment I almost wish you could see, if only to understand that you have failed. But you are a traitor, Walter – and, like all such men, you must die.'

So, this was it. While Rose could not kill so much as a beetle, here in front of her was a man capable of murdering thousands of innocent people. He would not hesitate to kill Walter. He would not hesitate to kill her.

'Get up,' Otto commanded.

Walter slid off the end of the pallet to stand next to the window and Rose moved to his side.

'All day I have watched you,' Otto said to Rose and his eyes roamed over her body as he spoke. 'In Hyde Park and by the Abbey, I watched you. In the train and on the coastal path. And all that time, I imagined this moment.' He reached a hand towards Rose's face and she felt the icy chill of his fingers as they slid across her cheek. 'I think I will enjoy you,' he murmured. 'I will enjoy you very much indeed.'

And it was in this moment, while Otto focused on Rose, that Walter sprang to life. Moving swifter than she thought possible, he grabbed the strap of Otto's pack and swung it towards him. The pack connected with Otto's hip, not hard enough to knock him off his feet, but enough to send him off balance. He staggered sideways, the pistol going off, the bullet flying past Rose to lodge itself in the window frame.

Otto reached out to the wall to steady himself and Rose felt Walter's fingers tighten round her own.

'Now!' he cried.

In the instant it took Otto to regain his balance they were at the open door, flinging it wide and charging through it, then veering away from the glade and into the trees where there was no light and a bullet would be less likely to find them.

They crashed through bushes, Walter holding fast to Rose's hand. It was impossible to move in the thick undergrowth, in the deep darkness, without making a noise. Impossible to know where they were, or whether they were going round in circles.

They ran for what felt like hours and then they paused, sliding behind a tree, listening for Otto in pursuit.

Rose held her breath. For a second there was nothing, but then she heard him, picking his way through the forest, coming for them, calling to them through the black night.

They ran on, painfully aware of the noise they made, and each time they paused it was the same: a few seconds of silence and then the sound of Otto in pursuit, the crunch of his feet growing louder, closer.

They zigzagged between towering trunks, hand in hand, constantly fearful that a sudden flash of moonlight through the trees would be enough to give Otto a clean shot. And each time they halted to listen, Otto called to them, his voice growing ever closer: 'Walter, I can hear you...'

They broke out onto the pathway they knew so well. While it was exposed, at least they could move faster now. Walter's long legs made him a good runner, though he still favoured his healthy ankle over the weaker one. Rose struggled to keep up, Walter almost dragging her along behind him.

'We've lost him,' she cried with the last of her breath, 'I think we've lost him...'

Walter stopped running and they stood together at the edge of the trail, holding their breaths, listening. Hoping.

Then shots rang out through the forest and a bullet struck a nearby tree. Walter tugged Rose sideways off the path, pulling her down into the undergrowth. They peered out, watching as Otto appeared on the trail, slowing momentarily and gazing around before whirling past them, his white hair blazing like a beacon in the darkness.

'He will see his mistake very soon,' Walter whispered, 'and he will turn back.'

Rose pointed through the trees. 'Badgers made a path down there,' she said. 'It's faint, but if we follow it, we'll come out further along the coastal path.'

'No.' Walter's tone was grim. Determined. 'We cannot keep running. This has to end tonight.'

It took Rose a second to understand what he meant.

Escaping wasn't enough. For the sake of the innocent people whose lives might be at risk from him in the future, Otto had to be stopped for good.

'Come,' Walter said. He took her hand again, leading her a short distance back along the trail, until it opened up to reveal the Thunder Oak. 'Up here,' he said. 'Quickly.'

Rose saw the sense in this. They could hide in the branches, in the spot where lightning had once severed the great trunk. Hide until Otto realised his error and doubled back along the trail, towards the cabin.

They would be the hunters that way, not the hunted.

But what then?

Walter hoisted her into the branches. Above them, clouds parted, revealing the brightness of the moon and bathing the small glade in an eerie, blue-white glow.

'Climb higher,' Walter said and she did so, to make room for him in the elbow of the great trunk. Rose thought of how she had played in the tree as a child. How she had sobbed there after her father died, and how she and Evelyn had screamed with impotent rage into the shivering branches after Norman had taken their father's place.

And she thought of Walter, suspended from the topmost branches of the tree the night he landed in the forest.

She leaned down towards him to give him a hand up, but Walter did not move.

'You will be safe here,' he whispered. 'I love you, Rose. If you do not see me again, know that I have loved you since the first moment we met.'

Fear rippled through Rose as the truth dawned on her. Walter had never intended to hide with her in the Thunder Oak. He was going after Otto, alone.

There was no time to argue. No time for Rose to say she would not be separated from him again, that they would live or die together, because in that moment they both heard a noise.

Footsteps on autumn leaves.

Otto, doubling back.

Rose shrank into the shadow of the oak's spreading branches and Walter slipped out of sight behind the trunk, but Otto barely glanced around the clearing before continuing along the trail.

Walter ran after him and Rose was left alone in the stillness of night.

The glade was utterly silent. Nothing scurried, rustled or whistled, either in the canopy or in the undergrowth. There was not a single noise to be heard, no matter how keenly she listened, and she felt the strangeness of it.

As if everything living had departed, recognising the deadly conflict playing out for what it was – something unnatural, something alien to the forest.

Rose eased herself down through the branches of the Thunder Oak and when she reached the fissure in the great trunk, she jumped.

Walter was a trained soldier, a special agent capable of so much more than she was, but that had also been the case in King's Cross station and yet he had needed her. She could not simply wait for the danger to pass. Not if there was any chance Walter might need her again.

Rose listened, trying to figure out whether the two men were still close by, but she heard nothing except an owl, hooting softly, far off.

Then a shot, in the darkness.

She stumbled onto the trail and broke into a run, charging through the trees with no thought of her own safety now, thinking only of Walter, who might be injured, bleeding, somewhere up ahead.

Or worse.

She came to a standstill on the edge of their own glade and peered out.

The two men were fighting in a shaft of moonlight by the old well, Otto's hand still holding the pistol. As Rose watched, Walter twisted the smaller man's arm, lifted it and shook. Otto howled in pain, loosening his grip on the gun. Walter jerked his arm a second time and the pistol flew through the air, landing with a clatter on the edge of the clearing, steps from the spot where Rose now stood.

But Walter had no need of a gun. Otto might be faster, but he had strength on his side. As Rose looked on, Walter lifted Otto off the ground as if he weighed no more than a child, lifted him high, one hand hooked under the smaller man's arm and the other clasped tight round his neck.

Otto was choking, the gargling breath coming in bursts from his constricted throat. Rose knew what it would mean to Walter, to take another's life. How it would haunt him for the rest of his days. And as she thought this, Otto flailed madly with the hand that had held the pistol seconds before, only there was no madness to his flailing, for he was reaching around even as Walter strangled him, plunging a hand down towards his belt and withdrawing something sharp, something long and metallic.

A knife.

Time stopped for Rose and she pictured everything before it happened. The swing of Otto's long, white arm, rising in an arc above the heads of the two men. The downward plunge. The blade slicing through Walter's shirt, through his flesh and into his heart.

Then time was moving again and Rose saw herself as if from far off, stepping out into the clearing, crouching to scoop up the pistol. As Otto's dagger arced through the air, in the instant before it began its downward path towards Walter's chest, she moved forward, calmly and without hesitation, depressed the trigger of the gun and fired.

Later, Rose would not remember the sound of the pistol firing, nor would she feel the jolt against the palm of her hand. She would not recall the sight of the two men, slipping to the ground. All she would remember was the wild flapping of a hundred wings as a murder of crows lifted up from the treetops and the black smudge of their bodies, like bullets against the darkening sky.

THIRTY-FOUR

EMMA

June 1990

The door to the cabin opened, swinging inward.

'Tristan!' Emma cried, calling him over from the well.

Tristan hurried to join her and they stood together on the threshold of Great-Aunt Rose's home. Emma felt a twinge of guilt, as if going inside would be an invasion of someone's personal space. She knew enough about her great-aunt by now to appreciate that this cabin had been her refuge from the world, but not enough to understand why she had needed one.

But the old woman was dead now. The cabin belonged to her.

Tristan rummaged in his pocket and Emma felt him press something into her hand. "Here, take this torch," he said, and when she hesitated, he added, gently, "go on."

Emma stepped inside.

She swung the weak beam over two comfy armchairs, hand-made throws tossed across their backs. A pretty corner table with a stained-glass oil lamp in the centre. A fireplace with a basket of logs beside it. Doors stood on both sides of the old cabin, leading to the newer additions. Through the left one, Emma could see a kitchen table and an old stove. The door to the right stood closed.

She heard Tristan strike a match behind her and turned to see the oil lamp burst into flame. He replaced the lampshade over its chimney and a warm glow spread around the room.

Emma gasped.

Every inch of every wall was filled with paintings. Beside the door, a long canvas ran from floor to ceiling and on it an image of the old tree where they had seen the badgers. The words *Thunder Oak* were written across the top of the canvas in letters that resembled a bolt of lightning.

There were other paintings of forest life, too. Fungi in dazzling colours, a red squirrel peeking out from a knothole in a trunk, ravens and robins, even a black beetle, its tail curled like a scorpion.

But most of the paintings were not of nature at all.

They were portraits of a man with weathered skin and gentle eyes, at different stages of his life. In one, he was about the same age as Emma, his face handsome, a suggestive glint in his eye. In another, he stood among the wildflowers Tristan had showed her just that evening, only the flowers were huge in proportion to his body, growing in riotous profusion all around him. In a third painting, he was middle-aged, sitting in the fissure of the old oak tree.

There were images of the man resting in a chair by the fire, sleeping in bed. Images of him chopping firewood and standing on the roof, a hammer raised above him like a sword.

In a tiny painting by the closed door, the man was very old. *This one is the best of all*, Emma thought, moving closer. Such kind eyes and a face that still burned with life and energy. Rose had captured something about the old man's personality in his now-wiry eyebrows, the thin, grey beard and the wrinkles that resembled the bark of the old oak tree.

Whoever this man was, Emma thought, there was no doubt her great-aunt had loved him very much and known him well, for each painting was a celebration of his life.

She looked around the cabin again.

Two armchairs. Two side tables. Two coasters, each made of painted wood.

She moved to the closed door and pushed it with her hand.

A double bed, with two pillows. Two narrow wardrobes. Two woollen dressing gowns hanging side by side on the wall.

Great-Aunt Rose may have been a recluse, but she had not lived her life alone.

Emma felt warm breath on the back of her neck. She turned to see Tristan, his eyes shining in the near darkness of the small bedroom.

'So much love,' he whispered. 'You can feel it, can't you? They loved each other very much.'

'Who was he, do you think?' Emma asked, but instead of replying, Tristan moved closer. She felt his arm slide round her waist, his fingers stroke hair back from her cheek. He leaned in, his face quivering with emotion, placed a hand on the back of her head and gently guided her lips towards his.

For a split second, Emma wanted to. She might have kissed him, allowed him to lead her to the bed, let desire plunge her into a new version of herself.

She could have done it. She wanted to.

Almost.

But as Tristan pulled her towards him, Emma probed the longing she felt, rising inside her, and realised something she had not known, had not let herself see until this moment.

While she felt attracted to this man, who flouted convention and lived the life he was meant to live, it wasn't Tristan she longed for.

It was Mike.

Emma placed her hands on Tristan's chest and pulled away, gently but firmly.

She didn't have time to address his hurt and confusion. Didn't have time to explain that she knew where she wanted to be right now, and who she wanted to be with, and it wasn't here, and it wasn't with him.

There was no time for anything because in that moment the door to the cabin burst open, revealing a huge, shadowed figure on the threshold.

Not a ghost, but a flesh-and-blood man.

Emma would have known him anywhere. She had seen him at all stages of his life, from his early twenties to his seventies. She knew the expression he wore when he felt proud, jubilant, playful, loving, passionate, at peace. She knew how his brow furrowed while he slept.

It was his face that stared down at them from every wall of the cabin.

But now this old man wore an expression that appeared nowhere in the paintings around them. He looked saddened, beaten down and exhausted by grief.

But he didn't seem surprised to see them there.

He moved slowly towards them both, where they stood in the doorway to his bedroom. 'My name is Walter,' he said, looking at Tristan, 'and I've been watching you for some time.' He shuffled around his living room, lighting more lamps, building a fire. Only once did he turn, looking right at Emma, and his eyes misted.

'You look so much like my Rose,' he said.

Walter indicated the two armchairs and they both sat down, watching as he put a match to the fire he had built. He moved through to the kitchen and returned with a stool, which he took for himself.

'This is your home,' Emma said, though she didn't need to.

The way he moved through the space showed his familiarity with the little cabin and his fondness for it. It occurred to Emma that he must have built the two additions, he and Rose together. They had patched the roof after winter storms, filled the window boxes with flowers each spring, cooked endless meals together in the kitchen, spent a lifetime of pleasant evenings side by side, staring into this fire.

And along the way, Rose had made art, sending her work out into the world, and Walter had cared for his wildflower garden tenderly and with skill, quite possibly teasing back species from the brink of extinction.

They had lived as a part of the ecosystem, here in Silverwood Vale, giving more than they took. And they had lived at the centre of each other's lives.

Not small lives, Emma thought. *Lives full of purpose and love. Magnificent lives*. She pulled from her purse the tiny black and white photograph of Rose and passed it to Walter, perched on his kitchen stool. The flames danced between them, flickering across his ancient face so for an instant he seemed like a young man again.

'You can keep it, if you like,' she said.

Walter gazed at Rose's young face and said nothing for a very long time.

He passed the photograph back to Emma.

'I have her here,' he said, tapping the side of his head. He moved his hand down, to his heart. 'And here,' he added.

'You're living in the cabin alone now?' Tristan asked.

'I do just fine,' Walter replied. 'This is my place and my life. My Rose is here and I'll not be parted from her.' He paused. 'Sometimes things have to change,' he said, 'but there are some things that need to stay the way they always were.'

'Why wasn't your name on the deeds?' Emma asked. She thought of the papers sent to her by the solicitor. Her conversations with Mildred and Mrs Foster. People had seen Rose occasionally, in the town. She must have bought groceries, visited the doctor, shopped for clothes. And she had posted her paintings, presumably to collectors all over the country. But no one had ever mentioned seeing Walter. 'Does anyone even know you exist?' she asked, tentatively.

Walter said nothing. His shoulders were shaking and he was gripping the sides of his stool tightly. Emma wasn't sure whether her question had angered or upset him.

'Do you know about the parachute in the root cellar?' Tristan asked. 'Do you know what's wrapped inside it?'

Walter's face briefly flickered alarm and then his features relaxed, as if he was deciding none of his secrets mattered any more.

This changes everything, Emma thought as she gazed at the old man, who was clearly struggling to regain control of his emotions. She wouldn't be going to London in the morning and she wouldn't be selling Silverwood Vale. Whatever the law might say, she had no right to it.

And while she expected to feel disappointment at losing the money for her condo, this wasn't what she experienced at all.

What she felt was relief.

Walter trembled on his stool. His mouth opened, but no words came out. They had gone too far, she realised. Asked questions he wasn't ready to answer.

Emma was as curious about the parachute and the bones as Tristan – but she couldn't bear to see what they were doing to him. Perhaps Walter would share his stories in time, but he wasn't ready to do so today.

She stood up. 'I'm so sorry we came into your home,' she said. 'And I'm so sorry for your loss.'

Walter's chest was heaving now, sobs breaking from him. Despite all his efforts at self-control, his grief was obviously as raw as the day his Rose had died.

'I live here, in the forest,' Tristan said, hesitantly. 'On your land. I think you already know that.'

Walter nodded, his head bent to hide his tears.

'So if ever you need anything at all...'

They turned to leave, but at the last moment, on impulse, Emma ran back towards Walter. She crouched down beside his chair and placed a hand gently on his arm. 'I'm glad my Great-Aunt Rose didn't spend her life alone,' she said, awkwardly. 'I'm glad you had each other for all those years. And I hope my life has as much love in it as yours did.'

The old man said nothing, only sitting in silent thought, his head bent, as Emma returned to Tristan's side. Then they left him in his home, with the ghost of his life's love for company, and headed out into the darkness, closing the door softly behind them.

Emma took the lead, walking softly and silently down the narrow trail, through the trees. It occurred to her that she could hear night noises around her now even without stopping. She was walking the way Mike might have done, each footfall chosen with care, moving with an awareness of the world around her.

When they came to Tristan's caravan, they stood together by his fire, in awkward silence. The flames had died back, for he had scattered the logs before leaving, but the embers still glowed, giving off a little light.

'It was Walter's voice I heard all those times,' Tristan said at last. 'His wailing, not the wailing of a ghost. And it was his face I saw in the moonlight.'

He stuffed his hands deep in his pockets, looking at the fire, not at her.

'I'm sorry, Tristan,' Emma said. 'Back in the cabin, I didn't mean to...'

Tristan shrugged. 'It's okay,' he said, though she knew she had hurt him. 'Do you want me to walk you back to Lowbury?'

Emma said, 'No. I'm going to be fine.'

'You were planning to sell Silverwood Vale, weren't you?' Tristan asked, unexpectedly.

Emma looked at him in surprise.

'You were going to sell it and someone would come here and destroy it all.'

There was a chill in his voice, a bitterness, and Emma thought what it must have been like for him, all that evening, spending time with her when he had already guessed what she planned to do.

'Was that why you showed me the badgers?' she asked. 'Was that the only reason you tried to kiss me? Because you were looking for a way to change my mind?'

Tristan shook his head, vehemently. 'No,' he said. 'It wasn't, honestly. I did those things because I wanted to.'

Emma knew he spoke the truth. She suspected Tristan was incapable of lying. 'I'm leaving in the morning,' she said gently. 'I want to go back home.'

'Right.'

'And I won't be selling Silverwood. Not now. This is Walter's land. I'm sure he won't mind if you keep on living here.'

Tristan turned to her. 'If we hadn't met Walter tonight,' he asked, 'and if you had left Lowbury without ever knowing he existed, would you still have sold this place? Would you have let them destroy it all?'

Emma recalled how she had viewed the forest as malevolent when first she saw it. A tangled mess of useless land that would be improved by a little tidiness and order. Then she thought of all she had seen and heard in Silverwood Vale over the past few hours. How the forest was bursting with life. The ancient trees, holding fast their secrets. The ghost orchid. The nightjar and the badgers.

But she had wanted the money so very much. The financial freedom it would have brought her.

What would she have chosen to do, if there had still been a choice to make?

'I don't think I could have sold it, not after everything you showed me,' Emma said. Wanting to be completely honest with him, she added, 'but I suppose we'll never know for sure.'

A silence fell between them. Tristan threw a log half-heartedly on the burning embers, but the fire didn't take.

'Walter knows things he isn't saying,' he said suddenly. 'He knows who the bones belong to in the root cellar and how they got there. He could tell us why he's spent a lifetime in this forest and why no one seems to know he exists. So many secrets and Walter could take them all with him to the grave.'

'But I don't think he will,' Emma said pointedly, intending to throw down a gauntlet. She stepped away from the fire and away from Tristan. 'Thanks for everything. You know, for the badgers, for all of it...'

'Goodbye,' Tristan said, adding nonchalantly, 'and good luck with your novel.'

What novel?

Emma wondered if Tristan was throwing down a gauntlet as well, but she didn't ask.

She walked around the back of the caravan and picked her way slowly down the old logging track. The trees didn't feel like a malevolent presence any more. In fact, Emma felt comforted, knowing they gathered around her in the darkness. It occurred to her that the lives of each of the trees stretched out for years before and after her own, and she was just a small part of their story.

But as she stepped onto the moonlit coastal path, pausing to watch stars spangle on the sea, and as she turned to look back at the black expanse of Silverwood Vale, it was Walter's words that she pondered.

Sometimes things have to change, but there are some things that need to stay the way they always were.

THIRTY-FIVE

ROSE

October 1940

Rose dropped the pistol.

Both men lay still on the ground before her and for one terrible moment she thought she had killed Walter as well as Otto. That the bullet had passed through both of their skulls.

Then Walter was pushing aside Otto's body and struggling to his feet.

'Walter...'

The word was a plea for help, for support. Her legs felt suddenly weak as she stared down at the dead body. *I have killed someone. I am a killer.*

He was beside her in an instant, this man for whom she had taken a life, holding her tight, supporting her.

'I did this,' Rose whispered, and everything about her felt unfamiliar as she spoke, even the sound of her own voice, as if she had become someone else in the instant the bullet left the gun.

'You saved my life,' Walter said. 'If you had done nothing, I would be dead now and you would be about to die, and Otto would be alive, to go on killing.'

But Rose barely registered his words. In that moment, all she knew was that the world was such a brutal place it had left her with no alternative but to take a human life.

I thought I could never kill, and I was wrong.

She was shivering with shock, whole moments passing as she pressed her cheek to Walter's chest and looked behind him at the dead man. She thought of a game she had played with Evelyn in the branches of the Thunder Oak, just after their mother had married Norman, when all they could feel was raw rage.

What could you kill for, Rose?

I could never kill.

If Norman hurt Mother, Evelyn said, *maybe I could kill him.*

I could never kill, Rose repeated.

If I had children one day and someone tried to harm them, Evelyn said.

Rose shook her head. *Not even for that.*

Or if I fell in love with someone and a bad person threatened him.

Rose said, *Even then, I could never kill.*

She had been so sure, and so wrong. There was a reason she could kill and he was holding her in his arms right now, this man whose life she had saved.

She blinked back to herself.

'We will get through this together,' Walter said. 'It is a terrible night, but we will deal with Otto now and tomorrow will come. Do you understand?'

She nodded.

'Wait here,' he said.

He peeled himself from her and hurried inside the cabin, leaving Rose alone with Otto's body. She wanted to ask his forgiveness, even though it was too late, but then she thought of the thousands in King's Cross station that he had been about to murder. She recalled what Otto had said – how he had trailed them both through London, spying on them, desiring her – and she felt a sudden chill. She imagined Walter dead by his hand and she thought of what her fate would have been, in the minutes or hours before Otto killed her, too.

Perhaps she did not need his forgiveness, after all.

Walter emerged from the cabin carrying in his arms the folds of the parachute. Something about his expression had changed. He looked puzzled. Astonished, even. He glanced over his shoulder.

'Rose,' he said, 'inside Otto's bag...' But he didn't finish his sentence. He looked at Rose's expression and something about it must have told him that this wasn't the right time.

They rolled Otto's body into the parachute and half dragged, half carried it to the back of the cabin. Rose stood by numbly, shivering with shock, while Walter opened the great wooden trapdoor leading into the root cellar and together they lowered the heavy silk bundle down into the earthy darkness. Walter smashed the cellar's ladder into pieces and tossed them down after the bundle. Then he closed the trapdoor, binding the handle with cords from the parachute. They covered the trapdoor with earth, so that things might grow on top of it, hiding it forever, and over the earth Walter piled branches. Finally, he dragged on top of it the fallen bough of a tree.

By the time they had finished, it was as if Otto had never existed.

As if no one could ever know the truth.

But I know, Rose thought.

And the shivering came on again, even worse than before. She recalled the man who had built their little cabin, the veteran with shell shock, and wondered if this was how he had felt, day after day, for years. Trapped inside a nightmare.

'Rose?'

She could hear the concern in Walter's voice.

'Everything is too dark,' she said, and her teeth chattered as she spoke.

'It will be daybreak before you know it,' Walter said.

'I need light now.' She struggled to speak. 'It's all too dark.'

She didn't mean real darkness, she meant the darkness of a world at war. A world that had made her a part of itself, no matter how much she wished it otherwise.

Walter led her back round the cabin, away from the root cellar. 'Look,' he said, pointing up through the trees, 'the sky is already turning grey. Before you know it, the sun will rise.'

When she said nothing, only trembled, he took her by the hand and led her, stumbling, down the trail they had run along in fear of their lives a short time ago.

They passed the Thunder Oak, continuing onwards to the coastal path, to the dunes. Out in the open, Rose could see that Walter was right: the night was almost done, the stars that shimmered on the water blinking out one by one. Already, the faintest light hovered on the horizon.

Walter sat her down on the dunes, dropped onto the sand beside her and held her close. Rose thought, *I want my mother*, and all of it came flooding back. She felt it more deeply than she ever had before, the pit of unshed tears in her stomach, weighing her down.

'On the night when you met Otto in the castle,' she said to Walter, 'Norman threatened me. I think he would have hurt me badly, as he hurt my mother for so many years, but she had put a sleeping draught into his whisky. It was the last thing she did, before she left for the hospital. And so, before he could do his worst, he fell asleep.'

It was her final secret. The last thing she hadn't told him.

'Your mother protected you,' Walter said. 'She must have been strong, just like you. She loved you and perhaps she even saved your life.'

Rose could see that, as he spoke the words. Her mother's love. The way they were alike, neither of them knowing the strength they had inside them, not until it was almost too late. It occurred to her suddenly that in Rose's shoes, her mother might have done exactly as she had done.

'Mam...'

And then she was crying, tears bursting from the pit inside her, and it felt so good to let it all out at last. She cried with grief for her mother and she cried for Evelyn, the sister she had loved so much – the sister who had left them both. She cried for herself, for the girl she had been, naively thinking there was nothing in the world important enough to kill for, and she cried with regret, for all the things she had never said to her mother while she had the chance.

She cried out all her tears, releasing the unbearable pressure inside, and all the time Walter held on to her. Held her together.

When at last her tears were spent, they sat in silence, watching the breakers on the beach, the grey of the sea pulse and heave.

Rose felt so much lighter now, with the tears gone. Light as air and ready to move forward with whatever their lives could be.

She eased herself out of Walter's embrace. 'We have to decide what to do,' she whispered to him. 'As soon as Silverwood is sold, there will be people everywhere. We can't let them find us.'

'There is something—' Walter started, but Rose interrupted him.

'I can never go back,' she said.

'You won't have to,' he told her. 'In the cabin—'

'No,' Rose said, 'you don't understand. I'm not saying I can't go back to Norman, though that's true as well. I mean more than that. Lowbury, London, all of it... I don't want to be in the world. I don't want to be a part of the war, of all the—'

Walter said, 'Rose, back in the cabin, when I looked inside—'

'I'm going to smash that radio, Walter. I'm done with it all.'

'Will you let me speak!'

She fell silent. Looked at him. Saw an expression on his face that surprised her. Hope. Excitement, even.

Walter said, 'When I returned to the cabin to fetch the parachute, I opened Otto's pack. It's full of banknotes, Rose. Stuffed full of English banknotes. He must have received them from Germany, for his next mission, whatever they intended that to be. And it must have been something huge. Germany must have been planning something terrible, for there are hundreds of pounds in there. And no one knows the money exists.'

'No one knows?' she asked, astonished.

'The banknotes would have been used to fund death and destruction, had Otto lived,' Walter said, 'and no one else this side of the Channel even knows they exist.'

Rose thought about this.

'We can hardly give it back,' he prompted, gently.

Over the past weeks, Rose had learned to follow her own intuition and mostly things had turned out well so perhaps in this moment, too, her intuition could be trusted.

Sometimes, you had to do a small wrong in order to achieve a greater good.

'We should use the money to buy Silverwood Vale,' she said. 'We can protect it forever. Stop them from destroying it. Then we could stay here – couldn't we? Fix up the cabin, make it ours. Live in it together, just the two of us.'

Rose felt a ripple of joy sweep away the last of her sadness. She wondered if perhaps they had more to live for than the present at last. If the two of them might have a future, after all.

She took Walter's hand. They closed their eyes and together they listened, separating the sounds into layers. Waves washing onto the beach, soft and rhythmic. The trees of Silverwood Vale, whispering behind them. And a single nightjar, calling in the forest, as the sun rose on a new day.

THIRTY-SIX

EMMA

October 1990

...they listened, separating the sounds into layers. Waves washing onto the beach, soft and rhythmic. The trees of Silverwood Vale, whispering behind them. And a single nightjar, calling in the forest, as the sun rose on a new day.

Emma lifted her pen from the page. She flexed her wrist, stretched her fingers and gazed out of the window. The sugar maples were blazing red under a dazzling October sky and Mike was drifting across the still lake in his new canoe, towards their dock. She knew the expression on his face as he looked up through the maples, watching a red-tailed hawk ride the currents. It was the same expression she had seen on Tristan's face, the night they watched the badgers, and on Walter's, while Rose painted him standing among the rare wildflowers he had worked so hard to save.

Mike was a man in love with life, and here, in the midst of nature, he was more alive than she had ever seen him.

Emma looked back down at her manuscript. She aligned the papers carefully and wrote 'The End' in giant letters across the final sheet. Then she placed her pen down on the desk.

Her Secret Soldier, she had written in looping, calligraphic text across the title page. 'Secret soldiers' was how the British had referred to their spies during the Second World War and while Emma had no idea if the Germans had used the same term for their spies, it seemed fitting for Walter.

Maybe no one would ever read her novel, she thought, but if it did find a publisher, she would be the only person to know that Great-Aunt Rose had really existed and that the story was based on truth.

Along with Tristan, of course. And Mike. She shared everything with Mike, as she always had.

Beside the manuscript on her desk sat the letter that had arrived from England just that morning. With a heavy heart, she unfolded the single sheet of paper inside and read Tristan's words slowly, for the second time:

> *I hope you have everything you need for your novel, because I'm sad to have to tell you that I won't be able to ask Walter any more questions. We spent many happy hours together as he relived his life with Rose and last night he died peacefully in his sleep. It was not unexpected, as you know. I do not think he had any desire to live on without his Rose and telling his story for your benefit, so the truth might be known – that was his final purpose.*
>
> *Just last week, the* Guardian *newspaper published their article on Silverwood Vale. They included photos of the wild-flowers I showed them, but the reporter did not name the location, just as she promised. She called her article 'Walter's Place'.*

Emma smiled, just as she had the first time she read that paragraph, thinking how wonderful it was that Walter's name was finally attached to the forest he loved, after a lifetime of anonymity. But it was the last few sentences of the letter that Emma dwelled on as she read it through again:

When I told Walter that you planned to bequeath Silverwood Vale to the Woodland Trust, I believe he was happy for the first time since Rose's death. And I'm happy too. It's time for me to move on, Emma, but I can do so knowing that Silverwood Vale has a real chance of remaining wild, well into the future.

Emma put the letter aside and watched through the window as Mike pulled his canoe up against their dock. Turning to look at the walls of their new cottage, already adorned with Mike's photographs, she wondered whether a visit to England might be possible in a few months. She knew how badly he wanted to visit Silverwood Vale.

Waving to her husband through the window, she pushed back her chair and stood up. She looked down at her manuscript, the first draft now complete: Great-Aunt Rose's story, and Walter's too.

'Mike!' Emma called. He waved to her as he stepped up onto the dock. She noticed again how free of tension his face was, now he no longer had to deal with life in the city.

She hurried into the kitchen, past her white faux-leather sofa, which looked far better in their country home than she had ever imagined. She grabbed a bottle of her favourite Chardonnay and two glasses, eager to celebrate her accomplishment with Mike. But before pouring the wine, she hesitated, noticing for the first time how empty the wall seemed between the kitchen door and their table.

It was the perfect spot for Great-Aunt Rose's painting of the Thunder Oak.

Emma filled both glasses, calling to Mike as she pulled back their screen door. Then she ran out into the sunset to join him.

A LETTER FROM JULIE

I want to say a huge thank you for choosing to read *Her Secret Soldier*. If you enjoyed it, and you would like to keep up to date with all my latest releases, just sign up at the following link. Your email address will never be shared and you can unsubscribe at any time.

www.bookouture.com/julie-hartley

Growing up in Lincolnshire, a child of avid hikers, it always seemed to me that Britain had a wealth of unspoilt countryside; endless public footpaths that traversed wild moors, overlooked spectacular coastline and meandered through cool woodlands. Then, two years ago, I read Raynor Winn's excellent memoir, *Landlines*, and realised just how much of that wilderness is in the process of being lost forever. According to the Nature Conservancy Council, only 3 per cent of Britain's natural grasslands remain and many of our ancient woodlands are now too small to sustain viable populations of declining species. When I moved to Canada, I fell in love with that country's stunning wilderness, too – but before long, I realised that wild places in North America are as threatened as they are everywhere else. Over the past years, so much rare beauty has been lost to industrial development and urban sprawl.

I have always been fascinated by the human urge to both destroy *and* create. We produce magnificent buildings, inspirational music, poetry, performance, art – and we have an endless capacity to love, which is also a form of creation. Yet there is no escaping the devastation we wreak upon one another and our world. Rose embodies both these aspects of our nature. She is a child of wilderness, capable of self-sacrifice and great love; an artist and a pacifist. Yet she has no choice but to be drawn into the world the way that it is. By protecting Walter, she betrays her country in a time of war. And she discovers that, when compelled by desperation, she is just as capable of destruction as everyone else.

In Emma, I wanted to explore the barrier we so often erect between ourselves and the natural world. It is this barrier that allows us to wipe out what we should cherish; we fail to appreciate the critical importance of what we have, until it's too late. Emma looks at wilderness and sees a malevolent force, separate from who she is. She has a great deal to learn from Mike, the love of her life! Nature is not something to like or dislike, something to visit or avoid. Nature is our planet and our survival; it has the capacity to inspire wonder and wisdom, to educate, heal and transform. Wild places enlarge us and make us capable of monumental things: great love, deep nurturing, endless creativity. Nature isn't only something we *need*, it is what we *are*.

I hope you enjoyed *Her Secret Soldier* and, if you did, I would be very grateful if you could write a review. This can make a real difference, as it helps new readers to discover my books for the first time.

I love to stay connected to my readers! You can get in touch on social media or via my website.

With endless thanks and warmest wishes,

Julie

KEEP IN TOUCH WITH JULIE

www.juliehartley.co.uk

facebook.com/juliehartleywriter

amazon.com/author/juliehartley

HISTORICAL NOTE

In September 1940, Hitler ordered that a network of spies be established across Britain and Operation Lena was the result – a mission botched so completely that historians now wonder whether there was a deliberate attempt by German intelligence officers to sabotage the planned invasion of Britain. The secret agents who landed in rowing boats and by parachute knew little of the British way of life, so it was impossible for them to blend in, and most were captured within days. One spy was even arrested for cycling down the wrong side of the road! Another was apprehended after ordering a pint before pub opening hours, a detail I borrowed for this novel.

If Operation Lena had been well executed, it is unlikely that Walter's duplicity would have gone unpunished by Germany, but the mission was a short-lived failure. Even as spies like Walter were parachuting into Britain, Hitler was beginning to accept he lacked the air superiority to invade and the Nazis were turning their attentions to the Soviet Union instead.

The Treachery Act of May 1940 made provision for the

execution of enemy agents found on English soil, but in reality this did not always happen. German spies often came under the control of the XX (Twenty) Committee, known as 'Double Cross', and they were used to pass false intelligence to the German Abwehr. But Rose and Walter could not have known this. They would have assumed that, in the event of capture, Walter faced certain execution.

The London Blitz began on 7 September 1940, with the Luftwaffe conducting bombing raids on the city for fifty-six of the fifty-seven nights that followed. The result was heavy loss of life and the destruction of thousands of homes, often in the poorest neighbourhoods. The spirit of Londoners throughout the Blitz became the stuff of legend; had they lost heart, support for Churchill might have waned, with disastrous implications for the war effort.

During the Blitz, tens of thousands of people sought shelter nightly in the London Underground. While there are stories of people being killed in the stations when the streets above suffered a direct hit, there is no record of a bomb ever being planted *inside* a station – though it is not difficult to imagine the devastation, nor the effect upon morale, if such an explosion had occurred. Since it is not known that German spies ever planted or defused a bomb on the London Underground, I had to rely on research to piece together descriptions of the explosives and timing device that might have been used if such a thing had ever occurred. In particular, I would like to thank Scott Bowman, as well as the Imperial War Museum, for their assistance.

Finally, this novel was inspired by my passion for ancient woodland, a glorious part of Britain's natural heritage that is under constant threat. An ancient woodland is defined as one that has existed continuously since at least the 1600s, which means such places remain relatively untouched by human activity. They are home to thousands of native species, many endangered, and they now cover less than 2.5 per cent of the land. Silverwood Vale may be fictitious, but there are plenty of ancient woodlands in Britain that can be enjoyed and must be cherished. You can learn more about them by visiting the Woodland Trust at www.woodlandtrust.org.uk.

ACKNOWLEDGEMENTS

I would like to thank Nina Winters and Susannah Hamilton of the Bookouture editorial team, without whom this novel would never have seen the light of day. Thanks are also due to my talented students in the Centauri Arts Writing Salons and the Centauri Arts Writing Retreats (Mexico, Costa Rica and England) for their endless warmth, inspiration and support. I would also like to acknowledge the folks at the Halls Island Artist Residency; the opportunity to spend two uninterrupted weeks writing on a deserted island is not one that comes around often.

Enormous thanks are due to my family and friends: to my wonderful parents, Hazel and Dave, and to my sister Sharon, who was the first to hear most of this story during our 'Costa Rica Storytimes'. Reg and June, Yvonne, Nikki, Jane, Joanne – thank you all. Without your support, I might have given up long ago.

Finally, and always, endless love and thanks to my dear husband Craig, who never, ever stopped believing, and to our wonderful daughter, Aislyn. Without the two of you, nothing is possible.

PUBLISHING TEAM

Turning a manuscript into a book requires the efforts of many people. The publishing team at Bookouture would like to acknowledge everyone who contributed to this publication.

Audio
Alba Proko
Sinead O'Connor
Melissa Tran

Commercial
Lauren Morrissette
Hannah Richmond
Imogen Allport

Cover design
Debbie Clement

Data and analysis
Mark Alder
Mohamed Bussuri

Editorial
Nina Winters
Ria Clare

Milton Keynes UK
Ingram Content Group UK Ltd.
UKHW021538050924
447875UK00004B/157